The Chimes in the Tree

The Chimes In The Tree

In **Book One**, Katie Windsor was chasing her cat, Green Eyes, through the forest, when he seemed to run directly into the Great Oak.

Hearing her cat's cries, Katie cautiously approached. Her fingertips touched the bark and then her hand vanished inside of it, and then she too, *entered the tree*.

Once inside, Katie learned that the Great Oak is a portal to another world, and that she is that world's *Lost Princess*, though an evil sorcerer, named Lord Osiris, wants her dead, so that he can rule Chaparral.

In **Book Two**, Katie struggles to control her otherworldly abilities. But what can you do when, *conceal it, don't feel it,* no longer works? In Katie's case, Robur, The Wizard, summoned the teenage version of Katie's grandmother to help her control her newly found magical powers.

However, the *Mother of Bones* is intent on bringing her son, Osiris back from the grave. It would seem she might just have the perfect spell to do so, after all.

In **Book Three**, we find Katie saddened by the loss of her beloved professor, but still anxiously wanting to get back to *The Academy of Enchantments and Other Magical Studies*. However when she finally returns to Chaparral, big surprises await Katie Windsor and her beloved cat, Green Eyes.
In this...

The Final Book In The *Chimes In The Tree Series...*

The Forever Spell!

The Chimes in the Tree (The Forever Spell)

A Novel
Written and Created
by Jazan Wild

Artwork by
Iwan Nazif

Colors by
Yuan Cakra

Narration by
Simon

Editing by
Sharon Levesque Barnes

"THE CHIMES IN THE TREE:
The Forever Spell"
Book Three in *The Chimes In The Tree* Series.

A Production of Carnival Comics ®.

Wild would like to give a special dedication to…

All the outsiders!

To those who dare to be different…

Those who dare to march to their own drummer…

Those who dare to dream!

To all of you, this book is your book.

I, myself, was one of those outsiders, when I was growing up.

And proudly, I still am an outsider, today.

And to J.K. Rowling, whose storytelling in itself, is the very definition of enchanted. Her words have opened wide the creative doors of so many young readers, as well as those readers, young at heart. Thank goodness that Joanne - the young, down on her luck writer, did not give up on her dreams and against all odds, saw those dreams through. The result of her having done so, is that now we ***all*** *live in a much, much more magical world.*

This Slytherin, for one, is eternally grateful!

CONTENTS

THE PROLOGUE

"YOU CAN'T JUST LEAVE IT THERE"

The sky above darkened. It turned grey so quickly that no one escaped getting drenched unless you were one of the lucky few who happened to be near some sort of shelter when the clouds rolled in. Three unsuspecting girls playing in the nearby forest were not so fortunate.

The shade that naturally existed inside the belly of the *Great Oak* acted much like an umbrella and hid any forewarning from the girls who were presently climbing upon its branches. It was only when a kitten tucked inside one of the girl's sweaters - he had grown almost too large to conceal himself, as he once could - poked his head out and meowed with displeasure at being struck by a droplet of water, did they all begin to realize a storm was bearing down upon them.

"What is it, Midnight?" Cynthiana asked of the cat.

Just then she and the other girls noticed a crackling sound encroaching like a monster through the forest coming directly at them.

"Grab onto the *Great Oak!"* shouted Cynthiana.

Kadence and Hailey listened to their cousin and each wrapped their arms around the thickest branch they could find. Together they held on for dear life, as the wind ripped through the old oak. To the frightened girls and the lump tucked inside Cynthiana's sweater, with its claws dug into the wool fabric, it felt as though the tree's roots might give way and they'd all be carried away to another world. But rest assured the *Great Oak* was strong, though it too, was struggling. All cried out for help.

Not too far away, an elderly gentleman lifted his head after being awakened by the rattling of the walls that lined his study. He had drifted off while reading a dusty old weather-worn book. Suddenly there was a thud upon the floor, as the book crashed at his feet. The old man reached for his cane and darted towards the nearest window. There, he looked out to see a blackened sky with a twirling funnel of wind heading unswervingly towards the forest where his grandnieces had been playing right before his eyelids had grown heavy.

"The girls!" he cried out.

With a quick clank, thud, clank, thud… the girl's uncle with cane in hand, made his way down the hallway, almost ripping the door off its hinges, as he exited the house. As the old man flew across the yard, he appeared to move more like a man of an age, which was decades younger than his present outward shell would suggest. As he reached the tree line of the forest, his cane fell away. The footprint pattern upon the ground would suggest that not only did the elderly gentleman ditch his walking stick, but he might also have tossed aside… the old man facade, as well.

Broken branches, uprooted brush and all sorts of shrubbery soared through the air, attempting to unfasten the girls from the oak. The rain pelted them so hard that they couldn't even see the wind born objects that were hitting them, until they were a mere few feet away. Each one of the cousins was losing their grips. However, the girl with the whitest knuckles was Hailey.

"I can't hold on any longer," she cried out.

"You have to," demanded Kadence. "Don't you dare let…"

She was cut short before she could finish the sentence, though. In horror she watched as Hailey's fingers lifted from off the bark. As Kadence reached for Hailey, she lost her grip, as well.

"No!" screamed Cynthiana as her cousins succumbed to the whipping wind. She too extended her hand out, while still gripping the oak tight.

Odd, though… as she reached out for the girls, it was as if the world itself went into slow motion. Cynthiana thought her eyes were playing tricks on her, because instead of Kadence and Hailey being swept away, they just seemed to dangle, hanging in midair, like marionettes with invisible strings fastened to their backs.

In that brief moment, Cynthiana concluded that her cousins must be stuck on a couple of strong branches. Or maybe... just maybe, the *Great Oak* actually grabbed them with its twig-like fingers, saving them from certain death. The blinding rain made it too hard to see things clearly.

Still, Cynthiana continued to reach for them all the same. Then a loud cracking sound rose up from out of the thunderous storm. It diverted

Cynthiana's attention just for a second… and in that brief moment whatever kept Kadence and Hailey in place, snapped and they started to drift away,

"No!" Cynthiana cried out again.

What happened next was unclear. Through the rain, Cynthiana heard that same loud cracking sound directly where Kadence and Hailey had disappeared into the murk. Just before they were consumed by the ravenous wind, it was as if a shadow from out of the forest grabbed them each by the garments they were wearing and pulled them forward, back to the base of the *Great Oak*.

Cynthiana wiped the water from her eyes and then looked again towards the ground, the very spot where her cousins just were.

They were gone.

But the storm remained.

"Kadence! Hailey! Where are you?" she called out in desperation.

And then another sound caught her attention. It was an eerie but soothing sound, even as it clanked, metallically. She looked up and through the shaking leaves hanging on a branch, for a split second, she thought she saw where the melodic tone was coming from. There, she believed she saw a set of wind chimes hanging overhead… near to the branch she was clinging onto. And then as quickly as she saw it, the chimes disappeared from her line of sight, as she was overcome by the same shadow that grabbed her cousins. Abruptly it grabbed her too.

The large shadowy figure swooped in and snatched Cynthiana. She felt a large claw like hand upon her neck, gripping her by the shirt collar. Head held forward, she squinted and braced for impact. It felt as though she had fallen and the ground was coming up quickly. The last thing she remembered was seeing the trunk of the tree, thinking she'd smash into it.

However, when she opened her eyes, she saw her cousins huddled in the dark.

"Kadence! Hailey!" she said, as she raced over to them.

"Cynthiana!" they said, and threw their arms around each other.

"I thought we were goners," said Kadence.

"Me too," replied Hailey.

Cynthiana looked around, puzzled.

"How did we all get in here? And where is here?" she asked.

Just then a voice called out from deep in the darkness.

"Girls! Can you hear me? Girls!"

Suddenly before them appeared a familiar figure.

“Uncle Simon!” they cried out, and ran over and hugged him round his waist, gripping him tight.

“How did you find us?” asked Cynthiana.

“I was about to ask you the same thing,” replied their uncle. “I saw the storm, and went looking for you. The winds got too strong, so I took shelter in the old Winslow Salt Mine. And then I heard voices in the darkness. I followed them and low and behold… here you are.” He looked at all his grandnieces and smiled, “I found you.”

“Hold on,” said Cynthiana with an inquisitive look upon her face, “we were by the *Great Oak*, not any caves.”

“Yeah, that’s right,” added Hailey. “Kadence and I were swept away in the wind when some shadowy creature grabbed us.”

“Same here!” demanded Cynthiana.

“Monster, you say,” replied the old man, with widened eyes.

“Not a monster, but a sort of a big strong thing, shadowy for sure,” explained Cynthiana, as her cousins nodded in agreement. “I mean, I felt its claw-like hands carrying me.”

“What did this creature’s face look like?”

The girls looked at one another and then glanced side to side, “Well, I mean… I ah, didn’t see its face,” said Cynthiana.

“Did either of you two see its face?” asked the old man turning and looking at Hailey and Kadence.

Both girls shook their heads side to side.

“No, but there was so much rain and wind it was hard to make anything out,” reasoned Kadence, as if she was trying to convince herself.

“Well, that might solve the mystery. Perhaps the creature was just the gusting wind and the claw… broken branches caught in your clothing.”

The girls’ uncle bent down and picked up some bits of tree lying nearby and nodded his head as though finding a puzzle piece with the correct edges.

“But how did we get here?” asked Cynthiana, not yet convinced, or willing to discount her own senses.

“I would surmise, that it might have been the strong winds that carried you further than you thought,” the old man replied, trying to sell it.

Cynthiana squinted and gave her great uncle a look that spoke without words. Though the word she would have said, would have been… really? In a manner that would suggest that his summation was more fanciful than what actually happened.

Seeing his grandniece’s expression, he quickly tried to divert the girls’ attention.

“I’m just so thankful that you are all alright. I think you had guardian angels watching over you and they brought you here, to safety. So now we have to stay in here and wait out the storm.”

“For how long?” asked the girls.

“As long as it takes,” replied their uncle. “We have no choice. You can still hear how heavy it is outside.”

“Let’s go back to the opening of the cave, and see?” asked Hailey.

A panicked look fell over the girls’ uncle.

“No, no, no, you could still be hit by flying debris,” he said unconvincingly. The old man shuffled a bit and then popped up and said, “I’ve got an idea. How about a story?”

Cynthiana’s eyes lit up, and she turned to Hailey and Kadence, who also had glowing grins.

But then Cynthiana, paused. As if to say not so fast, there was a little more negotiating to be done.

“Uncle Simon, we will stay in here quietly. But only if you tell us what happened to Princess Katie after Osiris came back. I mean you can’t just leave it there. You just can’t.”

The little girl stuck out her hand with steadfastness and asked, “Deal?”

Her uncle with a grin, looked down and grasped her tiny hand giving it a good firm shake and replied, "Deal."

Uncle Simon paused and reflected for a moment, possibly just for effect.

"Now where were we, again?"

The girls all contributed together to reply to their coy uncle, "Osiris and Hathor came back from the dead. The *Mother of Bones*, the *Dark One's* mother, turned to dust inside the *Witch's Glass.* And…"

Suddenly sadness crosses over the girls.

"Professor Hopingráve, she… she…"

"Right, right," said Uncle Simon, sensing the girls' despair. "Correct you are. I do recall it all, now. Thank you for refreshing my recollection."

The kindly old storyteller looked around for a rooted stump to sit upon. Finding one, he said to himself, "That'll do."

His knees creaked as he lowered down and with a deep breath in and a sizable exhale out, it was clear the tale was about to begin. He cleared his throat and looked out upon his audience of three. The storyteller's eyes connected with Cynthiana's excited gaze. He said, "You were right, my dear, I can't leave it there. That would not be fair to Miss Katie Windsor,

Miss Eshe Leota, or to the late, beloved, Professor Hopingráve, and of course, above all else, it would not be fair to… you."

CHAPTER ONE

"WHERE'S THE WIZARD?"

Summer was ending and fall was right around the bend. It would not be long before the leaves would start falling again in the town of Windermere and Katie Windsor was anxious to escape to another place, another world, onto another adventure. It had been almost three months since she had returned to the old Windsor farmhouse and each day seemed to grow longer as she waited to hear from anyone on the other side of the *Great Oak*.

The magical spell that Robur the Wizard, had placed upon Katie's family and all of the townspeople, so that Miss Windsor could attend, *the Academy of Enchantments and Other Magical Studies,* had been fulfilled. It was the spell that left mere shadows of Katie and her cat to walk in their footsteps, while both were away on Chaparral.

As Robur's incantation went... "Shadows on high, now bid you adieu, spirits it does split, splits them in two!" And the spell did just that, exactly the way Eshe and Robur planned. Like the ancient wizard, the magic he used was old and came with conditions, as all spells do. As he relayed to Katie upon casting said spell, "It is how it is, with magic. You get, you give… it's all a balancing act."

The give part that the impatient *Princess of Chaparral* agreed to was that for the protection charm to continue, Katie had to return to Windermere for at least 13 days every year. If not adhered to, Katie's shadow would fade and the *Great Oak's* portal between the worlds would shutter. The contract, of sorts, would not expire until 31st of October on Miss Windsor's18th birthday, as long as these conditions were kept.

Katie waited the first 13 days, biting her nails down to nubs. While she knew that she and Eshe had agreed to spend the entire summer back in their respective home worlds, there was a hope that someone would send word of any Chaparralian goings-on, via the *Great Oak's* leaves. Or maybe even a quick drop in by one of *the Seven*, poking their animal shaped heads through the bark just to say hi, and see you soon.

She went to the forest and sat under her favorite tree, waiting for any sign from the other side. Yet the only thing that moved was the wind through the leaves, dangling from the branches. They seemed to be laughing at her. On this day however, the sound emanating from the oak was more of a meow, rather than laughter.

"School's about to begin, and I did my time, Simon," said Katie, staring up at the cat just overhead. "I mean, Green Eyes."

"I know," said Green Eyes, through *skull-speak*. "Master Robur must have his reasons."

"It would be nice to actually be at the academy for opening day. Heaven forbid I'm made to use that rusty old bicycle handlebar to fly around the halls again... Eshe could barely hang on. Not to mention that we had to beg the professors to let us in their classes, cause they got so sick of the ruckus."

For a moment, a smile crept over Katie's face as she reminisced. But it faded as quickly as it arrived. She turned her head away and spoke to the tree more than responding to Simon.

"You know we share birthdays… *Haunt-O-Wick Day*. I… I, miss her, very much."

There was silence and she appeared to fight back a tear, before abruptly rising to her feet and turning her back to the oak.

"I hope it won't be Halloween before anyone decides to invite me back," Katie said angrily, as she walked out of the forest.

Green Eyes followed. But he stayed quite a distance behind.

As Katie reached the Windsor farmhouse she was greeted by several of her sisters playing in the front yard.

"Where have you been?" asked Violet. "Oh wait, let me guess."

Libby, Ruby, Annabelle and Jessica, joined in with their sister in conjecturing. In unison they spoke... "Up a tree?"

It was rather obvious that they had offered this summation before.

Katie retorted with a well-worn offering of her own.

"Oh, shut up, you gits!"

Ruby and Jessica looked at each other in mock outrage.

"How rude!"

Libby pretended to clutch a set of imaginary pearls, “Why I never.”

Violet just glared.

“You know tomorrow is the first day of school, and you haven’t set out your clothes, or readied your belongings yet,” said Annabelle.

Katie just stormed past the girls without engaging any further, and headed straight up the staircase. As she climbed the steps nearing the top, she muttered under her breath, “That’s because I don’t want to go!”

Katie slammed the door behind her. To her surprise a small voice arose from the other side of the bed.

“I don’t want to go either.”

Katie rounded the foot of the bed to find her youngest sister sitting on the floor, legs folded with her head in her hands crying.

“Daisy, what’s wrong?” asked Katie.

While all her other sisters had a tendency to get under her skin, Daisy always found a way into Katie’s heart. Theirs was a special bond.

“Why don’t you want to go? You love school.”

Daisy continued looking at the floor as she replied.

“I didn’t say anything, because, I didn’t want to make things worse. And you… you didn’t seem to care. I guess you had your own troubles.”

“What are you talking about, Daisy?” asked Katie, not following.

“Well, something happened just before summer break. I just pushed it down and swallowed it. The next year seemed so far away. Now it’s here and I have to face it. I have no doubt it will be the same thing all over again.”

“Daisy,” reiterated Katie, more forcefully and becoming ever more concerned, “tell me what happened?”

Through a tear soaked face Daisy said, “It was Mabel Wythenshawe and her cronies. At recess, I was playing hopscotch with Isabella Jenkins, when Gertrude and Priscilla grabbed me. Isabella yelled at them to let me go.

“Good for Isabella,” said Katie. “I always liked her.”

“Well, then Mable pushed her into the dirt. I bit Priscilla on the arm and ran straight at Mable, and shoved her as hard as I could. I told her to leave my friend alone. Even though she’s much bigger than me, I stood up to her. Like, you used to do.”

Daisy looked Katie in the eyes, which made her lower her head in shame. Even though it wasn’t really her, but just a mere shadow of herself to which Daisy was referring to.

“What did she do next?” asked Katie, despite the fact that in her bones she already knew the answer.

"She hit me."

It was Daisy who now looked ashamed.

"I fell to the ground, and when I started to well up, Priscilla and Gertrude laughed at me. They called me, Krazy Katie's crybaby little sister, over and over again; I was so embarrassed when I saw how Isabella was looking at me. She started to cry. Mable turned on Isabella and said, don't either one of you two little brats dare think of telling anyone what happened here today… if you do, we'll get you, and it'll be worse next time, I promise. That's when Mable bent down and whispered in my ear, and there will be a next time, especially for you Krazy Katie's little crybaby sister. Your sister may have checked out… lost her marbles, whatever. Either way, we finally put her in her place. We're gonna make sure you're put in yours, too."

The blood under Katie's skin began to boil. Her fist clinched tight, at the thought of Mable Wythenshawe hitting her sister. Suddenly Daisy heard a rattling sound. She looked upward toward the window and noticed a small crack begin to appear in the center of the glass.

"What's that?" Daisy asked, as she turned to her sister. In that brief second she noticed Katie looked different, almost entranced. Before she could finish asking the question though, there was a blast of wind carrying shards of glass, which had exploded out of the bedroom window.

"Aaahhh!"

Daisy screamed and shielded her face expecting to have the bits of glass spray overtop of them both. However, when she peered through the slats of her fingers, the sight she beheld caused her to gasp.

Though it was only for a brief moment, Daisy saw it. Frozen, hanging in the air, was the broken fragments of glass that she was concerned about. She removed her hand which was covering her face and reached out to touch the sparkling mist. Before she could touch it however, the shattered bits of window fell to the floor, encompassing them in a circle. It was as if an invisible dome of protection had formed around them, because it had.

"Katie, how?" asked Daisy.

In an instant, Katie saw flashes of last year's meltdown where her anger led to the schoolhouse being burnt to the ground. However, she quickly caught sight of Daisy's expression… that and all that she'd learned at *the Academy of Enchantments and Other Magical Studies*, helped suppress her rage, despite the instantaneous outburst.

Just then Charles and Abigail came running into the room.

“What the heck happened?” asked Charles.

“You girls alright?” added Abigail.

Katie and Daisy looked at each other. Katie fully expected her youngest sister to shout out; well she...she’s being a witch again. Instead she just said, “Yes, we’re fine.”

“What was it, a bird or something?” asked their father rifling through the glass on the floor with the tip of his shoe.

“Must have been a sudden wind gust, I think,” added Daisy, with a squeeze of Katie’s hand.

This warmed Katie’s heart, at least enough to calm her rage. Behind those emotions though was a heavy layer of guilt, feeling that somehow Mable’s bullying of Daisy, was her fault. Obviously this mere shadow of herself had a few things to learn about not only sticking up for herself, but also for her little sister.

There wasn’t any time to ponder that though, as the sound of many footsteps rapidly ascending the staircase could be heard.

“Oh no,” said Libby, “she’s up to it again.”

“Figures,” added Violet.

“No girls,” said their mother, stopping them in their tracks, “this was a gale, a rogue blast and nothing more.”

She said the words but Katie could see in her mother's expression that she didn't quite believe them.

"Now you lot…" added Mrs. Windsor, "make yourself useful and go get a broom and pan and clean this mess up."

The sound of groans and snide comments filled the room.

"Well, can you do some Voodoo or something and fix it, so we don't have to clean up your mess?" asked Ruby, looking at Katie before stomping her foot.

"And why do we have to go downstairs and get a broom? Don't you have one in the closet, to fly around on, under a full moon?" added Libby.

These words were instantly followed by Annabelle and Jessica howling like a wolf.

"You idiots can't even keep your banter straight. Witches don't howl at the moon, that's werewolves," said Daisy. "Morons."

Katie smiled her sister's way, as Mrs. Windsor yelled, "I agree with Daisy."

"Huh…" gasped the sisters in unison.

"Now that will be enough, girls," added Mr. Windsor. "Mind your mother and get this tidied up while I go into town and get some glass."

As the sisters stomped down the stairs, echoes of that's not fair and we didn't break it, could be heard.

Abigail sensing that something more might have occurred knelt down by her two daughters.

"Is everything okay girls?" she asked.

Katie looked to Daisy, searching for permission to perhaps confide this secret about Mabel Wythenshawe bullying her to their mother. However, Daisy subtly shook her head, in a manner that let Katie know, that it was not okay to do so.

"We're all good, mother," replied Katie.

"Daisy?"

"Yeah, all good," smiled Daisy.

"Alright then," said Mrs. Windsor, and she gave each of them a kiss on the forehead. "Just thankful you are both not hurt."

As she left the room, Katie whispered into Daisy's ear.

"Thank you."

Daisy just smiled.

Katie could hear that her sisters were about to begrudgingly make their way back up the stairs, so she knew time was short.

"Don't you worry about a thing," said Katie and gave her sister a hug.

"You leave Mable Wythenshawe and her goons to me. I'll figure something out."

At that moment Green Eyes, who had been silently sitting in the corner of the room, made an awkward sound for a cat. It sounded like a dismayed grunt of sorts.

That night it seemed like the sisters would never fall asleep. Each was excited about seeing their classmates again. Daisy, however, remained noticeably quiet. Well, at least noticeable to Katie.

Just about when Katie was ready to admit defeat and head down the stairs to sleep on the living room sofa, the sandman did eventually come, and all the sisters drifted off to dreamland. In fact, it seemed like they all fell into a very, very deep sleep at the same time, observed Katie somewhat perplexed. Precisely at the same time, actually. Unexpectedly a glowing white stream beamed out from under the closet door, and then it suddenly burst open. Floating forth from the darkness was the lantern, with flame burning bright. A voice emanated from the lamp's core.

"I thought they'd never stop talking," said the familiar voice. "That's why I used the slumber charm on them. I couldn't take waiting in the in-between any longer."

"Eshe, is that you?" asked Katie.

From out of the lantern emerged the younger version of Katie's grandmother.

"Katie, I missed you!" said Eshe.

Katie leapt up, knocking Green Eyes off from the foot of her bed. She ran over and hugged Eshe so tight that she could almost hear Aker saying, easy, easy… you're coming off a bit needy. But she didn't care. She missed her best friend. She missed her a lot.

"Are your things packed?" asked Eshe. "You ready to go?"

Eshe grabbed the lantern, which had begun to lower itself towards the floor.

"I've been waiting to hear word, from Robur, one of *the Seven*, or anyone, quite frankly," replied Katie. "It feels like I'm forgotten when I come back here… like no one cares."

"I promise you this," said Eshe and with her free hand she squeezed Katie's upper arm lovingly, "Katherzine Granxor, you will never be forgotten."

"Yeah, but Katie Windsor might be," said Katie with an air of melancholy, before continuing. "Nevertheless, you are here now, and I am over the moon to see you. I didn't even know if you were coming back or if you'd have to stay in your own time period. All kinds of thoughts go through your head when you have too much time to think. What if Robur changes his mind? What if someone or something casts a more powerful counter-spell? Or even the enchantment just fades. You know even the best of magic spells, wane eventually."

"Same here," replied Eshe, trying to reassure Katie, "I had the similar fears, too. I didn't know for sure I'd be coming either until the wizard showed up," said Eshe. "That's the way Robur likes to do things. I'm sure he has his reasons."

"He always does," added Katie, then she looked a bit crestfallen. "So he couldn't be bothered to come here tonight, I guess?"

Eshe looked a bit uncertain as to what to say.

"Well, after what happened to Professor Hopingráve, I kind of expected he'd be a no show," said Katie.

"It's no one's fault what happened to her," said Eshe. "She died protecting, what she loved most - us - her students."

"I know you're right," said Katie. "It's just seeing Robur carrying her to her resting place, over and over again in my mind. It makes me wish that there was something more I could have done, more that I should have done. And I sometimes think that maybe the wizard wishes I had too."

"That's crazy," said Eshe and then she raised her eyebrows and looked to the floor, realizing what she had said.

Katie gave a subtle grin and replied, "So I've been told."

"Well then Krazy Katie…" joked Eshe with a grin of her own, "now that we can go, we should be doing just that… and get going. I mean, remember what we got for being late to term last year."

And they both looked at each other and laughed, and said together in harmony, "The rusty old handlebar!"

"Swear I thought that wretched thing was going to kill us both," added Eshe, holding her stomach as if she'd eaten something foul. "Can't do that again. No way."

Eshe then noticed Green Eyes, who had just jumped up onto the window sill.

"Good to see you again, Simon," said Eshe.

He meowed and then looked to the forest. Katie got the hint. It seemed that Simon was anxious to return to Chaparral, as well.

"I'll gather my things," Katie said, and went to the closet and fetched her chimes, staff, broom and wand. She struggled to bundle them all together, gripping them tight.

"Here let me help you with that," said Eshe, and she took out her wand and started to cast the same spell she had used to conceal Katie's wind chimes, while fleeing the crumbling *Witch's Glass.*

"Conceal-mentiosa!"

However before she gave the wand a final twist of the wrist, Eshe's eyes suddenly widened, and she noticed something that stopped the stream of magic before it could be cast.

"You have a new wand and broom?" she asked.

"That's right, I haven't seen you since Robur gave them to me," Katie replied. "I had almost forgotten. When I returned, he did greet me, sort of, if only for a second or two."

"Really," said Eshe, surprised.

"Once I stepped through the portal, he was there. He cast the *Wandrous* spell on me, the beam of light found the *Great Oak* and *voila*… a new wand and broom."

The matter of fact way that Katie recounted the story left Eshe a bit taken aback. She could sense Katie was hurt.

"Well, there had to be more than just the old guy popping out of the bushes and yelling boo at you," Eshe said jokingly. "Did he say anything?"

“He told me to believe in myself, that’s magic no one can give you, yada yada yada. He then told me that he was sorry he wasn’t there for me last year. Well, low and behold, he seems to be starting this year off so much better.”

There was an awkward pause before Eshe broke the silence.

“Okay, shall we go then?” she asked.

The three of them, Green Eyes, Katie and Eshe started towards the window preparing to exit, when Katie turned around and caught sight of her sisters sleeping. There with the moonlight shining onto her face was Daisy. Instantly a wave of guilt rushed over Katie. Eshe noticed.

“Is everything alright?”

“I can’t do this,” replied Katie softly. “I can’t leave her.”

“I don’t understand,” said Eshe, with a puzzled look upon her face.

“It’s Daisy, my little sister, she needs me to be here tomorrow. The same bullies that gave me a hard time have decided to turn their attention onto her now… and that just will not do.”

Katie then told Eshe the details of what happened. After she finished retelling the tale, she paused and looked towards Daisy imagining her sweet little sister having to face the same torment that she endured for years... and facing it alone. It caused a lump in her throat and she had to fight back tears.

“She turned to me for help and I can’t let her down," said Katie softly, but determined. "She trusted me. All of me must be here for her, not just that mere shadow of myself that Robur’s spell created. Seems the wizard forgot to give it… a spine.”

“What do you intend to do… not attend the academy this year?” asked Eshe.

“I want to go, of course," replied Katie. “I just -“

Katie stopped mid-sentence not knowing how to finish the thought.

Then Eshe made a mischievous sound, “Hmm…” followed by, “No, you’re going. We can manage both things. Get there on time and also manage a bit of mischief, though we might just be cutting it close.”

Eshe then raised her eyebrows and said, “I’ve got an idea.”

By *skull-speak* something was communicated between the two. With a bit of a grin Katie looked at Eshe and she returned a lingering glance that signaled that the two of them had an unspoken understanding.

“I sometimes forget that you got all of her, my grandmother's, memories in you,” said Katie.

“I have them, yes, but it’s not like you'd think,” explained Eshe. “As with any memory, it lies dormant and even forgotten, until an event, a need, or even a certain smell, awakens it. Just so happens, that this situation has recalled a good one, indeed.”

With a plan put forth and seemingly ready to be implemented, and the sleeping spell sprinkled upon the sisters still in full force, all had a restful night. As an extra safeguard, should Abigail or Charles unexpectedly wander in to check on them, Eshe slept in the chair with a cloak of invisibility overtop of her.

Early the next morning at sunrise, Green Eyes woke Katie and Eshe with a soft meow as he sat upon the window sill.

“Alright, alright, I’m up, already,” said Katie.

She looked across the room and noticed Eshe’s head emerging from under the invisible blanket. She was wiping the night away from her eyes. Still, it appeared quite comical, as her head looked like it was floating in midair. Katie chuckled and felt warm inside seeing her friend and yes, also her grandmother, there in her room.

“Good morning,” said Eshe with a yawn.

“Morning,” replied Katie, with a whisper. “We better get moving before my sisters’ wake up.”

“Oh, no worries there,” said Eshe, as from under the cloak appeared a wand. “That won’t happen until I use the counter spell.”

“Eshe,” said Katie, in a mock scolding tone.

“What?” replied Eshe. “I wanted to sleep in... didn’t you?”

The two girls tidied themselves up, and prepared to depart. Katie wrote a note explaining that she left early because she was eager to get to school, and then fixed it to the mirror that sat just above a chest of drawers, so that her sisters wouldn't be suspicious of her not being there. She quickly gathered up her belongings, before opening the window where Green Eyes loved to sit upon its sill.

Instantly the cold morning air gushed inside, filling the room. After looking to make sure the coast was clear, Katie released the broom from her grasp and it floated out the window, where it waited patiently for its riders to board, hovering two stories above the ground.

“Ready?” asked Katie, as she leapt onto the broom.

Eshe nodded and turned towards the sleeping sisters and gave a wave of the wand. A sparkling mist began to fall over the beds, as Eshe sprung out of the window landing just behind Katie. She was followed in short order by Green Eyes. He was clinging tight to the straw end of the broom. As they soared away, Katie and Eshe could hear the sisters waking.

"Hey, where's Katie?" asked Daisy.

"Probably up a tree," responded Libby, Ruby, Annabelle and Jessica in unison.

"Jerks," mouthed Katie under her breath.

"There's a note on the mirror," could be heard as the broom flew out of earshot of its riders, and headed down the dirt path going towards town.

Not much later, walking down the pathway, approaching, was Mable Wythenshawe, Priscilla Pattensworth and Gertrude Moore. Mable was striding in the front of the pack, of course.

Ahead of them was little Daisy and her friend Isabella Jenkins playing hopscotch, just as they had been doing months before, in the account told to Katie the night before. They were just outside the old schoolhouse, where most of the children took their recess.

"Well, well, well, what do we have here?" asked Mable. "Now this looks familiar."

Priscilla and Gertrude once again moved in and grabbed Daisy, as they had done before.

"Get off of me," said Daisy.

They pushed her back and forth between themselves, before Gertrude knocked Daisy to the ground. Mable glared at Isabella stopping just inches from her face, as if daring her to speak.

"Do you have anything to say?" asked Mable.

Isabella submissively lowered her head.

"Good," said Mable, while Priscilla and Gertrude laughed maniacally.

Feeling satisfied the three girls started to walk away and towards the schoolhouse when a small voice got their attention.

"Actually, yes I do have something to say," said Daisy. "You smell foul. I believe it is the lingering odor from the outhouse you fell into last year."

Mable turned around and stormed directly at Daisy, with Priscilla and Gertrude trailing in stride just behind.

Suddenly just before Mable got into striking distance, Daisy threw her hands up and said, "Wait, wait, wait, there's more but it's a secret."

Daisy gestured for Mable to lean in. Possibly having let curiosity get the best of her, Miss Wythenshawe did just that, and moved in closer.

"See, you were right, it was my sister that used witchcraft to dump you into that hole," whispered Daisy into Mable's ear. "She could do that because she's a witch."

“I knew it!” snarled Mable, and she reared back her hand readying to strike the little truth spiller. Odd thing though, as her fist was about to come in contact with the side of Daisy’s face it stopped mid-blow… frozen in air. This gave time for Daisy to finish her thought.

“Ah, but who said she is the only one?” grinned Daisy, with the wave of her hand.

As she did this motion, a strong wind funnel emerged from out of thin air, and lifted Mable upwards. Daisy guided Miss Wythenshawe like a kite, overtop the same outhouse that she was already intimately familiar with, and dumped her into it again. Just as before, she smashed through the roof, disappeared down the darkened hole, before landing with a syrupy thud, followed by cries of disgust and anger.

With looks of horror mixed with a touch of, déjà vu, written upon their faces, Priscilla and Gertrude began running down the dirt path hoping for a clean getaway. That’s when Isabella Jenkins just seemed to apparate in front of them, stopping them in their tracks.

She stood tall, for a girl all of four feet, in Sunday shoes. Isabella did not say a word; instead she simply took her two pointer fingers and twirled them upward, much like a master composer in an opera hall.

The crazy gusting wind understood her gesture completely, and it obeyed. Instantly Priscilla and Gertrude lifted off the ground and soared directly towards Mable's wailing. And just like that, there were two more sticky plops.

Daisy and Isabella walked overtop the wreckage and stared down into the hole.

"Just so you know," said Daisy, "we can do this and worse anytime we feel like it. So stay on our good side, or else. Alright, then?"

"Yeah, what she, said," added Isabella.

Hurriedly, the two little girls skipped along happily, as they disappeared into the forest, which lined the schoolyard before anyone could get a good look at them, because just then a crowd started to gather seeing the destruction and having heard the screams.

Amongst the people arriving to the first day of school, was the teacher herself, Mrs. Charlotte, wanting to get everything in order before the children arrived.

"Oh dear heavens, not again," said Mrs. Charlotte, inching closer to the blackness. "Is anyone down there?"

"Yes," cried Mable, followed by the wails of Priscilla and Gertrude.

"I might have known, as much," said Mrs. Charlotte to herself.

"It was that Windsor girl and her friend," said Mable sobbing.

"Who, Katie?" asked the teacher.

"No, Daisy and Isabella Jenkins."

"What those two little sweet girls did this, to the three of you?" said Mrs. Charlotte in disbelief. "Impossible."

"It's true! They're witches!" screamed Mable.

"Witches, both of them," demanded Priscilla and Gertrude. "They are!"

As it just so happened, Mrs. Charlotte looked a good ways down the dirt pathway and saw all the Windsor girls walking towards the school. Coming from another direction entirely was Isabella Jenkins with her older sister, Mary.

"So you are telling me that Daisy, who is up the road over there, and Isabella who is way over there… and both are just now coming near the yard, did this to you, and then disappeared, before magically reappearing now beside their family members, is that correct?"

"It's true!" demanded Mable. "It's true!"

Just then the Windsor sisters, excluding Katie, came into earshot.

"Do you know anything about this?" asked Mrs. Charlotte of Daisy.

"Of what? The outhouse?" answered Libby.

"Did you destroy it?" asked Mrs. Charlotte, feeling foolish as she did so.

“No ma'am. We didn’t smash it. We just got here,” replied Daisy.

“Miss Wythenshawe says you caused this, Daisy,” said the teacher. “She said you pushed her in.”

Daisy’s eyes widened and a grin crept over her face as she looked towards the hole. Funny, an odd thing had occurred just as Daisy had neared the old schoolhouse, though she was not going to mention it, especially not at this moment. But for just a split second, she swore that she saw two people who looked exactly like herself and Isabella Jenkins running through the woods. The version of herself even smiled and gave a wink in her direction. However, when she blinked the mirage was gone. So she thought no more of it.

“Ha!" chuckled Daisy to her teacher, unable to contain herself. “So you're saying Mable Wythenshawe is in there! Well, I didn’t do it, I promise.”

“But I wish I had,” she added under her breath.

“How could little Daisy do that to a big bully like Mable?” asked Ruby, covering up her little sister’s unhelpful, yet true comment. “Besides, she’s been with us all morning.”

“Where’s Katie?” asked Mrs. Charlotte, noticing the Windsor girls were one shy of the normal count.

Just then the teacher noticed Katie was coming from the direction of the library. Once Mrs. Hall had her tea in hand, she’d opened the doors a half hour early for any students wanting to get a jump on their studies.

“Ah, there she is,” added Mrs. Charlotte, to herself. “We’ll just have to toss this whole mess up to that wicked foul wind, again, it would seem.

“No! They’re lying - they’re all witches! Witches!” screamed Mable from inside the muck.

“I think the gassy fumes have gotten to the girl,” muttered Mrs. Charlotte, before speaking clearly. “Just hold on, Mable, and we will get the three of you out of there.”

“Ha!” snickered Daisy. “I didn’t know that particular outhouse, could hold so much -”

Quickly Libby and Abigail placed their hands overtop Daisy’s mouth before she could finish her thought.

Mrs. Charlotte suppressed a giggle while acting as though she did not hear the comment, at all. The teacher then turned to a student, “William, be a dear and get the rope from the storage.”

“Yes, Mrs. Charlotte.”

"And Gracie…" started Mrs. Charlotte.

"I know, I know," said Gracie, "hose, bucket, water and soap. I remember from last time."

Gracie's words were drowned out by the whimpers and cries seeping up from the shadowy hole, also seeping was the smell. The opposite emotion filled the forest near the *Great Oak*, as the figures of Daisy and Isabella emerged in the clearing. They were somewhat out of breath, yet still finding enough air to laugh.

"Did you see their faces?" asked the one appearing to be Isabella.

"They will think twice before they mess with either of, us... I mean, them... again," replied the face of Daisy, as it morphed into Katie.

"We can thank older Eshe for that spell," added younger Eshe, just having shed the appearance of Isabella. "It's a doozy."

Suddenly the familiar sound of the chimes filled the forest. Jumping down out of the branches of the *Great Oak* was Green Eyes.

"Meow."

"Yes Simon, we are ready to go," replied Katie.

"We are running late," said Eshe, and she paused and grasped Katie's hand, "but it was worth it."

And she smiled at Katie, and Katie returned an appreciative grin.

With that, Green Eyes entered into and through the bark of the *Great Oak*, followed by Katie and Eshe.

When the resonating bell was stilled, they were gone, and there was only silence remaining on this side of the tree.

CHAPTER TWO

"NO SUBSTITUTE"

Darkness surrounded Eshe, Green Eyes and Katie as they entered the tree. Suddenly their feet lifted off the ground as they were all moving quickly through the portal as the roots, which were hanging like stalactites, brushed over-top of them. As before, the speed to which they were travelling through the portal continually excelled as they pressed onward, which caused them all to hold on for dear life. Katie also started to get that nauseating feeling in the pit of her stomach. While it was evident to Katie that they would not be exiting out on Robur's side of the *Great Oak*, somehow this route also seemed strangely familiar to her… too familiar, in fact. It was exactly like the hellish roller coaster ride from the year before, with the same twists and turns, thought Katie to herself. And the same exit, as well.

"Ouch! Dammit," exclaimed Katie. She landed tail first onto the hard surface made of stone. Her epiphany came too late, her wind chimes rattled and clanked from the impact. "Yeah, that never gets old," Katie added.

"Well it appears we are back at *the Academy of Enchantments and Other Magical Studies,*" said Eshe.

"Hey wait," said Katie rubbing her backside, making her way to her feet, "Aker said this portal was closed, that's why we had to travel to Robur's *Great Oak* by dragon at the end of term."

"I did say that," said a voice in the shadows, now stepping into the light, "but I lied."

"Aker!" yelled Katie and ran over and gave him a huge hug.

"I know, I know… needy," said Katie. "But, I don't care."

“Well, princess,” grinned Aker, “I knew you needed a bit of a pick me up, and riding away from the academy on a dragon… I mean come on, how cool was that?!”

She hugged him again twice as hard.

Green Eyes morphed into Simon and walked straight at the fox-man looking as if he was about to give him a good thrashing.

“You mean to tell me that I had to cling onto a dragon’s back hundreds of feet in the air, for nothing? So you could have a joy ride?”

Aker put his hands up to shield himself, “Whoa, whoa, flying on a dragon is never for nothing. We looked good up there, old friend. Can't deny that, am I right?”

The fox-man patted Simon on the shoulder, but the cat-man protector shrugged away shaking his head in disbelief.

Eshe interjected, more to switch the subject, than to actually offer a greeting.

“Good to see you, Aker.”

“Likewise, Lady Eshe. My pleasure, indeed.”

Simon muttered under his breath as he walked towards the doors at the end of the hallway. It sounded like… “Sahti is right, he really is just a gigantic -" But before he could finish the sentence Simon pushed open the door and returned to his cat form.

"He'll get over it," said Aker and rolled his eyes. "Come on, you guys are just in time, to only be a little late."

Katie and Eshe gathered their belongings and followed Aker down the hallway.

Through *skull-speak* Eshe heard Katie's thoughts.

"I know," said Eshe, "I thought he might be too."

Katie lowered her head and nodded, "As we always say, the old wizard has his reasons."

As they passed through the doorway and out into the *Great Hall*, the passageway sealed itself behind them and disappeared.

Katie turned back from eyeing the portal as it evaporated and she began scanning for Green Eyes. But his white fur was nowhere in sight. That doesn't mean he wasn't there. Because the hall was packed with students all dressed in the colored robes of their respective houses, hurrying on their way to their respective classes. There were a couple of lads with heads of jackals laughing loudly as they passed. A group of girls thin with long necks like flamingos giggling in stride after them. Another student who appeared to be part porcupine came rolling through the hall curled up in a ball with spikes protruding out of his red garments.

"Ouch! Hey watch it!" said a tall girl who appeared to be part giraffe. She had just been bumped by porcu-boy.

"Sorry," he said as he rolled on.

Overhead, were a troop of young gorilla-boys leaping from the top of the staircase to several chandeliers. They were following each other one after another, after another. All made long throaty belches as they swung by.

"You there!" said a familiar voice now emanating out of a cloud of smoke that rapidly appeared. "You lot need to keep it down. And do not break those chandeliers. They're as old as this academy."

As the words spoken began to trail off, a pointed hat materialized from out of the fog. It lifted to reveal Headmistress Valborga with her chin stuck outward and sporting a no nonsense expression, which was also as old as the aforementioned hanging crystal.

"Really," she muttered to herself out loud, "you'd think this place a jungle, not a refined institute of higher learning, by the way some of you treat it."

The headmistress stepped forth from the dissipating smoke while in full stride. To Katie's surprise Green Eyes was walking briskly beside her slick blackened boots. Just then Headmistress Valborga spotted something that caused her face to grimace, even wince in pain.

"Aker," she said.

"Headmistress," replied the fox, "it's a pleasure."

"Well it's something, alright," glared the headmistress, before quickly turning her attention to Katie and Eshe. "Miss Windsor, I found your cat, or rather he found me."

"Thanks," replied Katie, puzzled with a glance towards Green Eyes. Through *skull-speak*, she almost asked did you seek out the headmistress to have a private conversation and what was that conversation about? In the end, she thought better of it, realizing that Valborga would have most certainly been aware of a student using such a manner of communication in front of her. Katie did not have much time to contemplate the matter as the headmistress's gaze had just found Eshe.

"Miss Eshe Leota, I see you are back with us, this year."

Eshe looked at the headmistress in the same manner as the headmistress had just looked at Aker. The two of them seemed to pick right up with the same, *you could cut the air with a knife*, vibe, they had shared the year before.

"Should I not be here…" asked Eshe, sternly, before adding a delayed, "Headmistress Valborga? I do know that the wizard thinks I should be here."

Aker then added in, "As does, the old guy, in regards to me… especially under the present circumstances, with Osiris," started the fox-man, before stopping himself from spilling too much information out into the open air. "Well, anyways, he wanted to make sure I watched over the portal until our two students here, arrived. And make sure that they did so safely."

"Yes, I was just made aware of that," said the headmistress, and then muttered out loud, "a little forewarning would have been nice, being I have an entire academy with many charges under my care."

Headmistress Valborga gave a scolding glance at Green Eyes, which made Katie bite her lip even harder now. It would seem Green Eyes, might have had some communications with Robur which he had not disclosed.

“Let’s just hope this year will be a little less eventful than the last,” said the headmistress, while staring directly at Eshe in a game of who will blink first.

“I hope so as well,” replied Eshe.

It felt as though someone had hexed the clock ticking in the *Great Hall*, and made each second feel like an eternity. Luckily someone broke the spell.

“Oh please, boring,” said Aker rolling his eyes with a yawn. “When has any year in this academy been uneventful? I personally saw it as my job to make sure that didn’t happen while I was here.”

The headmistress lifted her gaze off of Eshe, and raised her nose upward at the fox-man.

“Finally, something we agree on,” relinquished the headmistress, “You have a point. Every year has its challenges. Right now, your challenge is to get to your first class. Usually tradition dictates that the student petition each professor to have them add you to their roster, however, since you both missed orientation, and how hard last year was on you both… well anyways, I took liberties. Here are your schedules.”

Eshe actually thought she saw a glimmer of emotion in the headmistress’ eyes.

She handed them each a piece of rolled up parchment with a red ribbon tied around the center. Both girls were about to unfasten the binding when a bell rang out.

"No time to peruse it now, it is almost noon. You both have to rush to the atrium for *Magelic Botany*," said Headmistress Valborga, and she instantly noticed the look of grief that fell over Katie and Eshe's faces. However, the headmistress did not give an opening for the obvious questions that were swimming around in both girls' heads.

"Hurry girls, can't be late on day one," added the headmistress, "First impressions are essential, so make it good."

She then turned and glared at Aker, "A bad one can leave a taste that lingers for many moons."

Aker put his hand to his chest and dropped his chin, as if to say without words, who me?

A plume of smoke appeared just before the headmistress. She turned away from the fox, and lifted her nose upward as if stepping away from a foul smelling garbage bin.

"Zelma, I'm truly hurt," said Aker in a mocking tone, as the headmistress disappeared into the mist. He was performing a bit which elicited a few giggles from Katie.

Then abruptly a sharp pointed stream of energy emerged out of the dissipating smoke and zapped the fox on his big toe, which made him hop up and down. A few words followed the bolt.

"*Now* you truly are… hurting," said the vanished headmistress, as her words echoed where the smoke just was. "There's a difference."

"There's no difference between you and an old bag, you, you, you old bag," muttered Aker as he had to stomp on the fuming foot with his non-smoldering one.

"We have to run," said Katie trying to not let the fox see her suppressing a laugh. She looked towards Green Eyes, "See you in the dormitory, later."

Green Eyes gave a parting meow, and darted off.

Katie then reached over to the fox, who was still concerning himself with his aching foot, and gave him a quick hug. "I better see you soon, okay?"

"You bet, prin-" Aker stopped himself. "I mean, Miss Windsor."

Eshe gave a wave, "See you soon."

As they rushed away, Eshe turned to Katie and said, "All the sudden I'm hungry for bacon."

"Right?" replied Katie.

“Really,” said Aker overhearing them as they exited.

“Sorry,” chuckled Katie, as she disappeared from sight.

As they turned the corner leaving the *Great Hall*, the hallways were packed with many students who were racing in all directions.

“We’re never going to get to the atrium in time on foot,” said Eshe. “It’s just too crowded.”

“Well, we’re no longer first-years, so brooms it is,” smiled Katie and she jumped on her broom and ascended upward.

“Good point,” replied Eshe, and followed suit.

As they soared overhead of many students below, suddenly Katie noticed something in the distance coming at them at a rapid rate of speed. Whatever it was closing in upon them, was moving wildly, erratically.

“What the heck is that?” asked Katie.

“Oh crap, I know what it is,” said Eshe.

At that moment a metal clicking, ringing high pitched bell sound rang out, as well as a circus clown horn which seemed to squeeze itself a few times in succession. The sounds blended perfectly with the screams of horror, which was being emitted by the two new students that were holding on for dear life.

As the object came better into view it was clear to Katie now as well, that it was… "The handlebar," said Katie, as she swerved to get out of the way.

"Whoa," said Eshe pulling up just short of crashing into a wall. "Damn thing is going to kill someone one of these days."

The rusty old handlebar seemed to smile as it flew by, though the two students were a little green in the gills, though that might be because they appeared to be part aquatic.

Katie smiled back and waved.

Eshe of course, did not.

After a few more twists and turns, they found themselves nearing the atrium just in time to almost be late. Ahead of them was the same slick marble floor that the old handlebar had thrown them onto, the year before, and at the end of the hallway stood the finely polished wooden door.

Katie recalled, the first time she laid eyes upon Professor Hopingráve… it was right here. Upon the marble, Katie had laid flat on her back looking upwards, having come to a crashing halt at the foot of the door. Today as she reflected, she could almost still hear it creak open to reveal the professor in a long black draped trench coat, a buttoned up blouse, with firmly pressed wrinkle free skirt, and glossy black boots close to Katie's head.

While on that day the professor wore an expression of mild disgust, it was hard to believe that just a year later Katie would be remembering the same woman, whom she thought she'd despise, as one of the bravest soul's she had ever known. Then the scene from that dreadful night flashed across her mind, and she saw herself with tears falling from her eyes as she lay atop Professor Hopingráve's lifeless body. Even the smell of the burning oak wood re-entered her nostrils. Her chest tightened as she once more felt the tension as the gathered crowd of students and professors parted as the ghostly image of an old man in a long white robe appeared in the middle of the atrium.

The pain on his face, made her feel a fresh wave of guilt all over again. As she thought of the wizard bending down and picking up Professor Hopingráve's body and carrying her to the last mausoleum, kissing her and saying goodbye, she concluded that it was no wonder, that he no longer cared to be bothered with the girl that cost his true love's life.

Katie just couldn't shake the feeling that she failed to be the heroine, it seemed she was expected to be. Instead, she let her emotions get the better of her. In the end though, she thought to herself as she dismounted her broom and pushed open the large wooden door, well, that's why I am here, at the academy… I want to be stronger next time when I have to face the darkness that I know is out there. And that darkness I know all too well... his name is Osiris.

As Katie and Eshe entered the atrium the rest of the class were already present.

The first couple of students they spotted had red robes. They noticed Katie and Eshe, as well.

"Well, of course these two would have to make a scene by being the last to arrive," grunted Tamrah lifting her rhino-horned nose upward. Though she gestured as if she was speaking to Kilmon, her words were loud enough for all to hear. And all did hear, and the entire room turned around.

"No dragons available to fly you in today?" asked Tamrah. "I'm sure the headmistress wouldn't mind opening the glass house roof so you could make the grand entrance, you so desire."

Katie and Eshe both felt a bit embarrassed, and both thought the same thing… thanks Aker. However before either of them felt obligated to respond, another voice spoke up.

"Eshe, Katie, I missed you both!" said a girl in black robes, with the features of a panther with ice blue eyes, as she pushed her way past Tamrah and Kilmon and threw her arms around both of her fellow bunk-bors. "I was wondering when you'd arrive."

"Vexika!" said Eshe and Katie at the same time with warm grins.

"Well quite frankly, we were wondering that, too," added Katie.

"Whatcha mean?" replied Vexika with a puzzled look.

Eshe shot Katie a glance that said… we still have secrets to keep. Actually she did say it through *skull-speak*, so Katie returned a stern look, being they weren't supposed to use that form of communication unless absolutely necessary. It would seem that both would have to re-acclimate to being back on academy grounds.

"Oh you know, there's always drama when you go home to spend the summer with the family," said Katie, trying not to show any signs of deception. In truth, she was bored to tears dying to get back.

"Tell me about it," grinned, Vexika. "I've got seven stupid brothers, each dumber than the one that came before. Always one of them in your way, and causing trouble. Prayed for a sister, but oh well."

She paused and her eyes glistened, "Well… now I've got two of them, the both of you." And again she hugged Katie and Eshe tight, as the mock sound of someone gagging emanated from exactly where Tamrah and Kilmon and others in red robes from the *House Stormander*, were standing.

"Ignore them," said Vexika.

Suddenly she noticed that Katie was already doing that, ignoring them. Her gaze was fixed on the eighth mausoleum that was just past the *Stormanders* and to the left.

"I know," said Vexika, "it's still all too sad, isn't it?"

"Yeah, it is," replied Katie, feeling a fresh wave of heat rushing over her again.

"I wonder who they are going to get to-" started Eshe, but stopped herself before saying replace, having noticed the expression on Katie's face, which had her think better of it. "Well, you know… teach the class this year."

"Don't know," replied Vexika. "Got everyone talking, though… a lot of guesses, being tossed about in the halls. It's a mystery. And it seems we will be the first to find out, being this is the first class of the semester."

Katie didn't seem curious at all. To her, this place was Professor Hopingráve through and through; the marble, the perfectly kept plants, the eight mausoleums, the atrium glass and the trees. At that very second something odd caught her eye. Katie had spotted a tall tree standing in the exact place that the Nyx Erebos had burned down.

"I see they got another oak," said Katie inquisitively. "It's remarkable how much it looks like the *Shadow Tree*."

That's because they are one in the same, said a voice that echoed overhead and all around.

Katie looked at Vexika and asked, "Did you hear that?"

"Hear what?" replied the panther-girl.

"I heard it, too," said Eshe.

The two of them eyed one another and somehow the both of them were drawn to the tall oak.

"Hey, where are you guys going?" asked Vexika trying to keep up.

Eshe and Katie seemed possessed as they moved through the gathered students.

"Hey, watch it!" bellowed Kilmon with his long pointed crocodile-like snout. "Damn normals … they think they own the place."

"Seems this year will be no different," added Tamrah. "It's what you get when you let the wrong kind in."

If Katie and Eshe heard the *Stormanders* say this, they didn't show it. They stayed on course to the tree. Once there, they both stopped just on the outer edge of its branches.

How can this be the same tree, asked Katie using *skull-speak. We watched it burn to ashes.*

We did more than that, said Eshe using *skull-speak*, and she looked at Katie, and continued… *We used it to find the Mother of Bones' cave.*

Does that mean the pathway to the Witch's Glass is back as well, asked Katie through skull to skull communiqué.

No, answered another voice, inside Katie and Eshe's minds. *The portal was rerouted to somewhere else, somewhere more pleasant, indeed.*

"It can't be you… can it?" asked Katie out loud.

Vexika, having just caught up with them, gave Katie a worried glance. However, before the panther-girl could ask who she was talking to, the answer formed.

Just then, a murky figure leapt from out of the top of the oak, and landed next to the *Shadow Tree.*

"It's good to see you all," said the ghostly figure of Professor Hopingráve, to the gathered students. She grinned, giving a slight warm wink in Katie's direction.

The entire class collectively gasped and then broke into applause. It seemed the entire academy was cheering. In fact, a few owls might have soared out through the open glass shingles on the atrium, so as to alert the rest of the magical community.

Katie couldn't hold it back; she had tears fill her eyes. And before her lips could ask how, it seems her mind had already offered up the question and the professor heard it.

"I know you all have a lot of questions," said Professor Hopingráve. "However, today I am here to teach. Though, I will say this… we live in a world of magic, and nothing ever really dies. It just changes, and lives on in another form."

The professor gestured towards the eight mausoleums.

"In my many lifetimes, I too have existed in many forms. Now on this 9th life, I enjoy an ethereal existence. In fact, the roots of this oak sought out my soul; crawled its way over to it actually. And in doing so, it made me part of itself… made me *the Spirit of the Shadow Tree*."

The professor gave a glance towards Katie and Eshe, and using *skull-speak* said, just like another spirit, who is dear to me, inhabits a very similar oak.

“Since the *Shadow Tree*, has indeed risen from the ashes, like a phoenix, and now stands tall once more here at the academy... I saw no reason why a ghostly version of myself, couldn’t or shouldn’t do the same and be your teacher.”

With these words more cheering broke out. It felt more like a rock concert than the beginning of a new semester. Every other professor in the academy as well as its headmistress had now filed into the glasshouse to witness their beloved *Magelic Botany* teacher’s return.

Moved by the outpouring of emotion, Professor Hopingráve paused, holding back tears of her own. Where there was just cheering and happiness in the room, a serious tone arose. At this point it seemed that nearly the entire student body was present. They were hanging on the professor's every word.

“For someone who has lived so many lives, I have rarely found that anything in the magical realm is truly a coincidence. And I do not believe my return is one either. Though, I could not in good conscience stand before all of you and carry on with a charade, all the while knowing that there is danger lurking just outside our gates.”

A stunned hush fell over the atrium, as Professor Hopingráve continued, "It was no mysterious fire that burned down the *Shadow Tree*, and took my life. It was an attack!"

A few round of gasps and gulps rippled throughout the student body. The professor continued, "And while many of us have chosen to keep secrets in the belief that it spares you, our students, from the harshness of the world outside these walls… I… I cannot do so any longer."

The professor's eyes once again met Katie's, and suddenly Katie felt a warm heat churning under the collar of her school uniform.

"See, an evil force had found a way to use the *Shadow Tree* as a portal. And the name of the evil is quite familiar to you all. It is well known amongst all *magixians*. The attacker was a powerful sorceress known as the *Mother of Bones*; she is the mother of the one they call… Lord Osiris, the *Dark One*."

Terror filled the eyes of the all too recently happy students. Even Headmistress Valborga looked concerned, but it was clear to Katie, at least, that the headmistress and the professor must have had a conversation about this not so impromptu orientation. Like Professor Hopingráve, Katie also did not believe in coincidences.

"See, many, many years ago a dark alchemist who served the royal family was banished to the *Forbidden Caves* of the *Great Valley* at the foot of *Clarion's Peak*, beneath the castle's dungeons. He tried to raise a dark army to do his bidding and in so doing regain his freedom from his fiery prison. But he was stopped by the Princess of Chaparral and *the Seven*. And I know you all have heard talk of the great battle of *Clarion's Peak*. It's not just rumors, the battle happened. Osiris was indeed defeated and presumed dead."

The professor paused, and she could see that Katie and Eshe had blush red cheeks. They looked as if at any second their clandestine cover would be exposed to the entire student body.

The ghostly professor continued, "As I am living proof – in a manner of speaking – that all things can return in various forms… Osiris is back, as well. Before the *Mother of Bones* met her demise she was able to free the *Dark One* by conjuring up the most forbidden of spells. In doing so, the *Shadow Tree* was sacrificed... lost. It was this dark magic that also took my life. It was in this magic, and this magic alone, to which lies the blame."

Katie lowered her chin, somehow knowing that the professor was saying this for her benefit. As if clairvoyant, Professor Hopingráve, could sense Katie's guilt over not being able to save her that night, and wanted to let her know it wasn't a burden she had to carry any longer.

"Professor Toohasi and I fought to keep these attackers from entering our academy. We knew we had to close down the portal by which they would gain access... the *Shadow Tree.* In so doing, it was through the oak that I had a window into the sorceress' efforts. A seer in all of my lifetimes, I have been, so I was not surprised to foresee death, however, this was the first time I had foreseen my own. I knew it was at hand. Frightening, even though I had died before; still, frightening no less. Yet, I also knew how many would perish should the *Mother of* Bones dark desires come to fruition."

For a moment Professor Hopingráve, reflective as though she was reliving the event once again, in her memory, gave a melancholy look towards Professor Toohasi, which contained a bit of a grin as she recalled her owl-like friend standing firm by her side… true to the end.

The professor lifted her chin back up firmly and concluded, "It was in these final moments of my life that I saw the best of us."

Professor Toohasi sheepishly looked towards his feet, embarrassed.

Professor Hopingráve, continued, "But I also saw darkness as well. I witnessed the *Dark One*, Osiris escape through the *Witch's Glass* and he transformed into a black fog, before drifting into the forest just below the *Forbidden Caves*.

The last thing I felt coming through my connection with the *Shadow Tree*, was his anger. The *Dark One* will not go away quietly into the night. He has returned. We got lucky once, I fear the next attack we might not be so fortunate. As your professors, we must not only protect you… but prepare you, as well. So with that, let us begin."

As the class was coming to a close, Katie and Eshe tried to make their way to the front of the room in hopes of getting some one on one time with the ghostly professor. Katie had a million questions tumbling like bingo balls inside her head. However, as the ending bell rang out, Professor Hopingráve abruptly thanked everyone for the warm reception upon her first day back from the grave, as their new, yet very familiar, teacher of *Magelic Botany - The Study of Magical Plants*. She then reminded the class to read the first chapter of *Deadly Herbs... Friend or Foe - Depends On What You Know*, by next week, and to be prepared because there would indeed be a quiz. With that said, the professor leapt straight up into the air, with her shadow fighting hard to stay attached to its maker, and returned to the inner dwellings of the newly risen *Shadow Tree*.

“Professor,” started Katie, but her call was drowned out by the clapping of all the students. Though there were a few moans and groans about the assignment, of course.

“Well, I didn’t see that coming,” said Eshe.

“No, not at all,” replied Katie still fighting back tears, with a sizable lump in her throat.

“It’s only day one and already there’s more excitement than the last few months combined,” smiled Eshe with a hand on Katie's shoulder.

“I have so many questions, though,” replied Katie. “Eshe, I know you said that before the shards of the *Witch’s Glass* faded, you saw Cassandra, the *Mother of Bones* die while trapped inside. We now have absolute confirmation from the professor that Osiris did indeed, make it out, in some form or another. However, the question I have is whether or not Professor Hopingráve or even Robur are aware of the fate of Zalika. Did she survive, too? Or did she perish within the *Witch’s Glass*, alongside Cassandra?”

“That is a very good question,” said Eshe, with a nod of the head.

“Well, it would be nice if someone, with an answer, would stick around long enough to let me ask it,” said Katie in frustration.

CHAPTER THREE
"TOGETHER"

After *Magelic Botany*, Eshe and Katie finally unfurled the scrolls that Headmistress Valborga had given them. To their delight, they both had the same class schedules, and the classes were in the same order as the previous year. Katie instantly thought to herself, this is no coincidence. No, this was Robur's doing. He wanted to make sure Eshe would be near, should Katie be attacked. She wasn't upset; in fact, Katie thought it meant he still cared. Even though, she felt very distant from the wizard, presently.

Just then, Vexika peeked over Eshe's shoulder.

"Your schedules, let's have a look. Hey, we got almost every class together," exclaimed the panther-girl. "Well, all of them except for that one."

All three girls read the words out loud in unison.

"*Clandestine Studies*, taught by *Professor to be named.*"

Each girl wore similar expressions upon their face. Katie put it best, "What the heck is that?"

After thinking for a moment, she then added, "And when and where is it?"

"Guess, we'll find out," replied Eshe.

Just then, as if the scroll was listening to their conversation, the words appeared... *time and place to be determined.*

"Well, that's just lovely. Determined by whom?" asked Katie puzzled.

Vexika and Eshe both raised their shoulders in an, *i-dunno* manner.

Just then the bell rang out cutting the conversation short.

"What's next?" asked Katie while scanning the scroll.

"Professor Bokor," they all said together.

“I thought that *Voodoology* had to be scheduled at sunrise on the dot, because of the professor’s condition. You know being a vampire and all,” said Katie.

Eshe and Vexika both gasped slightly as did some passersby. Seems that the label, vampire, wasn’t used here quite as casually as it was on Katie’s world.

“Well he is one, right?” added Katie, in a *sorry* kind of way.

As if the scroll heard Katie’s question, the words *Voodoology - the study of Voodoo, Hexes, Curses and Dark Incantations, taught by Professor Barclay Bokor,* moved to the front of the list. The words… *Class begins at sunrise on the dot*, also appeared, with the tag line, *starting tomorrow. As for today, the class begins… now!*”

Right on cue, the warning bell rang out. The girls had but a few minutes to get to the professor’s study before the late bell would sound.

With brooms under bodies, and chasing down the black panther-girl’s tail as it weaved through the crowd of students, Katie and Eshe hovered overhead nearing the class.

“Oh no, that darn angry eyeball filled stairwell,” said Katie exhaustedly, so that both Eshe and Vexika could hear her frustration. “No matter how much I try to remember the correct combination, I always wind up stepping on an eye or two."

"Don't worry we'll do it, together," said the panther-girl. "Follow me."

When they reached the staircase because the well was tight, the girls had to dismount their brooms and put foot to pavement, of course. Vexika, being the cat-girl she was, just seemed to spring up the stairs with no problem and without one eyelid angrily opening.

"Just step where I stepped," called out Vexika from the top of the stairs.

Eshe did just that, and likewise left the lids undisturbed, as did a few other almost tardy students.

"Come on, Katie," called out Eshe and Vexika, cheering her on. "You got this."

Katie on the other hand… deep inside whispered words of doubt, and did not at all, feel like *she had this*. It seemed her fears did indeed prove to be prophetic.

"Hey, there! Watch where you're walking! Oh, it's you!" said a blinking, watering eye.

In an instant, several other eyeballs chimed in.

"Oh, great… she's back."

"She's much heavier then she looks."

"Indeed."

"How would she like a boot in the eye?"

Katie looked terribly embarrassed, as she ascended the well, stepping gingerly.

"Sorry, sorry," she kept repeating over and over, until she finally made it to the top and stepped through into Professor Bokor's dimly lit, dusty old study.

"To all returning students, welcome back to *Voodoology.* And to first-years… greetings, this is the study of voodoo, hexes, curses and dark incantations… and I am your guide into said darkness. I am Professor Bokor, and if you are faint of heart, please leave, while you still can, under your own power."

And with that, two first-years exited through the door. Within seconds, echoes of angry comments by trounced upon eyeballs filled the air, once again.

"Watch it, first year!"

"How dare you!"

The professor waited until the enraged stairwell quieted down to continue.

Katie grinned, as she looked upon the bat-like, wolf-like professor, with grey hair and long boney, well-manicured fingers. She was thinking how he was still just as scary as she remembered, and how much she loved it. *It was great to be back at the academy,* she thought.

Professor Bokor abruptly froze in his tracks and looked to the rafters, as if he had received a transmission from the great beyond.

"Yes, Miss Windsor, it is good to see you, too."

He smiled as much as his creature-like face would allow him to, when suddenly his eyes widened. The professor seemed to be receiving yet another transmission. He extracted his wand and gave it a twirl, which caused him to become a whirlwind of magic. As he had done before, when they first visited the professor's study, a bat-like creature emerged out of the gust, and soared directly at Katie and Eshe. In a puff of smoke, the wolf-man looking Professor Bokor was standing directly behind them, whispering in their ears.

"Miss Windsor, Miss Leota… a word, please."

The professor gestured for the girls to follow him, out into the hall, atop the stairwell. They did so, with curious looks upon their faces.

"What I have to say, is not meant for prying ears. So I asked to speak to you alone. A message is on the wind… someone or something reaching out to you, to your blood. It's not close. It is a message from far, far, away."

"What is the message, Professor?" asked Katie.

"That's the thing… it's not a communique of words, so much as a longing," replied Professor Bokor. "When I began to probe further within my mind, my soul… the window abruptly closed."

Eshe and Katie eyed one another with a healthy bit of skepticism and a tinge of concern.

"Well, I thought you should know," added the professor, and once again became bat-like, and returned to the front of the class. "Alright then, first-years tell me why you believe you can survive to the end of term, and should I allow you into this class?"

And with that another two pupils exited.

Katie whispered into Eshe's ear as they returned to class.

"Who or what is the professor speaking of?"

Eshe just raised her shoulders in a, *you've got me,* manner.

What could it be, thought Katie, to herself. But just then Professor Bokor began to demonstrate how to properly defend oneself against a werewolf attack. He was howling at a simulated moon which hung high just below the rafters in the center of the study. It was impossible for

Katie to concentrate on anything else, when the entire class, were atop their desks seeming to collectively be… barking mad.

“Hilarious,” mouthed Eshe, at Katie.

Katie just grinned, and the two were-witches grabbed their two crystal amulets each dangling from gold chains; Katie, the amethyst and Eshe the rose charm. Both girls lifted their chins, pursed their lips into circles and began howling, as well.

After *Magelic Botany,* all three girls made their way to the *Great Hall* for a quick bite to eat before rushing to their next class which started at sunset on the dot… as it read on the scrolls stretched out in Katie and Eshe’s hands… *X-chanted Warcery – The Study of Rivalry, Dueling and Combat. Taught by Professor Miron Montakha.*

The girls had the same schedules as the previous year, so as in the other classes they had just attended, there was a distinct possibility that two familiar faced *House Stormander* students might be in this class as well. They were right.

“Last year you both got lucky,” said Tamrah. “Care for a rematch?”

The croc-boy to Tamrah’s side, Kilmon, opened his jaw enough to show what looked like an endless row of sharpened teeth.

Before Katie or Eshe could answer, Professor Montakha stepped in to stop things from escalating, remembering the bloodbath that took place on the girls first day in his class a year earlier.

"Miss Badara, Mr. Kroy… that will be enough. You can fight alongside the rest of your housemates in the circle, in short order. More pressing matters are at hand. As Professor Hopingráve noted in her spiritual return today, the *Dark One* is indeed back and we must prepare you for whatever… come what may. Personal grudges will not serve you well in the face of such a dark threat. You must have one another's backs. With that said, prepare for battle."

The fiery phoenix-man spread his wings all ablaze and raised up in the air, and spoke with authority, "*House Zabar* to the left, *House Violeta*, to the right. You will duel in the center ring."

The violet-purple robed students went to one side and the silver robed students went to the other.

"I want to see what you returning students actually learned last year. And new students, we will see what you are instinctively made of when thrown into battle. Select your weapons from the arsenal provided to your side. Face off one on one."

All the competitors chose their weapons and gripped them tight. Some with shaky hands, some more steady,"

"You there," said the professor, "choose your weapon."

The empty handed student dug his clawed feet into the dirt and replied, "I'm good."

"Have it your way," said Professor Montakha, shaking his head, believing this would no doubt be a hard lesson learned for the student, but he did admire his courage.

"Be on your guard," screamed out the professor from the sky above, "and best of luck to you all! Now fight!"

The first-years were quickly knocked out in short order. All except one. He was the student that did not take a weapon in hand. It would seem that he did not need one after all. He was a tiger headed boy from *House Zabar*. While the others tapped out almost instantly, the tiger-boy stood tall with a grin that seemed more suited for a facial expression one would wear at an amusement park, not one in the heat of battle. All the same, the young student seemed to be relishing the defeating of each challenger. His clawed hands sent all that neared him soaring through the air.

“Who is this young warrior?” asked Professor Montakha, out loud, yet to himself.

Vexika, who had very good hearing, being part panther and all, seemed to have heard the professor’s question. Or at least, she echoed as much.

“Ah yeah, who is he, indeed?” she said ending with a growly purr, which made Katie and Eshe snicker.

At the end of the match, it was the tiger-boy first-year, who was left standing alone in the center ring. A true hush fell over the rather large class. Well, it was not a total hush, because there were quite a few groans, and rubbing of sore limbs amongst the unsettled dust.

“What is your name?” asked Professor Montakha lowering himself down to the ground, as his flamed wings and head, extinguished.

“Rah,” growled the tiger-boy, who still had an overflow of adrenalin flowing through his veins.

“Well done, young warrior, well done.”

Rah walked much like a tiger after a kill, as he left the fighter’s circle. His gaze caught Vexika’s eye, and for just a moment, there might have been the slightest of a grin.

But then it was quickly gone as Professor Montakha rose back into the air and cried out… "*House Hallox* to the left, *House Stormander* to the right."

Vexika, Katie and Eshe, and all the other black robed students lined up on one side of the circle, with chosen weapon in hand. On the other side were Tamrah and Kilmon, who were flanked by several red robed students.

The rhino-girl grabbed a double edged spear. While the croc-boy snatched up a club and smacked it into the ground so hard, it felt as though the challengers' circle shook, because it did.

Katie chose a staff, of course. Eshe grinned and followed suit, taking up a stick as well, while the panther-girl surprised everyone gathered by taking no weapon in hand, at all.

"Not you too, Miss Vee," said Professor Montakha.

Vexika's eyes tightened, though she did give a quick glance towards Rah, as he stood on the sidelines. She had his attention.

"So be it," added the professor, with his fiery wings spread wide. "On your guard… and… fight!"

Instantly Tamrah and Kilmon rushed towards Eshe and Katie, but it was Vexika who moved like the cat she was and circled around the two

Stormanders yanking their feet out from under them. Tamrah and Kilmon slid face first in the dirt coming to rest in a cloud of dust just before Eshe and Katie.

"That was very impressive," said Katie to Eshe, while looking at the rhino-girl, who was spitting dirt out of her mouth.

"Oh yeah, impressive indeed," replied Eshe unable to suppress a snicker.

Just then several blasts of energy struck Katie and Eshe, sending them flying through the air and knocking them outside of the circle before the match had barely begun. They were taken out by a red robed student who had the features of a tarantula spider with eight fur covered limbs, each holding wands. Salex Spix, had fired them all at the same time, and he looked rather pleased with himself for having done so.

Also rather pleased was Tamrah, but not for long. Because no sooner had a smile appeared on the Rhino girl's face, when it was abruptly wiped away as Vexika dug her claws into two of Salex's many arms, and her tail, acting much like a lasso, ensnared his chest. In what seemed to be one quick motion, she tossed the much larger foe like a shot put ball, sending him out of the ring, as well.

One by one the other students took one another out of the competition, until it was down to three. Two red robes and one black.

"You're going down," said Tamrah to the panther-girl standing in the center of the ring, as the rhino-girl and croc-boy circled her, waiting for the right moment to strike.

"Well, are you going to talk me to death, or are we going to do this?" replied Vexika.

Tamrah with double edged spear in hand raced towards Vexika. The croc-boy seeing this followed suit with his club raised high ready to bash the panther-girl.

However, Vexika remained calm, not at all like one who was about to be pummeled. Instead she glanced once again at Rah, and winked at him just a mere second before a spear was to pierce her heart and a club flatten out her head. It was hard for the naked eye to see what happened next, because she moved so fast. Still, all that were gathered did witness what occurred, and were left stunned.

The panther-girl lassoed the spear with her tail and grasped the club with her claws, and somehow used her opponents own ravenous force against them. She spun them in a manner that sent both spiraling through the air like Frisbees out of the field of competition, and into the loser's circle, if you will.

All gathered erupted in applause, all that were not wearing red robes, that is. Eshe, Katie and everyone else ran out and lifted Vexika onto their shoulders.

Standing on the side of the field was Rah, grinning and eyeing the panther, who certainly noticed.

"Good class! Good!" said Professor Montakha, as he lowered back to the ground. "These were hard fought battles. I am proud of you all. Now remember the lessons learned today."

He paused as the students hung on his words.

"You must have one another's back. Rage alone never wins. And the most important lesson is one that will serve you well until your dying days."

Again he paused.

"Of all the weapons you can choose to hold… belief in one's self is the strongest. Always."

With those words and a few more pats on the back for Vexika, the class was dismissed.

*

Later that evening in the girls' dormitory, Eshe, Katie and Vexika were catching up, and talking about their summer break. Katie of course, was being evasive about the particulars, but made it very clear that she was miserable the entire time, and couldn't wait to get back.

"I couldn't wait to return either. I just love being here with my bunk-bors again," said Vexika, throwing her arms around Katie and Eshe.

The panther-girl then scratched Green Eyes behind the ears.

"I missed you, too!"

Just then out in the hallway, Rangord, a student who resembled a wild boar, passed by the door. He was guiding a new group of first-years to the dormitory, as he had done the prior year for Katie and Eshe.

"Ah, I see that the two of you are back," said Rangord, with a sour look upon his face.

"Look everyone," he said out loud to the first-years. "We have the honor of being in the presence of two memory locks, experts. They took mere seconds to learn and master the locks and the spells that make them fly. Mind you, they did this on their first tries." The wild boar looking guide, then turned the Katie and Eshe and said, "Maybe you both should take over leading the group, being you are so much wiser and well versed in the art of well… everything magic, than say a simpleton such as myself."

The young man was the one whom had introduced Katie and Eshe to memory locks the year before, and he still seemed to be a sore boar, feeling that they had lied about their abilities, in order to mock him.

Katie seeing that Rangord's feelings were still hurt decided to take the high road. Eshe, however, was feeling a bit cheekier.

"I accept," said Eshe and took out her wand and gave her wrist a twirl. When she did this, the locks attached to the chests at the foot of their beds unhinged themselves and took to flight. Eshe's books, clothes and lantern lifted into the air. This was followed in short order by Katie's staff, broom, and wind chimes, amongst other belongings, too. All the items swirled around the room, as if they were caught up in a tornado. A smiling Eshe then gestured for the wind funnel and all its possessions to make their way into the darkened opening.

All the items gently placed themselves inside the chest. In fact the clothing which had been dancing about wildly, actually folded themselves, before landing atop one another in a pile.

Lastly, Eshe gave her wand a final twirl, and as she did so, the memory locks with fluttering wings returned to their respective chests, fastening themselves with a click and a tug for good measure, as they like to do.

The first-year students all began clapping, as did Katie and Vexika. Eshe looked over at Rangord and sent a wink in his direction, before taking a bow before the cheering crowd. The boar-boy's eyes tightened as his heated gaze found each of the first-years.

"Come along!" he barked and stormed off.

You could hear mumbles as he headed down the hallway, "Darn girls always make Rangord look foolish. Mother's right… witches be crazy."

Vexika, Eshe and Katie giggled, trying to suppress their snickering.

"That was bad, Eshe. Very bad, indeed," grinned Katie.

"What?" said Eshe. "He asked for it, didn't he?"

Vexika looked at Katie and the two of them shrugged their shoulders and nodded their heads in agreement.

"It's going to be a fun year," said Vexika.

"One to remember," agreed Katie. "I can feel it."

*

After Vexika's performance in the challengers circle, she needed to rest. Eshe and Katie felt tired, too. So with a couple of yawns and rubbed watery eyes… one by one the girls drifted off to sleep. Even Green Eyes kneaded the blanket at the foot of Katie's bed, before circling up to get some shut eye, as well.

The moon was high in the night sky when a magical alarm went off near the panther-girl. It was a translucent bird chirping as it flew around Vexika's head. Katie had one eye slightly open just in time to see her panther friend snatch the poor little innocent songstress into her paw-like hand, and squeeze it tight before shoving the bird into her mouth.

Instantly both of Katie's eyes opened wide and a grin crept over her face, as translucent feathers floated around the still slumbering bunk-bor.

Eshe looked over towards the scroll as she was waking up.

"Professor Toohasi," she uttered, *"History of Magic."*

The last class of the day would be the same as it was the year before.

Suddenly, Vexika, Eshe and Katie, all looked at one another, as light bulbs above them had just flickered on.

"*Professor Toohasi's Wild Brew!*" they all exclaimed in unison.

"Ah, I can almost smell it brewing now," added Katie.

“It’s almost midnight on the dot, now,” grinned Eshe, also seeming to be able to smell the grinds percolating, too. “We better get going if we want our cups filled hot, straight out of the pot.

Quickly the girls gathered their books, wands and the like and headed for the nearest open window.

“Hop on,” said Katie to Green Eyes. But he seemed content to sit this one out, feeling confident, knowing his charge would be watched over by the owl-man professor.

“Suit yourself,” added Katie.

Off went the three black robed *Hallox* students, each atop their own brooms. They shot off upward into the night, almost seemingly heading straight towards one of Chaparral’s many moons.

Steadily they climbed until finally reaching the birdhouse-like laboratory that sat high in the sky, at the very tiptop peak of the academy.

As they landed on the perch that led in the classroom, each inhaled deeply.

“Ah, that’s it! I can smell it!” exclaimed Eshe.

The girls’ feet seemed to carry them swiftly down the passageway and into the study, where to their surprise the room was already filled to the brim, so to speak. It would seem that all the other students had a bit of a craving overcome them, as well.

"Dammit," said Katie in *skull-speak* and out loud. "There better be some left."

"Ah, fret not, Miss Windsor, there is always a fresh pot brewing for my students," said the kindly owl-like professor as he lowered down from the rafters with a tray of several steaming cups of his famous *Wild Brew* coffee.

"Thank you, professor," they all said in unison, as each girl hurriedly reached for a cup. And as always, the first sip caused that bit of a lemon puss expression upon their faces, which was almost instantly followed by another sip and another.

"It's so good to see you back again, Miss Vee, Miss Leota, and Miss Windsor," said Professor Toohasi, warmly. "Quite the surprise our good friend Professor Hopingráve gave us this morning, I'd say, would you not?"

The girls each nodded in agreement, busying themselves with their coffee.

"That's the thing about our magical world," continued the professor. "Charms and curses come and go. Wizards and witches rise and fall.

Even the most powerful incantations fade away, eventually. But one, only one spell that I know of, endures the test of time."

"Which one is that, professor?" asked Katie, intrigued.

"Why, *the Forever Spell*, Miss Windsor. *The Forever Spell*."

The professor paused, as if he just remembered something important he needed to do.

"Ah, more about that later; I've got to wind it back. Yes, yes… go back to go forward, after all. Would you not say?"

The three girls eyed one another with grins, as the owl-like professor raced down the steps between the rows of students, which led to his desk. To the side, somewhat in the shadows, was the very same grandfather clock that was destroyed – turned to ash - the year before.

In fact, Katie gasped upon seeing the clock. She blurted out a very reasonable question through *skull-speak*… "How is that possible?"

The professor seemed to have heard.

"Oh, yes, yes, some of you might have noticed that our time keeper has returned to us," said Professor Toohasi, matter-of-factly. "Well, when the *Shadow Tree*, from which the original clock was made, was destroyed it took its descendant with it. And when the tree grew again, and resurrected our cherished professor of *Magelic Botany,* well…she, now being the spirit that oversees and resides inside the oak, saw fit to craft me, or rather us, another time piece."

He paused, stepping back to give the clock a good once over from top to bottom, before adding, "And what a fine job our professor did, indeed… perfection, right down to the hour hand."

The professor again looked as though he just remembered the very thing, he had *just remembered* a moment or two earlier.

"Oh yes, the hour hand," said the owl-like professor as he pointed his wand at the hour hand. Instantly the numeral 12 descended to where the numeral 11 was located, and so on which made room for numeral 13 to take its place atop of the clock. "Now that the magical, yet hidden *Witching Hour* has been invoked, we can begin."

The professor stepped in front of his desk and eyed the full house that sat before him.

"I know there is much talk about what took place at the end of our last term, and just what dark forces have returned. Well, while I can't give any guarantees as to what the future holds, I can say that all of your professors, myself included, and all the faculty here at, *the Academy Of Enchantments and Other Magical Studies* will always be by your side come what may. We will face tomorrow, together."

Eshe and Katie gave an appreciative smile in the direction of the professor. For he had been the one, standing arm and arm, hand and hand with Professor Hopingráve as she took her dying breath on that cursed night. Both professors were fighting desperately to keep the *Shadow Tree* from burning to the ground, and by extension, causing the collapse of the portal and all those who had ventured into that dark alternate world.

Again the professor looked as though a thought inside his head suddenly jumped out from the shadows and kicked the side of his skull.

"Oh, that's a great idea," said Professor Toohasi, seemingly replying to his own thought. "Since this is the first day of the semester, let's do an aerial tour of the grounds, for the benefit of our first years."

The professor lifted his wand and cast a spell. The ceiling obeyed and opened itself wide. As the moonlight found its way into the darkened study, a certain face caught Vexika's attention. There on the other side of the room, was Rah, the tiger headed boy from *House Zabar,* in his silver robe. Vexika grinned, and he gave the slightest wink in return. Katie noticed, and nodded towards Eshe, who tried to hide a smile.

The moment was broken by the owl-like professor lifting up into the air, flapping his wings gently.

“All first years, double up on the brooms with our returning classmates,” he declared. After looking around the room to see everyone was paired up, that needed to be. “Alright then, we fly!”

The students all ascended through the rafters. Some of those who had not flown much over the summer break barely missed the wooden support beams. Once the class was high in the night sky, the owl-like professor spoke on the history of the academy, its four house founders, and of the *Krantiza Bridge*, during the great Chaparralian revolution. These were the same topics he covered the year before. Still Katie, Eshe and the rest of the returning students hung on every word, for Professor Toohasi is quite the storyteller. Well, all except Vexika and Rah. It would seem the two of them never heard a word the professor said. Professor Toohasi might have noticed as well.

“Miss Vee, what did the kings and queens who led the uprising against creature-kind believe or fear that the *hybrid magixians* would someday destroy?”

“Ah, ah,” stumbled the panther-girl, before someone in a red robe from *Stormander* whispered something in her ear. Suddenly Vexika blurted out a reply.

“The moon,” she said.

Professor Toohasi's eyes actually widened to the size of two moons upon hearing this. Instantly laughter erupted from atop every broom. Especially from Tamrah, who was the one who offered up the helpful suggestion to the panther-girl.

The owl-like professor gathered himself, and replied.

"Good guess, I suppose. However, the answer is… that the kings and queens feared that the *hybrid magixians* would destroy their territories using sorcery. But close."

Vexika bore a sheepish grin, knowing she had been busted.

Once the laughter died down the tour resumed. Next, the professor took his pupils to the edge of the forest, not far from the spot where Eshe and Katie had come eye to eye with the one who resembled Hathor, the crow-woman, the previous year. The professor told a little bit more about all the charms and protections that surrounded the academy; even mentioned that recently some unnamed students had been cloaked from a would-be intruder. The owl-man eyed Katie and Eshe, but did not call them out by name. Still, the girls knew to whom he was referring.

As the professor was speaking of the incident, without warning, Katie had a wave of emotion that swept over her. In a flash, she vividly saw Professor Hopingráve and the *Wandrous Reading* that gave Katie a wand

and a broom from the *Shadow Tree*. Then the vision moved to the story Professor Toohasi recounted of, having an antique shopkeeper, gift him the grandfather clock with the number 13 atop the time piece. Katie through her mind's eye could see that it was the *Mother of Bones,* in disguise.

The vision next shifted to Katie seeing the one who appeared to be Hathor, entering the academy through the clock. Lastly she saw Professor Hopingráve standing, but just barely, as she fought hard to keep the portal through the *Witch's Glass* open, before the entire *Shadow Tree* had burned to the ground. She watched as Professor Hopingráve collapsed, as a branch near to her snapped sending leaves still smoldering floating downward.

Suddenly Katie could see inside the *Shadow Tree*, inside the collapsing world, inside the witch's cave. There was the *Mother of Bones*. Katie witnessed firsthand the fight between her Aunt Zalika and the *Mother of Bones*, to get Osiris out of the glass before he was trapped inside its shards forever. Through the closing portal she saw Osiris make his escape, followed instantly by her aunt, the crow-woman. But then she saw something else. As the *Mother of Bones* was falling backwards away from the opening, she heard the old woman speak words of old, some sort of spell. Her descent into darkness stopped suddenly as her body crashed atop a pile of bones. Like the glass, the cave, and everything else in this otherworld, the old witch's skin began to crackle, whither and peel itself away from the body who had carried it for so, so long. In the end, all that was left were a few more bones for the collection. Eventually, they all turned to dust, as well.

This was the same vision Eshe had seen of the old woman's final moments. Though Katie did notice a particularly disturbing grin that was plastered upon her face before the *Mother of Bones* eroded away. That was not the kind of thing, one could forget.

Katie thought the visions were through with her, but she was wrong. There was one more. She was now outside on a riverbank, watching as Osiris was flung out of the *Witch's Glass* opening as it was closing. He landed hard upon the ground.

A moment or two later, a black crow soared out of the portal just seconds before it collapsed and exploded sending shards of glass flying through the air. The reflective bits of mirror were wobbling back and forth, as if in pain. Many pieces were already each turning to dust and fading with each passing moment.

Among the debris was a large portion of glass, which was the main remnant of what once was the entrance into the *Mother of Bones*' cave. On either side of the shard were two souls that Katie knew well. On one side was a weakened newly reformed Osiris, and on the other, was the black crow who had just landed and transformed into Katie's Aunt Zalika.

The two stared at each other as water flowed over the stone covered riverbed. It was the *Dark One* who broke the silence.

"Hathor, we can still rule this world… together. Come take your rightful place by my side."

Zalika's eyes glowed red, as she offered up her reply, "Don't you remember? You killed Hathor. My name is Zalika. Zalika Granxor!"

She spread her black wings out wide and cawed a fiery response at the *Dark One.* He barely dodged the blast in his weakened state. Osiris quickly transformed into a black mist and escaped into the forest just below the *Forbidden Caves*.

As Katie watched the *Dark One* flee, she noticed that her aunt winced. When Zalika extended her wings, it would seem that bits of the *Witch's Glass* had made its way into and under her skin.

Like everything with the mirror, it was fading. The glass was disintegrating, only leaving behind reminders in the form of gashes in the crow-woman's wings. Though one shard, did however seem particularly large and resilient. Even in turning to dust, this shard was bound to leave traces in the blood, not to mention, quite a scar.

Zalika shook it off, however, and abruptly transformed back into the crow. Katie watched as her aunt flew off into the moonlit sky. She almost started to call after her. But she knew these were only flashes of memories, still something hit deeper in Katie's soul. She knew this was more.

"Are you alright," asked Eshe, noticing an odd look that had fallen over Katie.

"No," replied Katie. "I've got to ask the professor something."

As the class had begun to exit the woods and head back towards the birdhouse like dormitory atop the academy, Katie approached the professor before he spread his wings and lifted off.

"Professor, can I ask you something?"

"Sure you can, Miss Windsor," he replied.

"Well, I was thinking… if the *Shadow Tree* could restore your clock, what else could it restore?"

The owl-like professor looked at Katie deeply.

"Hmm, that is an interesting question," he replied rubbing his chin for a moment. "You know, Miss Windsor, I sense you fear it might restore something dark, is that correct?"

"Yes, professor," said Katie. "The tree made my wand and my broom; well the ones that were destroyed. It also made your clock and the portals to the realm of the *Witch's Glass* through your clock and the tree itself. Could not, those things all be restored as well?"

Professor Toohasi looked concerned over the question and the threat that lay within it.

"All things are possible, for magic is a curious thing. However, Osiris' mother did indeed die, and in doing so, her *Witch's Glass* turned to ash. All of our elders and empathic seers, on that agree. So I feel secure in telling you that the clock and tree no longer pose the threat they once did."

"I too, believe that the *Mother of Bones* did die, professor," replied Katie, "but so did Professor Hopingráve. And yet…"

"Point taken, Miss Windsor, I will be on my guard to make sure the tree and its lineage does not repeat last year's events. And so will the spirit now residing in the tree, Professor Hopingráve," said Professor Toohasi, as he looked up to see all of his students already in flight, most nearing the tower upon which the classroom sits. "Now, we better going as well, before the *Witching Hour* spell deems us tardy."

Katie lifted up on her broom and followed as the owl-like professor soared back to his perch. Once inside, the professor spun his wrist with wand in hand, towards the grandfather clock. Almost as if it was waiting for him to return, the timepiece eagerly wobbled side to side before its numbers did a dance of their own and relocated to their normal positions on the clock face, as the *Thirteen O'Clock* went away, at least for the time being.

Since the *History of Magic* class begins and ends at midnight on the dot, due to the true *Witching Hour* spell, the girls returned to their dorm just minutes after leaving, even though it had been over an hour. Katie, Eshe and Vexika climbed into their beds to get a well-deserved night of sleep before having to attend *Voodoology* at its regular scheduled time at sunrise on the dot.

"What was it that troubled you, by the forest?" asked Eshe in a hushed tone as they lay down, pulling up their blankets.

"It was visions having to do with the *Shadow Tree*," whispered Katie back, realizing they could just use *skull-speak* but this form of communication felt more right in the moment. "I mean, don't get me wrong… I am beyond grateful and heart-filled that the tree brought Professor Hopingráve back to us. It even brought back Professor Toohasi's clock. Still, there is something everyone is overlooking. If good can come back… be brought back… then so can evil. Right?"

Eshe looked over at Katie and saw something she hadn't seen in her best friend before… fear. Sure Katie had been scared in the face of all the things she and *the Seven* had faced, but this was different. This was the sort of fear that those coming home from too many battles, too many wars brought with them. Eshe knew what was at the heart of this concern.

"Whatever it is, that will occur, we will face it together. You are not alone in this battle," said Eshe with a warm smile.

"Why am I so overwhelmed with this feeling of panic?" asked Katie. "I've never had these feelings before."

"Because growing up, you felt alone… you fought alone… you were, indeed, alone in many ways. Now you have us. You have family," continued Eshe. "But with that, you know you have so much to lose. But trust me, you won't lose us."

Eshe reached over and grasped Katie's hand.

"Together."

And in that moment Eshe not only looked like Katie's best friend, but shadows of her grandmother shined through.

In no time at all, Katie's eyes closed and she was off to another place… dreaming, or something very close to it.

CHAPTER FOUR

"OF TWO MINDS"

As Katie slept, she found herself drifting, soaring, and flying away. The wind carried her, as her wings were spread wide. She was a crow, a black feathered one that looked all too familiar.

Below, through the clouds she saw the castle atop *Clarion's Peak*. However, this journey was just beginning. What would have taken several weeks, as the crow flies, took only moments for this particular bird.

As she descended, what came into view through her red eyes was a place accurately called *the Outlands*. Here is where, nowhere is. Here is where, no one goes… and from here… no one returns. In this place of the forgotten, they like it that way. In this land there is a constant monitoring for use of magic which is implemented at all times, and in all areas. To say, magic of any kind, is frowned upon in *the Outlands*, would be a grave understatement. Fact is, they'll kill you for using it.

The crow glided down into what resembled an old western saloon in the pages of the books in Mrs. Hall's library. Without so much as a squawk, Katie perched herself in the rafters looking down on the motley crew of characters that lay below her.

"Who's that sitting alone in the corner?" asked someone resembling a Tasmanian devil, if there was a Tasmania on this planet. The devil part was accurate, though, as he had horns, tail and all. *Nothing about his appearance is friendly or kind, in the least,* thought Katie to herself as she sat with claws dug into the beam, overlooking the scene as it unfolded.

"Don't know," replied a jackal faced barkeeper, as he filled the devil-man's glass. "She entered the village a few weeks back. Keeps to herself. Usually spotted out on the edge of the forest, near the *Ruins of the*

Damned mining hole. Today is the first time she stepped foot through this door. Paid for her food, with a genuine bit of silver. Must have got lucky."

"Lucky, huh? Well, that luck just ran out," said the devil-man as he sprung to his feet knocking over the stool, sending it to the floor, in a manner that let everyone in the bar know that *no good* was about to occur.

"Hey stranger!" barked the devil-man. "Heard you found something that doesn't belong to you! So give me the silver!"

The person in the corner stayed cloaked in the shadows, with head lowered.

"See, this is *the Outlands*. And that means our land… all of it! What's buried here is ours too. So last warning, hand it over!"

The shadowed figure lifted her head. Katie recognized her instantly. It was her aunt. It was Zalika.

"What's going to be buried here, is you," she said matter-of-factly. "Your last chance. Walk away and live. Or don't."

The man whistled and three more creature-men of various breeds, stepped forth to either side of him.

"You're dead!" said the devil-man.

And one by one the village's welcoming committee lunged at the crow-woman.

Katie, in bird form, cawed but couldn't be heard. She wanted to help her aunt, yet this vision or whatever it was, did not afford her that ability.

Zalika, knowing that using magic would almost certainly get her stoned, decided she'd have to fend off the devil-man and his friends the old fashioned way. As the first warthog looking bloke reached out to grab her, the crow-woman dug her claws into the outside of his arm and tossed him into the wall with a splat. The impact sounded much like a wet dish rag being slammed against a sheet of glass.

The next to try his luck, was a man with a vulture-like top half of his body. He spread his wings as his head extended out, with beak open wide, trying to bite Zalika's head off. The crow-woman grabbed the creature-man by his long neck and flipped him over onto his back. The vulture hit the wooden floor so hard that it shook the dust from the rafters.

The crow-woman quickly moved side to side just as a porcupine-like creature shot several spikes into the wall surrounding Zalika, almost impaling her. The crow-woman sprang off of a spike, using it like a pool diving board, and as she did so, Zalika picked up her chair and smashed it over the porcupine's head.

"It won't be so easy with me," said the devil-man, and with that he spun round like a tornado. As he did so, his spiked tail sliced across Zalika's face drawing blood.

The crow-woman transformed into the bird fully and spread her wings and lifted upward. The devil-man's tail kept spinning through the air, hoping to rip out another chunk of flesh from Zalika. The crow flew through a tight opening where there was just enough room for the bird to squeeze through. However, as the tail kept attempting to strike again, it unknowingly wrapped itself around one of the beams, causing the spinning beast to be tightly bound and tied up to the wood. The crow then circled around quickly and flew directly at the devil-man's face. As the bird neared, it transformed back into Zalika, who landed a kick to the jaw, which knocked the horned one, unconscious.

The crow-woman then walked out the swinging front door of the establishment. Once outside Zalika transformed again into a bird and took to flight. Katie flew after her aunt trying to keep up as they soared towards the clouds just above the mining hole that the barkeep called the *Ruins of the Damned.*

As she neared the tail feathers of the crow in front of her, Katie called out through mind-speak to her aunt… *Aunt Zalika, it's me, Katie!* Upon hearing the words the crow suddenly appeared disturbed as if a worm of some sort had crawled into her ear. Abruptly the crow turned its head while still soaring forward, and eyed the very area where Katie in bird form was flying. It was as if Zalika could see the translucent dream state bird following her. The crow squawked as it opened its mouth wide and turned on its invisible pursuer. Katie winced as her eyes closed, for it appeared as though the crow, was about to swallow her completely.

"Katie, Katie!" said a voice in the distance. It was intertwined with an eerie resonating melody.

With a gasp, Katie suddenly found herself sitting upright in her bed; sweat beading on her forehead and down her cheek. Dangling in mid-air, but not for long, was a set of familiar wind chimes. Just as Katie's eyes found the bells, they went crashing to the floor.

"Katie, we're here," said Eshe looking concerned, with Green Eyes at the foot of the bed.

"Are you okay? The chimes were ringing wildly, and you were calling out your aunt's name," continued Eshe. "I had to cast a quick silence charm and a sleeping spell to make sure the entire dormitory didn't come running.

Confused and struggling to hold onto consciousness, Katie spoke in a breathless manner.

"I saw her. I saw Zalika," said Katie.

"What?" asked Eshe. "You mean you dreamed about her?"

"No, I saw her," replied Katie, certain of herself. "It was this faraway place. Somewhere called *the Outlands*. I heard the devil-man call it that before Zalika knocked him out."

Eshe raised her eyebrows.

"Is she hurt? Is she okay?" asked Eshe.

"I don't know," replied Katie. "I could feel so much inner rage and turmoil."

Katie paused for a moment, seemingly searching through her own emotional recollection of the events that had just occurred, before continuing, "But the thing I felt the most, was shame."

"Shame?" questioned Eshe.

"Yes, shame and remorse," said Katie reflectively. "I tried calling to her, through *skull-speak*, but that's when I felt the anger give way to this rush of regrets."

“I felt that from her, too, when she was battling us inside Professor Hopingráve’s atrium. Zalika was battling the dark parts of herself even then, while struggling to escape out from under the *Mother of Bones’* spell,” said Eshe.

“She has been to hell and back, for sure,” said Katie. “I just don’t know if she will have the strength to resist Osiris, should he seek her again. She’s alone with no support at all. I could feel it. She is my aunt. She is a Granxor.”

Katie paused, as she searched for the right words, “I’m torn. Granxor or not… I can’t forget all the harm she’s done. I mean, look at what she did to you. She took your life. Or rather she is going to do that, in your future. She killed you, my grandmother. My friend.”

Katie stopped herself, not only because she was getting emotional but also because she noticed the look of sadness that had suddenly befallen Eshe.

“I’m sorry. I shouldn’t have said that,” said Katie.

“No, I already knew it. I’ve seen how I die. I watched Zalika at the Fountain of Life on your christening day, as she cast that evil spell. I’ve seen her, with my own two eyes, as she betrayed our entire family, and then turned into the crow and just flew away.”

Eshe sighed, "I have all of the older me's memories, even the ones that enrage me, which I can't bear to think about. Still, that same me, the one that lives in the older part of my soul is undeterred… it forgives her, yesterday, today and tomorrow, even if this me can't," replied Eshe.

Katie could still see she had touched upon a raw nerve.

"Well, we should get some sleep," continued Eshe, wanting to end the conversation.

"Yeah, we should," agreed Katie, thinking enough had been said, maybe even too much.

Just then, when Eshe was about to wave her wand and cast a counter-spell to rescind the sleeping spell that had silenced the dorm, a voice spoke up and filled the room.

"Before you wake everyone up, I've got a few questions," said Vexika, turning over in her bed. She had been listening to every word.

"How did you not fall under the spell?" asked Eshe, filled with surprise.

"Oh that," replied Vexika, rolling her eyes and twisting her lips, dismissively. "Child's play. Not to mention I have my own protective barrier that surrounds my bed. Had to do it, that sock thief, Rutellan, kept taking them off my feet when I was sleeping. You know how I always have a leg hanging out of bed. That squirrely girl is so damn mental for socks."

Eshe and Katie politely grinned, however collectively they looked like two deer caught in the headlights of an oncoming train.

"Now, did I hear you correctly, and I know I did," said Vexika, wiggling her black furry ears, which are known to hear a thousand times better than their human counterparts. "You two are actually Granxors? And, now it gets even better, as if that weren't enough… Eshe is somehow, your grandmother?" The last part of that statement ended with Vexika staring at Katie in a manner that made her feel like… well like, *Krazy Katie.*

"Well," started Eshe, but Vexika cut her off.

"I want to stop you there, before you give me some made-up excuse," demanded the panther-girl. "I want the truth, because that's what friends do. They tell each other their secrets. They tell each other the truth."

Eshe got ready to press on, when Katie spoke up.

"You heard correctly. It is all true. However, we weren't meaning to keep things from you. It's just that we were instructed to not tell anyone in the school, who we really are. Robur, the Wizard who carried Professor Hopingráve's body to the mausoleum the night she died, well he forbid us from telling a soul, for many reasons. The main one being that there are many protections around the school to keep dark forces from finding us."

Vexika said, "Hmm, that didn't work out so well, huh."

Katie nodded and pressed on, "It helped hold them at bay, until it didn't. And we all saw how that turned out. And the other–"

Eshed interjected, "The other reason is me. I need to have as little interaction with the timeline as I can, so that I don't disrupt the order of things, any more than I might have already done."

"But why did you journey here, in this time period, in the first place?" asked the panther-girl.

"Because I needed her," said Katie, with a hint of a protective spirit arising in regards to her best friend and grandmother. "I needed someone to help me on this path to controlling my magical abilities. And..." Katie paused for a second as a lump seemed to all of a sudden appear out of nowhere. "I needed family."

Eshe grabbed Katie's hand and squeezed it tight.

Vexika was touched by her bunk-bor's words, too. Then her eyes tightened, and much like Professor Bokor, the panther-girl tilted her head to one side as if she was receiving a message from the great beyond, too.

"Hang on, if you're Katie's grandmother, only the younger version of her from the past… well, doesn't that make you the biggest target, then?"

The girls and even Green Eyes all seemed to have their ears perk up upon hearing this question and letting it sink in.

Vexika continued with her train of thought, "I mean, if Osiris is out there, wanting to do you harm, Katie… then you being here, Eshe, is a huge risk, not only to the timeline, but to the entire Royal Family. See if the *Dark One* does…"

The panther-girl struggled to finish the sentence. So Eshe finished it for her.

"I know, I know. If I die here in this time period, then all the Granxors that came after me, including Katie would cease to exist."

It suddenly got very serious in the dormitory. The realization of this fact hung heavy in the air, leaving everyone who wasn't under a sleeping charm with little to say, until Katie spoke up.

"Well then, we are just going to have to make sure you keep doing the thing, we Granxors like to do," she paused for dramatic effect as Eshe, Vexika, and Green Eyes all eyed each other with curiosity, waiting for the answer. "Keep living," concluded Katie, "no matter what."

Eshe grinned.

Katie glanced from her young grandmother, sheepishly towards Vexika.

"Are we good?" she asked of her bunk-bor.

The panther-girl had a million more questions but thought that was enough surprises to take in for one day. So she graciously said, "Well, as long as there are no other big secrets being kept from me, we're good."

Katie and Eshe both turned towards Green Eyes, who also looked uncomfortable.

"Well," replied Katie.

"Well, what?" asked Vexika.

Just then Green Eyes morphed into Simon.

The panther-girl recoiled backwards in shock. So much so, that the hair on her body stood straight up, and she literally fell out of her bed.

"Who the hell are you?" she asked,

"I'm Simon… one of *the Seven*; *Protector of Princess Katherzine Granxor*. At your service, my lady," concluded Simon, with a bow.

As he leaned forward, the top of his head was met with a sizable book from Professor Toohasi's class, *Night Flight: What Moonlight Can Do For You.*

"How dare you!" said Vexika, "I change in here!"

Simon growled as he scratched his head, uncomfortably. As well he seemed a bit red in the face.

"My lady, I always turn my gaze out the window to the trees," the embarrassed protector, explained.

"Hmm," replied a perturbed panther-girl. "See that you do."

Katie and Eshe fought hard to suppress a snicker. Vexika noticed and just cut her eyes at them.

"Goodnight," she said in a huff.

With that, Simon returned to Green Eyes, as Eshe cast a counterspell to her slumber charm, but everyone stayed asleep just the same.

The next day and in the weeks that followed, Vexika became quite distant, despite Katie and Eshe's efforts to make small talk. The panther-girl was always rushing off to meet a friend, late to class or needing to see a professor, or something pressing. It was clear that she was hurt by being kept in the dark, by her best friends.

She gave Green Eyes the worst of it though. Vexika even hissed at him, when he passed the doorway as she was brushing her teeth. He seemed more content than ever to stay perched on the windowsill, with his gaze, more than ever before, fixed on the outdoors.

Katie and Eshe were also getting the cold shoulder, or at least it felt like that from Robur, whom had not made an appearance, at all. Professor Hopingráve's shoulder was less chilly, but still out of reach, all the same. It seemed that whenever Katie tried to get a moment alone with the returned from the grave, professor … the bell would ring out, and she'd already leapt into the air and back into the tree.

One question Katie desperately wanted to ask was in regards to… the mysterious *Clandestine Studies*, taught by *Professor to be named*, at a *time and place to be determined.* But again every time she started to ask the question, only a bit of a breeze would remain where Professor Hopingráve had once stood.

Together, Katie and Eshe did ask every other professor about the class, only to be met with, *never heard of it*, or *that's a new one to me*. When Professor Bokor was asked, he did put his hand up and turn his head to the side, for a moment, it seemed as though some important information would be coming in from the cosmos… but *alas*, he sighed saying *the transmission had been lost.* In the end, Professor Montakha's advice was what the girls heeded. *If it's an error in the parchment, so be it. Or since it is to be determined by someone else, let them determine it. Either way, be ready, and you will never be caught off guard.* But then Katie, thought to herself, that was kind of his advice for everything.

Besides the… *to be determined class* with a *to be determined professor*, the awkwardness between the bunk-bors, and the ever elusive ghostly professor, it was actually beginning to feel like a rather routine school year, Katie thought to herself. She and Eshe were both just so very happy to be back at the academy, happy to back in one another's lives.

Maybe this year is not going to be all out pandemonium, thought Katie to herself.

Maybe, replied Eshe, through *skull-speak*.

CHAPTER FIVE

"HAUNT-O-WICK EVE'S MAZE OF THE DEPARTED"

Decorations donned the hallways, as Katie and Eshe walked towards the main hall. It was a week before *Haunt-O-Wick*, and this was going to be Katie's first time celebrating the holiday.

"What do you think of our celebration of the departed?" asked Eshe.

"It's brilliant," replied Katie. "Very similar to our *Halloween*, only slightly different."

From the rafters hung bats, moons and stars, in a familiar fashion to what Katie was used to. She thought to herself, that Professor Bokor must fit right in with the holiday season.

However, Katie did notice a few things that were different. Instead of bright orange pumpkins, it seemed that on Chaparral, blackened gourds were the main staple. The stretched out, twisty, snake-like adornments for the most part, sported jack-o'-lantern carvings, with candles inserted in the belly, in the same manner as they appear on the other side of the *Great Oak.*

A certain bit of folklore, in particular, did catch Katie's eye. Quite a few of the decorations were adorned with this rather strange looking creature. It had the face of a wolf, or wild dog, with a long forked tongue, like a snake.

"What or who, is that creature, there?" asked Katie, pointing to a statue where the being was howling at the moon, amongst a field of gourds. "He looks like what is called a *chupacabra*, back where I'm from; a cryptid creature that is said to suck the blood of other animals."

"Ah, here he is known as… *Jixka, the Gatherer of Souls,* and he doesn't suck blood out of people, well, not that I know of, anyways," replied, Eshe. "No, he sucks your soul out, instead.

"Yikes," gasped Katie, in fake horror, playing along with the fun of the holiday.

Eshe nodded, before continuing, "Actually, it's his howl that rips it, your soul, right out of your body. He then stores them safely in his *Garden of the Departed.* Keeps them nicely tucked away inside the gourds. That's why there's a light on inside of them."

Eshe pointed at one of the gourds flickering overhead.

"They say when the light inside a gourd dances about, that it's crying for someone to let it out… and dying to let you in…" Eshe paused, before reaching out and grabbing Katie, "…to take their place! Bruh ha ha!"

Just then, Vexika happened by and noticed Katie and Eshe laughing, and turned her tail up, before walking in the other direction.

"Okay, I've had enough," said Eshe.

"Wait," said Katie, but it was too late, Eshe was already walking straight at the panther-girl.

"I'm sorry we didn't tell you, Vexika, but we were told not to say anything to anyone. Telling you would have put you and everyone in this school in danger. So, go on and hate us forever, but I wouldn't change a thing."

This time it was Eshe who stormed off in the other direction. Katie made eye contact with Vexika… and was about to say she was sorry, but she didn't. Because she agreed with every word Eshe said, Katie simply gave the panther-girl a conciliatory gesture, and then followed after her best friend.

After some breakfast, all three bunk-bors eventually wound up in Professor Hopingráve's class, though they did not enter together. Vexika, made sure to steer clear of Eshe, for she had not seen her angry like that before. Well, at least not with the heat directed at her.

The atrium was well decorated with ghosts, gourds, moons and stars. There was even a floating mist around the row of mausoleums, as well as spotlights illuminating the tombs, which gave the entire scene and even creepier feel to it. As if the everyday cemetery atmosphere of the atrium needed any help in doing so.

"Alright class, look alive," said a voice from out of thin air. From out of the mist, Professor Hopingráve just seemed to appear. "Or if you are really in the *Haunt-O-Wick* spirit, then well, don't. Look ghastly if you must."

Katie turned to Eshe and in *skull-speak* said, *"Did Hopingráve just crack of joke?"*

The professor looked directly at Katie and gave the slightest of grins and nodded her head as if to say, *yes I did*. She then cleared her throat, and redirected her attention back to class.

"Today we will cover some of the flora and vegetation associated with the holiday, and their, umm, darker roots."

After giving the origins of several plants, the story of *Jixka, the Gatherer of Souls* and his collections of gourds came up once again. Professor Hopingráve had a surprise for all of the students.

"Okay class, you might have noticed that the entryway into our class is a bit bare, in comparison to Professors Bokor and Toohasi's studies. Both do indeed have a tendency towards the grandiose, and much less of a proclivity towards subtlety. That being said, with the remainder of time we have left today, you will each be picking a gourd and carving your very own soul keeper. The best decorations, I mean gourds, will be displayed all along the hallway leading to our atrium.

The professor then mouthed something to herself that seemed to be, "That will show those show-offs, who has the most *Haunt-O-Wick* spirit."

The professor cleared her throat, before returning her attention back to those gathered before her.

"The best in class, will not only receive highest marks, but on this very *Haunt-O-Wick Eve*, this person will also be the first to enter the *Maze of the Departed*, to which I have been proudly put in charge of constructing for many, many moons, and this year will be no different."

The entire class gasped and seemed very excited at the announcement, all except for Katie, of course, who had no idea what the maze was about, being this was the first time she had ever heard of it.

Katie was about to ask about the *Maze of the Departed* but thought better of it, not wanting to stand out.

The professor then waved her wand in the air and from the far side of the atrium, several gourds freed themselves from the vine and took to flight. One by one they floated towards the class. The students began nudging their way forward, some jumped upward, trying to snatch the gourd they'd determined to be the best of the litter, so to speak.

One rather large gourd with the perfect round base was drifting in Eshe's direction, when she reached up to grab it, however she was surprised to find that another set of hands was grasping it, as well. It was Vexika.

The two bunk-bors both looked uneasy.

"You take it," said Eshe, breaking the uncomfortable silence. "Wouldn't want you holding a grudge."

The panther-girl tightened her eyes and replied, "No, you take it. Seeing it up close, it's not what I thought it was at all. Not at all!"

Vexika, leaped up and grabbed another gourd that was drifting overhead. When she landed, the two black robed students gave one another one last dagger-filled glance, before turning up their noses and walking away to opposite sides of the atrium.

All the students whittled and carved away on their gourds. With just minutes left before the bell, all the gourds were lined up in a row. Professor Hopingráve, with clipboard in hand and scribbling, much like a judge at a carnival pie baking contest, before declaring… "All the decorations will be displayed and the top three finalists are as follows. 3rd place is awarded to Miss Windsor, for this rather odd, yet unique soul catcher."

Katie had carved her entry in the same way you would have seen a scary *Jack-O-lantern* be adorned on the other side of the *Great Oak*.

"2nd place is awarded to ah… Mr. Rah," declared the professor, to the silver robed boy from *House Zabar* with the head of a tiger.

“Just, Rah, professor,” whispered Vexika. “Rah has no family line, to speak of.”

“Well, Rah, nicely done,” nodded Professor Hopingráve at the tiger-boy, who had created a soul catching gourd that looked like a bat with outstretched wings and smoke coming out of its glowing red eyes.

Vexika smiled sheepishly at the deep voiced tiger-boy, as well.

Now with only one ribbon left to hand out, the entire class was waiting on pins and needles. Professor Hopingráve started to speak, but stopped herself once or twice. She seemed very torn between two gourds. One was that of a wolf's head perfectly carved out of the darkened melon of sorts. The other was a black cat that was incredibly crafted and delightfully spooky.

First the professor began to place the ribbon on one entry, before turning to place it on another. After much internal debate, a deep breath in followed by a longer exhale… Professor Hopingráve, stood tall with her chin lifted readying herself to make a pronouncement.

“And the 1st place award, as well as the honor of being the first through the *Maze of the Departed* goes to… two students. It is a tie! The winners are Miss Leota and Miss Vee. Congratulations to you both.”

Most of the class started giving them claps on the backs. Some red robes looked rather displeased, and under their breaths, things such as rigged, and teacher's pets, were uttered.

"This should be an exciting *Haunt-O-Wick Eve* indeed," continued the professor. "For the first time ever, an actual spirit, will be overseeing this ghostly maze. And in another *first*, two souls will be entering the challenge at the same time, to launch the festivities. This will be a grand event. *Jixka, the Gatherer of Souls,* himself would be proud."

Eshe and Vexika's eyes met and they looked rather uncomfortable. Katie also offered up an expression one could only interpret as, *yikes*.

The week leading up to the entire academy's celebration of *Haunt-O-Wick* and the *Haunt-O-Wick Eve* party was intoxicating to Katie and Eshe, despite the in-dorm tension. In fact, Katie and Eshe had hardly even thought about Osiris, Zalika, Robur, *the Seven*, or even the mysterious *professor yet to be named*, in a class yet to have taken place. It actually felt like they were just students attending school. Both of them had not even mentioned the fact that their own birthdays were just days away as well, both having been born on this most spooky of holidays.

Katie thought to herself and to Eshe through *skull-speak*, as the two of them strolled together under the glowing gourds that lined the hallway, *everything feels just so right... I mean, dare I say it... I actually feel, normal.*

Eshe grinned and spoke her response out loud, "Yes, I know what you mean. It's nice for a change."

The last day of the school week, just so happened to be *Haunt-O-Wick Eve*, so throughout that day, all anyone was talking about was the *Maze of the Departed.*

The maze itself was constructed on the edge of the forest line behind the academy. For the best view of it, in its entirety, you'd want to be looking down upon it from Professor Toohasi's study. That is exactly why Katie and Eshe had stayed up late, trying to see if they could get a leg up on the competition before today's event. But both had no idea what they were staring at, or what they were supposed to do to win, or even what *winning* meant. Never had either ever entered this haunted challenge before, but still, as Eshe, put it... "One of us has to win this damn thing. It's our birthdays after all."

Katie just nodded her head in agreement, suppressing a bit of a chuckle, at seeing Eshe with her blood, good and riled up.

That day as the sun went down and the moons of Chaparral were mostly visible, despite quite a few eerie clouds drifting in the night, the entire school body gathered on the grounds. A makeshift announcer's podium stood in front of the maze. There was electricity in the air; so much so that it was as thick as fog, and coated every inch of the proceedings.

The students were all looking around, waiting impatiently for the celebration to begin. Chants broke out.

We see Jixka

Eyes like burning coals…

Open the maze

Or he'll gather our souls!

Suddenly, the academy bell rang out filling the air, in a long detuned tone. Emerging from out of the night, coming in every direction, was a parade of teachers with creature features.

Floating down from the north highest tower of the academy, with wings spread wide, was the owl-man, Professor Toohasi. Soaring in from the south of him, was the fire lit phoenix-man… Professor Montakha. From the west, flapped a bat, which transformed into *Voodoology*, professor… Barclay Bokor, who sports a *Haunt-O-Wick* aura about him year-round, being he's part vampire, part werewolf.

Rounding out the arriving faculty was the translucent figure of Professor Hopingráve, whose shadow raced overtop the crowd seconds before she landed on the podium, followed by, a rolling mist which formed into, Headmistress Valborga. She stepped out in her usual attire, of a crimson robe which cascaded in the night breeze, with a pointed hat, whose rim gave a half shadow over her serious expression.

"Welcome all to our *Haunt-O-Wick Eve's Maze of the Departed*," said Headmistress Valborga, and she had to pause as the gathered students cheered so loud it felt as though they made the ground shake. "This year is quite special. We have an actual spirit overseeing the ghostly proceedings on this fine hallowed eve. Without any further ado, I give you your *Master of Ceremonies… the Spirit of the Shadow Tree*, and much more to you and me… our beloved, Professor Hazel Hopingráve!"

The crowd erupted in thunderous applause, as the professor glided forward, to the center of the podium.

"Thank you all. Now, as in years past, this legendary maze continues to be a one of a kind, in that it changes and rearranges itself to cater to each one of its guests. So each one who enters will have a customized challenge, specific to the read the maze conducts on your very soul."

There were many oohs and ahhs, especially among First-Years who had not yet been through the maze.

"That's correct students, to all you newcomers this will be quite a chilling experience, indeed," said the professor with a devilish grin. "Let's hope you make it through the many traps and snares that await you inside… for *Jixka, the Gatherer of Souls* might be gathering you, and there is nowhere to hide… in this *Maze of the Departed.* So now it's time to open the gates! And if you make it through to the other side, you will have plenty of activities to try your luck at if you dare." said the professor, and she waved her wand in a twirling motion and a curtain fell from beyond the maze and you could see what appeared to be a carnival of sorts, come alive, with flashing lights, spinning rides, and an assortment of game booths of all manner.

As the professor turned away from the crowd to face the maze - and the carnival creepily fixed just beyond it - she abruptly paused. Her hand lifted upward into the air, as she appeared to have just remembered something very important.

"Wait! Wait!" she exclaimed. "Hold the gates. Pause the festivities."

While her body remained facing the maze, suddenly two eyeballs appeared to be poking out of the back of her head, like two gumballs that just rolled out of a candy machine. One eye was staring directly at Eshe, while the other eye had sought out Vexika. Then the rest of the ghostly professor spun back around to face the audience once more, as well.

"I almost forgot," said Professor Hopingráve, and she once again lifted her hands, and raised her voice to carnival barker levels, projecting fully to the crowd. "There was a contest held amongst all our Magelic Botanist's here in the academy to see who could carve the most haunting of gourds, and the 1st place contestant, would receive the privilege of being the first to enter the maze. It was a tie for the top honor. And so for the first time, we will have two souls enter the maze at the same time. Usually we let each student enter in five minute intervals. Some do indeed make it through before their time runs out… and they are greeted to a grand celebration… while others are… well tossed out in a most *Jixka* worthy manner."

Professor Hopingráve noticed a few first-years wince in fear, so she said softly, yet unconvincingly, "Don't worry, dearies, in good time, all recover, mostly."

Once again a wicked grin appeared on Professor Hopingráve's face, before pressing on, "Now, the two students who have gained first entry into the maze this year, will have five minutes to make it to the half point of the maze before we send in our 2nd place student, and then followed by our 3rd place student five minutes after that and so on and so on. We will keep the maze open to all souls straight on through the night and into *Haunt-O-Wick Morn*! *Jixka, the Gatherer of Souls* can never get enough souls to fill his gourds after all, can he? Now, let's welcome our winners to the stage."

Professor Hopingráve eyed Eshe and Vexika once again, as well as Rah and Katie. She then gestured for them to make their way to the front of the crowd and onto the podium.

As they made their way through the crowd, you could hear several unflattering comments, especially coming from those in red robes.

"Three from House Hallox, and that show off, Rah, from House Zabar."

"Seems the professor has favorites, doesn't it?"

"Isn't right, if you ask me."

Eshe and Vexika were first onto the podium. They both stared directly at Professor Hopingráve, avoiding eye contact with one another. Rah and Katie stood off to the side, giving space to the winners, though none of them felt much like winners due to the crowd's reaction to learning that they get to enter first.

“Alright, Miss Leota, Miss Vee… are you ready?” asked Professor Hopingráve.

Eshe wanted desperately to say, *no she was not at all ready*, being she had no idea what the heck she was supposed to do when they…

“Open the gates!”

Two very large rusty looking metal gates creaked open, letting a cloud of fog escape as it did so. Through the darkened misty night, the two girls stood motionless in their midnight-black robes looking in.

“Once inside the outside world fades away. No one out here can hear you and you can’t hear anything outside the grounds. It’s just you and whatever experiences the maze sees fit to give you, so… enter if you dare!”

The crowd all oohed and aahed at the spookiness they were anxiously waiting to enter into. The professor, could sense their eagerness.

“So without further ado, let the festivities begin,” she said and turned to Eshe and Vexika. “The clock is ticking. You have two tolls of the bell to make it through. One toll will sound at the halfway point and the second toll at the end. If you don’t make it to either point by the bell’s sound, you will be tossed into darkness, or you might just find yourself trapped inside one of *Jixka's* gourds. Go and may the spirits see you through!" declared the professor, with a wink of the eye.

Above the maze, towering high above the winding puzzle of shrubbery was a clock tower, whose minute hand started ticking on the professor's command.

"Here goes nothing," said Vexika, and she was swallowed up by the fog as she entered the maze.

"After you, I guess," mouthed Eshe to herself, and then she followed suit.

Once inside the maze, Eshe was trying to see where Vexika, had gone to. She figured her cat-like night vision would be a plus towards making it through the twists and turns. However, quickly Vexika's black panther tail could no longer be seen as it descended into the fog covered rows.

Eshe began feeling a bit of claustrophobia creeping in as she seemed to be bumping into walls of shrubbery at every turn. She could feel her breath becoming heavy and her heart rate started to increase. Her feet began to feel heavy, as the dark green walls actually felt as though they were closing in on her. That's when she realized that they were.

At first, Eshe reached for her wand, but something had wrapped itself around both of her hands. She got ready to scream but a vine had surrounded itself around her face, like a gloved hand over her mouth. Only a muted gasp escaped, before she was totally engulfed in the brush. It was enough of a sound though, that someone did hear her plea.

A figure leapt over the maze wall and landed where Eshe had just been standing. In an instance, a clawed hand ripped away many of the vines that were restraining Eshe's.

"Give me your hand," said the figure.

Eshe took the person's hand and was lifted out of the brush and found herself soaring over several rows of green and landing somewhere in the middle of the maze. The light revealed who had saved her.

"Vexika?" said Eshe, "I thought you hated me."

"Well, I do, but I love you too," the panther-girl replied with a grin, "And I'm not going to leave you stranded, when you need help, ever. I'll go back to being angry after we make it out of this thing. We are *House Hallox* after all."

Eshe took a page out of Katie's book and threw her arms around her bunk-bor's neck and hugged her tight.

"Thanks," smiled Eshe, sheepishly.

With that said, the two girls moved forward together.

Down one path to the left lead them to a dead end, so they began to double back to the center, when a voice behind them spoke.

"Vexika, you are going to help a normal, when they need you?" said an older panther-lady.

"Grandmother?" questioned Vexika. "But how? You're…"

"I'm what, dearie?" hissed back the cat-like woman.

"Dead," muttered Vexika, gently.

"Never you mind that," the old woman continued. "I warned your mother, that this place would make you soft. And soft you are! Now go, be on your way, be gone!"

The two girls started to do just that, when Vexika turned around and walked towards her grandmother.

"No, you be gone," she said sternly, and swiped her hand right through the vision.

"Come on," she gestured towards Eshe. And Eshe did the same, stepping through the mirage, which was cursing at them both as they did so. But, when passed by, the two girls went directly through to the other side of the once closed off, dead-end shrubby and just past the center of the maze, and a good thing too, because at that very moment the bell rang out. It had been five minutes and they had met the requirement to continue to the second half of the maze.

"I say we use the clock as a landmark to get us out," Eshe said, "Maybe, if we keep going towards it, it will lead us out of here."

Vexika nodded in agreement.

The panther-girl uncomfortably added, "About that, back there," she was a bit embarrassed by what had just been revealed to Eshe about the Vee family. "I'm sorry, for the things she said," she told Eshe. "The rest of my family doesn't feel that way. She always was a mean old thing."

"No worries," said Eshe with a conciliatory grin. "Believe me, I know about family secrets."

"Yes, you do," said an eerie voice coming from down and around the turn at the end of the row. "Come!"

Vexika looked at Eshe with great concern.

"I have a bad feeling about this," she said, "The hairs on the back of my neck are standing up. Let's find another way."

"I don't think we have time," replied Eshe. "If we are following the clock, it's this way to the tower. I'm sure of it."

She paused, giving Vexika an unconvincing grin, "It's only a game. I'm sure it'll be okay."

The panther-girl looked unsure as they neared the bend.

"Eshe, is that you?" said the voice. "Don't be shy, come."

Eshe stepped in front of Vexika to turn the corner first. When she peered around the corner, she gasped. It was a black mist hovering in mid-air. It began to take shape, in the form of a black crow.

"Come, follow me," said the eerie voice. "This way."

Vexika, shook her head, as if to say no.

"The bird seems to be headed towards the tower," said Eshe. "You know, it's probably just part of the maze; you faced yours to get us through the last challenge, now I have to face mine."

"So do you know this crow?" asked Vexika.

"I believe I do," replied Eshe as she took off after the bird, following it as it soared through the twists and turns. Vexika stayed hot on her heels as she did so. They chased it for what felt like an eternity. As Eshe rounded what appeared to be the last turn… the large clock tower finally came into full view. Behind it were the glowing lights of the make-shift carnival.

Eshe seemed unable to stop herself from going forward. Suddenly Vexika caught up with her and reached out and grabbed Eshe by the arm.

“Eshe, wait,” she said, out of breath. “I’ve been calling for you to stop chasing the crow. Didn’t you hear me?”

“What?” asked Eshe, appearing to be coming out of some sort of trance. “I didn’t hear you.”

Before them, the carnival was laid bare and empty. The clock tower was unusually still, as no ticking could be heard. A haunting feeling came over both girls, and it wasn’t a *Haunt-O-Wick* type of playful spookiness. It was darker.

“Come just a few more steps, and you are there,” said the eerie voice, in the direction of the crow, who sat on what would be the exit sign of the maze, and entry way into the carnival.

Eshe whispered under her breath as to not alert whatever, or whoever was lurking before them.

“I don’t believe this is just another mirage or memory, like yours.”

“Eshe, I have a horrible feeling about this,” said the panther-girl, but before she could finish the sentence a blast struck her.

Eshe watched as Vexika hit the ground. She lifted her head to see where the spell had come from. As she did so, the crow morphed back into the black mist before changing once more into something different. This time it formed the *Dark One*.

"Osiris," muttered Eshe, as she reached for her wand.

But before she could grasp the magical ember, both herself and the panther-girl lifted into the air and found themselves floating towards the dark misty figure.

"No, no, little girl, no need for that, no need at all," said the voice. "It will all be over very soon."

The evil grin on the *Dark One's* face seemed to grow as the two girls got closer to the exit point of the maze. However, before his grin could reach its desired width, and only a mere feet before Eshe and Vexika crossed the barrier, a roaring figure came leaping through the air and grabbed both girls in midair, landing well inside the grounds.

It was Rah, who had been let into the maze at the first bell toll. It seems he had heard Vexika crying out for Eshe to stop running, and knew something was wrong.

"You no good traitor!" cried out Osiris, and he cast the wickedest of spells. *"Kill-a-gra-mona!"*

Eshe, now having grasped her own wand, shot back a spell as well, *"Reflect-o-onis!"*

Most of the spell was returned back upon Osiris, however a bit of it hit Rah, square in the chest. Ever the brave one, he struggled to get back onto his feet and continue the fight, and protect Vexika and Eshe, and as he did so, a pain shot throughout his body. The tiger-boy clutched his heart before collapsing to one knee. Osiris, just stood staring back at the silver robed student with a maniacal grin.

Vexika cried out, "*No! Rah! Rah!*"

He glanced at her, with an, *it's okay,* expression, before returning his gaze upon Osiris. Still trying to protect, still trying to fight, Rah raised up and growled one last time, as if he could will himself back from the killing spell's wounds, but the damage was done. He fell to the ground.

Simultaneously, while this battle was occurring, the final bell sounded, and the 3rd place winner was let into the maze. Instantly, Katie felt that something was amiss. In her blood, something was stirring. At first, she thought it was just that the maze was dark and eerie, and that maybe this was the way you were supposed to feel in this wicked game. Then a flash of Eshe on the ground deflecting another spell from an opponent that she couldn't quite make out, crossed over her mind. She was seeing through Eshe's eyes, feeling what she was feeling, a sort of *skull-speak* only stronger. That's when she read Eshe's thoughts, as well. She heard the word... *Osiris*.

Without thinking about it, Katie's instincts to protect her best friend and grandmother, took over. Much like the night when she was chasing Green Eyes through the forest towards the *Great Oak*, Katie began feeling a transformation surge within her. She started running as fast she could through the maze, following the scents on the wind. Without knowing it, she was moving on all fours like a wolf hunting down its prey. But the maze, as it was intended to be, was tricky, and she kept hitting dead ends.

Finally, because she was still seeing through Eshe's eyes, she knew if she didn't get to them right away, they would perish... Katie let her inner were-witch come out fully. With the wave of her clawed hand she tore through the maze. If any wall of shrubby dared get in her way as she followed the smell of the battle, Katie cast the partition aside or ripped through it, if it didn't move quickly enough. In so doing, she cleared a straight path through the maze to the exit.

Just as Katie was about to reach the spot that she had been seeing through Eshe's eyes, she heard a friend cry out, as well as a familiar evil growl.

"You evil bastard! You killed him!" Vexika screamed.

The panther-girl began to cast a spell on Osiris, but he offered up one of his own.

"Lasso-na!" snarled back Osiris, moving faster than the newly formed body should be able to do.

A stream of magic had ensnared Eshe and Vexika, It had wrapped itself around their feet, like a lasso, and was dragging them towards the carnival entrance. Osiris bore a wicked grin, as he was using his wand to reel them in like fish on the line.

Still in a feral state, Katie almost howled out a spell, rather than just cast it, as she retrieved her wand from her under her robe, and commanded, *"Sev-in-fi!"*

Her wand shot forth a beam that sliced through and severed the bindings from Eshe and Vexika only feet before they reached the exit. The *Dark One* bore a surprised expression upon his face, which quickly melted into disdain, as he found the words to welcome the seemingly unwanted visitor.

"Katherzine Granxor, come to join your friends?" he asked. "Soon you will all be like that one!"

The *Dark One* aimed his pointy finger towards the lifeless body of Rah, and let out a croak filled laugh.

Katie felt her rage boiling under her skin.

"I see that I've angered you," said Osiris. "You look very different than before, little princess. Very different, indeed. You and I share that gene… the creature one. Come closer and I'll show you."

From out of Osiris' sides sprang forth six additional arms. The *Dark One* had a wand in each of his eight arms. All were now pointed at her.

"Rush-a-tonum!" she cried out.

One by one several of the rows of the maze nearest to them lifted and began to twirl, and one after another of these walls of shrubbery soared at the spider-like alchemist, keeping each of his arms busy.

With the *Dark One* busy for a mere moment, Katie, twisted her wrist and pointed it at Eshe and Vexika, who were both clearly injured from the duel with Osiris.

"Protect-o-sempra!"

A bubble-like shield encompassed them both, as well as Rah. She gestured with the motion of her fingers and the protective encasement carried them away, back towards the entrance. She did not want to risk another person getting hurt or dying. Especially, not Eshe and Vexika, who were two of the people she cared about most in the world…this one and the other one, on the other side of the *Great Oak*.

Eshe mouthed something to Katie like, *no don't do this*. Through *skull-speak* that was exactly what she said, a couple of other things added, to convey her displeasure with being escorted out of the fight. However an injured Eshe was about to lose consciousness, so she did the best thing she could, and warned her best friend and granddaughter.

"I can sense Osiris was trying to lure us outside the maze and into the carnival. Beware Katie!" said Eshe, through *skull-speak* and then like Vexika, she passed out, as well. However, before Eshe faded into blackness, she heard Katie mutter one thing. A spell. *"Mendi-o-so!"* And something hit the protective bubble.

Now it was just Osiris and Katie. Each on their side of a border so to speak.

"Come little girl, and face me," dared Osiris. "You remember the cave, don't you? Remember? It's where I killed that crow, right before your eyes. She cared about you, after all, did she? Her mistake."

The *Dark One* paused and then retracted six of his eight arms, as a staff from out of nowhere seemed to return one of his remaining hands. He swirled it ever so slightly and bits of the black mist appeared, forming a mirror of sorts. In the vision being shown, someone was bound and in chains, imprisoned.

Katie gasped, "Aunt Zalika?"

"That's right, girl. I tracked you when you used the chimes to travel to *the Outlands*. I had a feeling that you would lead me to her eventually. See, after I escaped the *Witch's Glass*, thanks to my mother's sacrifice, your aunt and I had a little chat. I offered for her to rejoin me, as I finish what I started in the caves beneath *Clarion's Peak*. I offered your aunt the chance to return as a leader in my Dark Army. She refused. Well moreover, she tried to kill me. The nerve of her."

Osiris' face shivered up as if he had tasted something foul.

"You did kill her, remember?" snarled Katie, her anger rising.

"I do," said Osiris.

The expression on the *Dark One's* face soured even more, when Katie said this.

"You defiant little brat... don't you see? The tree, its branches and all the fruit it's borne, must be destroyed. They must! What was true then is true now."

The staff in Osiris' hand pointed towards the barrier between them.

"All that is left to do is to come face me," said the *Dark One*. "Every moment you continue to hide behind these walls, know that your precious aunt, the one that gave her life for you, is suffering a fate worse than the death you witnessed her undertake."

Katie looked at Osiris defiantly and moved closer to the invisible line. The look in the *Dark One's* eyes glimmered with delight. However, just as Katie's foot was about to cross over beyond the school's protection, a kinetic lasso wrapped itself around her torso and pulled her backwards.

"Miss Windsor, step back," declared Headmistress Valborga, stepping out of a mist that just had rolled in, along with the entire faculty at the academy. "You won't be taking any of our students on this day."

All of the professors stood side by side with wands at the ready, except for Professor Montakha, who hovered overhead, with wings blazing a bright orange red. Still he was more than ready to engage, as well.

The *Dark One* glared at them, having ruined that missed opportunity that had his mouth salivating. He swirled his staff once more and the make-shift mirror showing Katie's aunt transformed into a black mist and dissipated into the carnival grounds, though Osiris' words lingered long enough to leave Katie with a final message.

"Remember what I showed you, little girl. Your poor weak Aunt Zalika is but a shadow of the once mighty warrior, Hathor. The powerful crow-woman is no more. She is as good as dead!"

Professor Toohasi was the first to get to Katie.

"Are you okay, dear?" asked the owl-like professor.

Katie didn't answer, instead she asked a question of her own, "Eshe, Vexika and Rah, how are they?"

"Alive, all of them… and in the infirmary as we speak, thanks to you," replied Professor Hopingráve, in her spirit form. "Very impressive, that mending spell you cast on them before sending them out of the maze. Very impressive, indeed."

"Osiris has my aunt," said Katie with a quiver in her voice. "He's going to kill her again."

"It is *determined.* It's time we begin," said the headmistress.

Katie looked at Headmistress Valborga puzzled.

"Begin what?" she asked.

Just then, from out of the portal window that suddenly appeared, stepped Robur, the Wizard.

"Katie, are you alright?" asked the wizard.

"Fine," replied Katie, curtly.

Robur could tell she was not pleased with him, having kept his distance from her, especially not being there to see her through the *Great Oak's* pathway at the beginning of term. She was determined not to give the old coot, as Professor Hopingráve liked to call him, the satisfaction of knowing she cared. In the end she couldn't help herself.

"So I guess it took Osiris almost killing Eshe and me, for you to bother?"

Robur gave a sheepish grin, which let Katie know that he wasn't going to discuss the matter here and now, but the point was taken, all the same.

Some of the professors who weren't in the loop, on Katie and Eshe being Granxors, like Professor Bokor and Professor Montakha had a bit of a puzzled look as to why the famous wizard was there. So Headmistress Valborga took the floor.

"Quickly, before the students make their way through the maze to us," demanded the headmistress as she removed her wand and pointed it to the sky. *"Protect-o-sempra!"*

Following the headmistress' lead, each professor lifted their wands one by one and spoke an enchantment into the night.

Professor Toohasi, *"Shield-amona!"*

Professor Bokor, *"Invis-ie-onish!"*

Professor Montakha, *"Conceal-mentiosa."*

And lastly, Professor Hopingráve lifted her wand and uttered a spell; however no sound could be heard to the naked ear. A blurring of her lips as she spoke the enchantment occurred, as well. Katie assumed this was to guard against anyone whom might by looking in by some magical means that the academy faculty had not considered, though, that would be very unlikely.

Katie knew the other four spells that the headmistress and the professors used, so it piqued her interest when one of them was concealed. She almost asked but as soon as the spell was cast, the headmistress continued in a very serious manner.

"We don't have time to go into great details at this most dire moment, just rest assured that Robur, is here to oversee the protection of two of our students, which have been, shall we say, cloaked in clandestine robes during their time here at the academy. And tonight has shown us just why we needed to be tight-lipped about this."

Headmistress Valborga looked to the professors who were unware of the girls true identities and took in a deep breath before revealing the truth.

"All I can say is that we have two Granxors amongst us at this school, and the darkest of forces wants them harmed."

While Professors' Bokor and Montakha, had surprised looks upon their faces, Professor Toohasi, rolled his eyes, which are almost the size of his entire head, and said, "Who… didn't know it?"

The owl-like professor's mannerisms almost got a smile out of Katie, almost. But then her thoughts returned to her aunt.

"What about Osiris, he has my aunt?" she demanded of everyone there, but was looking in Robur's direction. "I had a vision before this night… one where I went to a place called *the Outlands*, and I saw my aunt there. She then disappeared into the *Ruins of the Damned* when these men tried to kill her. I wonder if Osiris saw my vision too. Did he use me to get to her?"

"I don't know the answer. But that is why I am here," replied Robur, eying the headmistress. "We need to strengthen your ability to guard your mind from the *Dark One*."

"Yes, Miss Windsor, I summoned Robur to come the moment I knew this attack had occurred," said the headmistress. "The *class to be determined* must begin straight away… for you, and for Miss Leota when she heals. It is a class only for the two of you. The fates have spoken and it is clear to all, that your paths will cross with the *Dark One* once again, as it did tonight, and you need to be ready. You both need instruction which exceeds what the other students in this academy require. So, *Special Skills and Knowledge of Ancient Enchantments,* is a class designed only for you and your *special* needs."

Katie's expression bore that of a puzzle as its pieces started to fall into place. The headmistress saw this awakening happening, so she continued…

"And the professor *to be determined*, is..."

Robur, interjected, "It is I."

Katie's response was less than enthusiastic, to say the least.

Just then a voice added… "And me, as well, then."

The ghostly figure of Professor Hopingráve floated next to Robur, while keeping direct eye contact with Katie.

"There is no way I'm letting this old bag of bones, instruct you alone," said Professor Hopingráve, matter-of-factly. "The first of the week… nighttime… two turns of the clock hand, prior to Professor Toohasi's class."

The ghostly professor looked towards Katie, "Agreed?"

With a bit of a smile, Katie nodded her head in agreement.

She thought that Professor Hopingráve had added herself into the mix because she could sense that there was a bit of a rift between Katie and the wizard at the moment, and that having the professor there might make it a bit easier, under the serious circumstances.

"Good then, it is settled," added Headmistress Valborga. "All of this stays within those gathered here. No one else is to know. We stand between the world we know and the world the *Dark One* wants to bring. And it all starts with protecting this academy and those entrusted that reside inside its walls. And speaking of our students, I believe they are almost upon us."

At that moment, the students who had been outside the maze started trickling into the area where the battle had just occurred. The headmistress might have cast a spell or two that delayed anyone from finding their way there any sooner; however when three of the competitors of the maze come out injured in a protective bubble charm, it was clear that something out of the ordinary had occurred, something that was not related to *Jixka, the Gatherer of Souls Maze*. Word spread quickly throughout the crowd that there might have been an attack, and then someone uttered the name *Osiris*, and the entire school began pushing their way forward, despite any spells or enchanted barriers meant to hold them back.

“Calm down everyone,” said Headmistress Valborga. “We had a bit of an incident, but everything is under control. However due to unforeseen circumstances, we will be moving the festivities into the *Great Hall.* Professor Toohasi, can you go ahead of us all, and see that there is plenty of your *Wild Brew* for the students? And Professor, please get word to Mrs. Hogsworth to see if the cafeteria can whip up some Hallow-wick treats, as well, would you?”

“Yes, Headmistress,” replied Professor Toohasi with a nod and off he flew.

Many students disapproving groans and unanswered questions resonated throughout the crowd.

“Was there an attack?” asked one silver-robed student from *House Zabar,* having the features of a dark aye-aye lemur with large round brown eyes. Many other questions filled the night air as well.

“Was it, the Dark…” started another student from *House Violeta,* who had the look of a death's-head hawkmoth. She tussled with her purple robes, feeling that she might have overstepped.

A silent chill rushed over the crowd, having surmised what the rest of the question was. The headmistress finished the entire sentence before she answered it, as well.

"Was it Osiris? Yes, yes it was."

Headmistress Valborga gave a nod towards Professor Hopingráve and then glanced at Katie, before continuing. She seemed to be conveying that she had their backs; letting them know that they would not be fighting this battle alone.

"Tonight there was an attack by the *Dark One*. And for that reason, we would be doing you a grave disservice by concealing this fact from you."

The student body collectively gasped in shock and horror.

"We were caught off guard last year. We won't make that mistake again," said the headmistress.

From out of the crowd came another question, offered by a loud, yet familiar voice, "This is the second time there has been an attack, and she was at the heart of both of them!"

A mixture of a human hand and a rhinoceros hoof slid its way out of a red robe and pointed itself directly at Katie.

"It cannot be a coincidence. Osiris is after her! She is endangering all of us," said Tamrah.

The rhino-girl walked closer to Katie with disdain burning in her eyes.

"I think it's time to come clean. Why does the *Dark One* bother with you? What about the wizard showing up here again? One of *the Seven* flying you away from the school on dragons? Something's foul here!"

A murmur began spreading about throughout the students.

She's right.

The Dark One wants her, not us.

Why does he want her?

Rumor is, she's the one, they've been whispering about...

The long lost one.

Headmistress Valborga raised her chin high and lifted both arms above her pointed hat.

"Enough!" she demanded of the crowd, before turning her attention directly onto the *Stormander* rhino-girl. "Miss Badara, that means you, as well."

However, Tamrah decided to press the matter further, "But we all want to know, are the rumors true? Who are you really, Katie Windsor? Or should I say princess?"

Katie looked both defiant and uneasy at the same time. The wizard noticed the wand in her hand started to slowly turn upward. The headmistress and Robur eyes locked, exchanging a look that conveyed an agreement, which said that this was getting out of control, not to mention hitting too close to the truth.

Kilmon noticed Katie's subtle gesture, as well.

"You better be ready to use that stick, girl!" snarled the croc-boy.

"I said that will be enough!" declared Headmistress Valborga, emitting an enchanted power that no creature, witch or wizard would dare to challenge or take lightly. "Miss Badara, Mr. Kroy, stand down. We move forward together as an academy, if not… divided, we will crumble under its foundation. Now, tonight, is *Haunt-O-Wick Eve*… so to the *Great Hall*, with you all."

The seriousness of the headmistress' words must have broken through, at least for the moment, for the gathered crowd made their way inside the academy into the banal safety of its enchanted walls. As Professor Toohasi was overheard saying of this night after a few gourd-flavored cups of his special brew, "Well this has certainly been a *Haunt-O-Wick Eve* that we won't soon forget."

And he was right, thought Katie to herself, having been the one who was listening in. She would not be forgetting either, especially the look upon Zalika's face being held captive. Or the delightful grin fixed upon her captive's boney chin... Osiris.

CHAPTER SIX

"THE CLASS TO BE DETERMINED"

To Katie's delight, the following week found Eshe and Vexika on the mend from their injuries. Rah, however, was not so fortunate. He would have to spend several weeks in the hospital, according to Head Nurse

Moons. She had the features of a brown bear and the growl of one too, if you did not follow her orders.

"The three of you were extremely lucky," said Head Nurse Moons, when Headmistress Valborga was visiting the patients after the incident.

"Mrs. Moons, is correct. You were very lucky, indeed," added the headmistress. "You were saved because you did not cross over into the carnival grounds. Had you done so, you would have not had any of the academy's protections to aid you, and the *Dark One* would have been able to use his full force. I fear to say, the outcome would have been very different."

This confirmed that Eshe's instincts were spot on, when she warned Katie not to cross into the carnival.

Since the events of *Haunt-O-Wick Eve*, Katie stayed faithfully right by Eshe and Vexika's bedsides, only going back to the girls' dorm to shower and change clothes. Despite Head Nurse Moons adamant protests, she even slept in an empty hospital bed nearest to Eshe.

"Stubborn, that one is," muttered the head nurse, with recognition of similar qualities, which triggered a slight grin of admiration.

Over the next few days in the infirmary, Katie took the opportunity to fill in Eshe about Osiris showing her a vision of Zalika being bound and chained, held against her will by the *Dark One*.

"It could just be a trap," said Eshe. "He knows we're here and wants us outside the academy."

The time for Eshe and Vexika to leave Mrs. Moons care had come. Vexika made sure to let Rah know that she would be back to check on him, after each and every class. She then fluffed his pillow and gave him a kiss on the forehead before leaving. He didn't seem to mind at all.

Katie had also let Eshe know about Robur's visit and the fact that they would finally learn what the *class to be determined* was all about. With that being said, now that Eshe was all mended up, the headmistress was certainly good to her word, when she said that the *class to be determined* begins straight away… for you, and for Miss Leota when she heals. Because as the three bunk-bors reached the front steps of the infirmary and were about to exit, they were greeted with two familiar flying scrolls which had squeezed out of the storage chests at the foot of their beds, and flew to each them. Hovering before the girls, the scrolls unfurled themselves, with urgency.

"Okay, okay, I get it," said Eshe, "You want to be read."

Katie, Eshe and Vexika all read the words together in unison as they appeared, seems they would only reveal themselves when their recipient's eyes were fixed upon the parchment. Well plus one.

"The class to be determined has been determined. The teachers to be determined have been determined."

"I know, *Special Skills and Knowledge of Ancient Enchantments*, Robur, Hopingráve, and…" said Katie, impatiently.

The scroll seemed noticeably upset by their rude upstaging. They rattled rapidly waiting for an apology, which they got, after Eshe elbowed Katie.

"Sorry," said Katie with the roll of her eyes, "you were saying."

The words began to appear once more, now adding what Katie had just said to the parchment.

"The class to be determined has been determined: Special Skills and Knowledge of Ancient Enchantment.

The teachers to be determined have been determined: Robur the Wizard and Professor Hopingráve."

Then the words the girls had been waiting to read began to appear,

"And the time and place to be determined has been determined: Now, at the academy atrium. Hurry, you're late!"

The three girls looked at each other with widened eyes.

“You two better get moving,” said the panther-girl. “I want to hear all about it!”

“Right,” said Eshe, giving Vexika a hug.

“But we don’t have –“ started Katie, but before she could finish the sentence, the girls brooms, her chimes and Eshe’s lantern all came swirling through the air coming to rest in their owners hands. Their wands were already tucked away in their robes, as they carried them at all times, as any good witches should do.

Once the items were securely in the girls’ hands the scrolls once again shook feverishly. The word, HURRY appeared, just larger and bolder than before.

“Okay, okay, we’re going,” replied Eshe. “Quite pushy for parchment, you know.”

Katie and Eshe raced to the atrium. As they entered they expected to find at least one set of judging eyes fixed upon them, possibly with a stop watch in hand, as they broke through the entrance. Instead they found the greenhouse of a classroom empty, save the plants, of course.

“Oh good, we’re right on time,” started Eshe, but she was abruptly cutoff.

"You're late," said a voice as a shadow swept overhead. Before the gust of wind could finish moving through the girls' hair, a figure was standing before them.

"Professor Hopingráve," said Eshe and Katie, in unison.

"Good to see you are all better Miss Leota."

"Thank you, Professor," replied Eshe.

"And Miss Windsor, it's good to see you at all, after the events of *Haunt-O-Wick Eve*."

"Yes, Professor," replied Katie.

"This class is going to hopefully see to it, that it stays that way for both of you. I mean… living and all," the professor paused reflectively. "I do miss it so."

Just then an oval shaped portal of sorts opened up not far from the *Shadow Tree*.

"Speaking of dead things, here comes this old piece of driftwood," muttered Professor Hopingráve under her breath.

"Ah, I heard that Hazel," said Robur, as he stepped out through the opening.

"That's Professor Hazel, I mean Professor Hopingráve to you."

This caused both Katie and Eshe to try hard to suppress their grins, from turning into full blown laughs.

The professor cleared her throat as she rolled her eyes away from the wizard and returned them to the young witches standing before her.

"Let us begin," said the professor. "We have much to cover. Follow me."

Professor Hopingráve led the girls and Robur, as well, to the third mausoleum. She stood before it with a Melancholy look upon her face. The professor extracted her wand from her robe and gave her wrist a spin.

"Reveal-mentiosa."

The marble stone began to display a vision from many years ago. In was what appeared to be a young witch, who very much resembled Professor Hopingráve.

"This was my third life. Ah, I was so young then. This was many years before this academy existed. I was so happy then, with my family. But this was the day I lost my life."

In the vision, the young witch with rabbit features, was caught with her entire family and taken in cages to a center square where a crowd had gathered. Tears running through the fur covered cheeks of the young

Hopingráve, as she watched her parents beg for their children to be spared. The young version of the professor from another life, hugged her sister tight, as flames filled the make-shift window into the past.

"I looked away from my parents as they died, and I held my precious little sister as tight as I could, knowing what was to come next."

Katie and Eshe looked at one another in horror. The professor just kept looking forward not making eye contact with anyone, not even Robur when his hand loving resting upon her shoulder.

"This was my fourth life," said Professor Hopingráve as she stepped in front of the forth mausoleum. Again the professor twirls her wand and repeated the same process. Like before, a window formed as a vision from the past revealed itself. This time the version of Hazel Hopingráve had a family of her own, and they were huddled in the bows of a ship. She was hugging her children, which had similar animal-like features as their mother had.

"This was my family, my precious, precious family. How I miss them so," said the professor, with a lump in her throat. "We were fleeing our village, in hopes of finding a new home, where we could be among our own kind; a place where we would fit in, or at least not be in harm's way for not doing so."

The window was abruptly filled with several men grabbing Hazel, her husband and their children and bringing them to the deck as a storm was raging. Again you see the vision of another version of the professor holding her loved ones tight, as the window goes to black.

"Needless to say, what happened next," said Professor Hopingráve.

As the professor walked in front of each mausoleum, a similar fate repeated itself, right up till the eighth one.

"I am showing the two of you these visions for a reason," said the professor. "See my first and second life was filled with happiness, and in them I lived to a ripe old age. However, that was before… well before, creature-kind ventured into the parts of Chaparral where, our kind were considered to be *not normal*."

Katie and Eshe felt a rush of embarrassment wash over them, again as they had when they first entered the academy. It was an uneasy feeling for being more *normal* in their appearance, even though there was nothing *normal* about either of them.

Sensing this was the case, the professor quickly added, "I am not telling you these things to bring shame for anyone's features. But the reason I am showing you my history, is so that you can better understand what I am going to show you now."

With that said, the professor twirled her wand, and the eighth mausoleum's window to the past opened, revealing a recent memory. One Katie and Eshe knew all too well. It was the night that Professor Hopingráve, this very version of Professor Hopingráve, the one they know, lost her life.

The professor and Professor Toohasi were battling the fire as it was consuming the *Shadow Tree*. As the flames seemed to stretch all the way to the Land Of The Dragons, Professor Hopingráve would not yield to the heat or the smoke that was surrounding her. *We can't let it fall with our charges still inside. We have to hold the portal open as long as we can*, she demanded.

And then before Katie and Eshe's eyes, they watched as the professor's body lay lifeless on the ground. As the vision showed Robur walking out and carrying the professor's body to this very mausoleum, the wizard standing before Katie and Eshe had to look away. He couldn't or wouldn't watch it. Katie felt the same, almost wanting to ask, *why are we reliving this*?

It was almost as if the vision had heard Katie through *skull-speak*, because the scene instantly switched. In the window was a younger

Professor Hopingráve, only she wasn't a professor. She was a student. Katie and Eshe instantly noticed she was in red robes.

"Professor, you were in *House Stormander?"* asked Katie, before she could stop herself.

"Yes, Miss Windsor, indeed I was. But that is not the most revealing part of this memory."

At that moment a young boy with the features of a half spider, half snake-like face, also in red robes, entered the vision.

"Is that?" started Katie.

"Yes, it is Osiris," replied Professor Hopingráve.

"You knew him?" added Katie.

"I did, indeed. But that's not the point of this lesson, Miss Windsor. You will see."

She then gestured back towards the window to the past.

"Oh yes, I remember this day well."

Professor Hopingráve narrated the vision as it played out.

"A group of students from our house were on break, so we decided to travel into the village of Atra, which is a day's journey from the academy."

The vision showed Hazel Hopingráve and Osiris, along with several other *Stormanders*. Eshe and Katie's eyes widened as they watched Hazel and Osiris being very close with one another. It is clear they're good friends.

"Since we were on break, we did not have our wands or any other enchanted properties on our persons. It was frowned upon by the academy for students to perform magic outside of the school grounds, being we were all adolescents.

When we finally arrived at the village we were famished from the journey and found a pub that was serving the public meals. We were minding our own business when suddenly a group of students from the Academy of Excellence, otherwise known as Excel, which had a no creatures policy, approached us."

Professor Hopingráve, having given Katie, Eshe and Robur the backstory, let the vision take over telling the tale.

"Keep it down, half-breeds!" said one of the students from Excel, with brilliant blonde hair, sporting a blue sweater with the school crest embroidered upon it.

“You tell them, Kirf. This trash has no right to be in here,” said Dexin, a black haired boy wearing a matching outfit. In fact they all were matching in attire, and personality.

“These days, they will let anything in here, I guess,” added Rog, who was actually about the size of a young giant, himself.

All the students from Excel slapped each other on the back, seeming to be pretty pleased with themselves, when Hazel Hopingráve spoke up, as she kept one hand on Osiris’ shoulder holding him back from undoubtedly tearing into the troublemakers.

“We don’t want any problems. We’re just trying to enjoy our evening,” she said, firmly but politely.

“Look at that everyone,” said Kirf, “the hare can speak. What a good little bunny.”

Kirf reached out his hand to tickle behind Hazel’s ear. In a split second, six of Osiris’ arms came out of their concealed sockets to join the two that were already out. One arm grabbed Kirf’s wrist, another arm his shoulder, while yet another found his neck, lifting him in the air. With the sound of much crackling and snapping, Kirf’s arm, wrist and shoulder were separated from one another.

All the students from Excel took off running for the exits. Some made it, while others that Osiris got his many hands on, found themselves flying through the air, through a window, or crashing out on the street.

Swiftly word spread throughout the village, that the creature hybrids were attacking the upstanding students from Excel. The non-creature kind quickly swarmed the streets looking for the spider armed student and his friends.

The window to the past now showed the *Stormanders*, with Osiris and Hazel standing amongst them, in the center of the town square. With lit torches and stones in hand, it is clear that the creature-kind students were forcefully dragged to this location. The gathered crowd commissioned an impromptu trial and sentencing, which would all be carried out in one fell swoop.

"You creatures have come into our village to terrorize our good citizens! We must put an end to this here and now! You and your kind are not welcome here! It is time to make an example for all of Chaparral to see!" said the village mayor. To the side of the Mayor Wincer stood Headmaster Moron, who was the headmaster of the Academy of Excellence and a few of its professors, as well. They had quickly made their way out to the scene when informed of the incident.

As the *Stormander* students stood before the crowd, it was clear that they were getting riled up by the mayor's words. They were demanding a pound of flesh. Katie and Eshe watched as stones, sticks and various other items were being thrown at the students. Suddenly a rock strikes Hazel across the temple of the forehead. Enraged, it was taking several villagers to restrain Osiris and each of his eight arms as he attempted to tear into the person in the crowd who had thrown the stone.

"This is exactly why we banned these animals from our institution," declared Headmaster Moron. "Look at the beast, it is rabid! I say we put them all down!"

The crowd began cheering for the *Stormanders* execution. As the rocks and stones continued to fly, Hazel, Osiris and the others were being dragged through the mob, to a pile of wood with several stakes protruding out.

The villagers bound the *Stormanders* with thick knotted rope, as the crowd continued to cheer for blood, Mayor Wincer stepped forth, with torch in hand.

"I declare each of you creatures guilty of the attempted murder of some of our finest young citizens! Therefor you are sentenced to death by fire! Any last words?"

Suddenly from what appeared to be an ever-growing cloud of smoke, a voice spoke with an echo that reverberated throughout the village square.

"I have a few to say!"

A somewhat, younger appearing Headmistress Valborga flew out of the red mist on a broom with wand in hand.

"Rush-a-tonum!"

Out of the tip of the professor's wand came a spinning tornado that spun its way through the piles of wood freeing the students, as it also extinguished several flamed torches.

As the mist lingered, from behind Headmistress Valborga stepped out three professors from the *Academy Of Enchantments and Other Magical Studies*, all with wands in hand, spells dancing from the tips.

One was a younger Professor Toohasi, one Professor Bokor and the other professor, was an older creature-kind with jackal features. This was a professor that Katie and Eshe had never seen before. Professor Skark.

Most of the crowd ran for cover, while some of those without any magical abilities, continued to throw rocks and stones at the Head Mistress, and the other professors. While some *magixians*, who despised creature-kind and hybrids, pulled out their wands and began fighting.

Katie and Eshe were enthralled at the scene playing out before their eyes. To see Professor Toohasi and Professor Bokor in their prime battling was quite the sight to witness. The owl-man was able to deflect spells with his wings by using them as a makeshift shield. The blasts bounced off his feathers and were redirected in whatever direction the professor wanted them to go, most of the time the spells were returned to the sender.

Professor Bokor was equally impressive, as he seemed to move from shadow to shadow. From out of the darkness he'd emerge and snatch up his prey, raise them up high in the air, before discarding them, usually releasing them like a bag of bones, dropped on their fellow villagers fighting below.

The elder professor with jackal features, Professor Skark, was quite a bit more animalistic in his approach. He seemed to move on all fours, leaping upon his opponent with such speed, that most of time, they could not even get a spell out before they'd find their wand hand firmly fixed within the jaws of the professor. With the shake of his head, he'd cause the wand holder to lose his grip, and a good bit of flesh, as well.

As the battle raged on, Headmistress Valborga opened a portal back to the academy. Each of the *Stormander* students made it through as well as the professors… the last needing to enter were Hazel and Osiris. The headmistress held the doorway open to make sure that everyone made it through, even though killing spells were flying all around them.

Osiris was behind Hazel, in short making sure she made it through safely, when even with eight arms, a spell made it through and hit her in the back.

The younger *Dark One's* face changed. A darkness fell over him, darker than any evil that was already there. That or, something buried inside rose up in him. Either way, he changed in that moment. What happened next changed the entire world of Chaparral.

The headmistress looked down at Hazel as she lay near lifeless in one of Osiris' arms. As he held her, another one of his arms moved closer to the headmistress' wand hand. To the headmistress' surprise Osiris grabbed the wand from out of her hand. The young version of the *Dark One* gestured to Headmistress Valborga to take Hazel and go through and that he would hold off the pursuers.

Even though taking her wand was off-putting, the headmistress knew that if there was any hope for Hazel to live… she needed to get her to the infirmary right away. That being said, Osiris held the portal open, as

Headmistress Valborga stepped through with Hazel, expecting him to follow. However when she looked back the doorway had turned to black.

Present day Professor Hopingráve took over the narration once more as the window to the past also went black.

"Quickly the headmistress rushed me to the nurse's ward where they were able to use counterspells to bring me back to life, without me having to use one of my nine. Good thing too, or I might not have been there with you girls and the *Shadow Tree* last year."

"I don't understand," stated Katie. "So was Osiris a hero? He held the portal open, to help save all of you, correct?"

"Indeed, he did hold the open the door," replied Professor Hopingráve. "And yes, he stood for creature-kind and for me… but…"

Robur interjected, "But… Osiris is no hero."

The wizard looked angry, if not jealous, thought Katie and Eshe, too. The girls eyed each other sensing the uncomfortableness of the moment.

"Finish telling the whole story, Hazel," said Robur. "I believe the girls need to know."

With a tinge of melancholy, Professor Hopingráve pointed her wand towards the blackened window. Instantaneously color returned. The vision continued showing the portal closing before Osiris. With his back to the crowd, Mayor Wincer, Headmaster Moron, the professors from Excel, Kirf with his arm in a sling, as well as Dexin and Rog, were all moving in on this young version of the *Dark One*. After all, they believed him left behind, abandoned and helpless.

"Left you did they?" asked the Mayor. "Your filthy kind, have no loyalty."

"Serves you right," added Headmaster Moron. "Now you can receive your punishment with your back turned, like a coward, or you can face it head on. What will it be?"

Osiris with all eight arms stretched out wide, turned around slowly. One would barely notice the wand in the eighth hand, but it was there all the same.

"Firstly, I must confess, I was not left behind. I closed the portal. Slammed the door shut. And secondly, I choose *head on*. Your heads… on the ground!"

Osiris cried out, "*Sev-in-fi!*"

As if they were ripe fruit dropped in a blender, the spider-like Osiris not only took their heads, he took the entire village. The screams could be heard throughout the mountains and valleys that surround the village of

Atra, as well as the maniacal laughing of a madman, followed by the shouts of a command.

"Kill-a-gra-mona!"

When the vision finished Katie and Eshe looked horrified, yet through *skull-speak* Robur, the Wizard and Professor Hopingráve could sense the confusion that lingered about, too.

"He killed all those people," said Eshe.

"But they would have killed him," added Katie. "They would have killed all of you, too."

"Yes, that is true," said Robur. "However, we can't become just as heartless and cruel."

"Still, Osiris believes he is right to defend creature-kind," reasoned Professor Hopingráve. "And that was the goal of this lesson, this journey into the past."

Robur summarized, "If you wish to defeat your enemy, you must first understand your enemy."

To which Professor Hopingráve added, "Learn the ways you and your enemy are alike. Both of you two girls have proven you will stand up for and defend yourself and others when you believe you are just in doing so.

Maybe, just maybe your enemy believes that, also. The desired outcome would be to no longer have that person be your enemy."

Just as the professor finished the last sentence, the bell rang out.

"Well, ladies," said the professor, "that is all for today."

With a tip of her hat, and a half grin sent towards the kindly old wizard to her side, the professor with hare features, leapt into the air, as her spirit returned inside the *Shadow Tree*.

Robur, also gave a nod and disappeared back to his *Great Oak*, as well, particularly doing so before Katie could ask him any of the many questions she had rattling around in her head.

"But…" started Katie, as both spirits faded from her sight.

Katie looked towards Eshe, "Well, you can't fault a girl for trying. Still, I want answers. My aunt is out there, and she may need help. She may need us, her family."

CHAPTER SEVEN

"THE LONG-LOST ONE"

The wizard left the *Special Skills* class and immediately called a meeting of *The Seven*. Through the looking glass of several enchanted portals all the protectors united.

"It is good to see all of you, again," said Robur. "I asked to speak to you today, to inform you of quite a disturbance in regards to the *Dark One*. He attacked Katie and Eshe in the academy on *Haunt-O-Wick Eve*."

"And we are just finding out now?" said Wizlon, the Dragon, indignantly, being Eshe was his charge, and still is his charge in a different time period. "Is she okay?"

"Everyone is fine," replied Robur. "The protections in place at the academy held. However, it is clear now, that Osiris knows that Katie and Eshe are within the grounds. So he is trying to lure them out where they will be vulnerable.

In fact, he showed Katie a vision of her Aunt Zalika, being held hostage. I don't know if this is in fact the case, or a trick. The only way for us to know the truth, is for us to find her."

"So we are now going to go after Hathor?" asked Lore, the ape-man, not seeming to like the suggestion one bit. "Lore says no. She tried to kill us all."

"I understand, my brave friend," replied Robur. "However, we have to remember, this is Zalika and not Hathor."

"Birds of a feather, same, no matter what name," growled Lore.

"Lore has a point," said Aker, the fox. "I know, I'm shocked, too."

Lore gave the fox a look and a grunt that suggested at any second the ape-man might reach through the enchanted window and smash Aker over the head.

"Easy big fellow," said Aker. "I agree that we don't know if the crow-woman that came back through the *Witch's Glass* is actually Zalika or Hathor, or both, really."

"Well, that is what we need to find out," replied Robur. "And we need to know right away. I've been sensing that our Princess Katherzine is quite torn, about seeing her aunt in that way. Osiris can sense it too, I fear, and he will use it, no doubt. We are preparing her for the inevitable now. But we need time. And she needs to focus, so that when the time comes, she'll be ready."

"What do you need us to do?" asked Sahti, the snake-man.

"I need two of you to travel to *the Outlands*," replied the wizard. "Katie had a vision while sleeping, and traveled there by way of the chimes. She saw Zalika in a bar near the *Ruins of the Damned* mining hole. If Osiris saw this vision too, somehow, maybe he used it to find the crow-woman and capture her. If not, and the crow is still there, in *the Outlands*, then maybe we will find out just who it is that lives under the bird's feathers… Zalika or Hathor. I believe it to be Zalika, being she did indeed help her niece twice now, when it mattered most."

"I will go," said Lore. "If it be Hathor, I will finish the bird once and for all."

“My friend, you are needed here to keep your guard of the Royal Family,” said Robur. “Osiris knows that young Eshe is in this time period. If she does not make it back to her own time, the Chaparral as we know it could be lost, forever. So protecting the Granxors in this time period is essential, so that they are not used as pawn pieces to draw out Katie or Eshe from the academy.”

The wizard then made a gesture to the grizzly and the minotaur.

“That being said, I ask that Gennadius and Zoticus… that the both of you make your way to *Clarion’s Peak* to add extra security to the castle and its grounds. It is crucial that we know where all the branches of the Granxor tree are, at all times.

Simon, you of course, must continue your constant guard over Katie and Eshe at the academy. As well, I believe it is wise that you inform both of your charges of what I am about to say next, as it will keep them from becoming impatient.”

The lion-man nodded in agreement.

“Sahti and Wizlon,” continued Robur. “I ask that you both go to *the Outlands*. Wizlon, my old friend, being your dragon-kind can travel the long distance in a relatively short amount of time; I ask that you get there as soon as you can.”

"Of course, Master Robur," replied the dragon-man. "I will not let you down. We will leave straight away."

"Ah, that's right, I almost forgot," said the wizard tugging at his beard, with a finger pointed in the air. "Take Aker with you, as well."

"Aw, dammit," muttered Wizlon and Sahti in unison.

The fox-man, who had started to look a bit dejected from having his name left out, suddenly brightened. His ears and tail perked up, too, as if electrified.

"All right! Just me and my boys," grinned Aker, with a bit of a shuffle, wanting to reach through the portal and throw his arms around the dragon and snake's necks, like a childhood boy would do with his good buddies.

Sahti gave a side eyed glance towards the enchanted window, as a choice parting word slid out from his lips, "Moron."

On the morning the three protectors were set to depart, the skies were dark and pouring down rain. Wizlon, Sahti and Aker were preparing to take to flight on the back of a dragon named Wixaki. Being Wizlon still sat on the throne of the *Castle in the Sky* beside the lovely dragoness, Raka, commandeering a dragon to complete Robur's mission would not be a problem.

“It’s an honor for me to see that King Wizlon and his companions safely make it to *the Outlands,”* said the very large dragon that could easily fit all three passengers. Wixaki was also known to be one of the fastest dragons in the kingdom. So being the wizard deemed this an urgent matter, speed would indeed help.

“We should be there in no less than three to four weeks if the winds favor us, because the weather sure isn’t,” said a drenched Wizlon. “Is everyone ready?”

“Yes,” answered Sahti. “Where’s the -”

The snake-man was cut short as he spotted something *odd* approaching.

“Wait, don’t leave without me,” cried out the fox, who had three large coconuts which had tiny umbrellas and straws protruding out of them. He was sporting a sun visor and multicolored beach shirt and shorts.

“What the hell is that?” asked Wizlon,

“A dumbass,” replied Sahti.

The fox climbed on Wixaki’s back with a grin upon his face, which would have suggested that it was a perfectly sunny bright day, which it wasn’t.

“Let’s go,” cried out Aker. “Roadtrip!”

"Urgh," sighed both Wizlon and Sahti, as they climbed onto the large winged beast, as well.

As Wizlon surmised, it did indeed take every bit of four weeks to reach *the Outlands*, mainly due to the insistence of a stopover upon the island of Hercana to rest at the midway point, by the fox.

Just so happened that Aker knew exactly where this island was located. Seems Hercana was also known as the *Island of Debauchery*. Unsurprising to Wizlon and Sahti, the fox-man, was greeted with several warm embraces at the local hostel. In fact, everywhere Aker went on the island, everyone seemed to know him by name.

The day that the three protectors arrived in *the Outlands,* the sun was beating down heavily upon them. It seemed this part of Chaparral was always hot and dry, with a desert-like heat. Following the information that Katie had given Robur from what she'd seen in her vision, they made their way to an old dusty town just outside the *Ruins of the Damned* mining hole. As to not draw any more attention to themselves, Wixaki dropped them out of sight of any locals, and the dragon took cover in the hills.

"This looks like the tavern from Katie's vision," said Wizlon. "Remember, magic is forbidden here. That is the main reason it is such a long journey. The people and creatures that reside in *the Outlands* insist on keeping it very basic to say the least. So we will have to manage without the aid of any spells or enchantments. Even breathing fire is seen as sorcery. That being said, shall we go on?"

"Sounds like fun, after you," replied Sahti. "I have a bad feeling about this."

"Ah, what could go wrong?" said Aker. "It'll be fine. Probably won't even notice us."

Instantly the place went silent as the three walked in the door. Every creature-kind gathered by the bar turned around and eyed the protectors. Those who were seated eating, stood up or leaned out of their booths to stare at the strangers, as well.

"I think they noticed," muttered Sahti to Aker, under his breath.

Aker shrugged his shoulders.

"Drinks on the house," said the fox, loudly. "Slithers here, is buying."

The snake-man grunted as everyone remained quiet with all eyes fixed on their every move as they made their way inside.

"We are looking for the crow woman," said Wizlon, figuring they already had the place's undivided attention, might as well get to the point. “She might have caused quite a disturbance in your community recently.”

Aker shook his head with a wince, being that Wizlon spoke like a professor, which would not and did not endear him to this particular crowd.

A large man, with the face of an armadillo… shell as well, gestured to the jackal faced barkeeper to top off his drink. The entire pub seemed to be waiting to see what he’d say... and so he spoke.

“Who are you, and why should we help you with anything?”

With a large stein in hand, no one but the barkeep could see his face as it was shadowed. The back of his head was turned to the strangers, as his mouth lingered over his drink. Anzok was the head of the toughest gang of creature-kind in *the Outlands*. He was indeed the boss.

“We’re not looking for trouble,” said Sahti. “But we have reason to believe this crow-woman might need our help. So we need yours, if you would be so kind.”

“Huh, kind,” huffed Anzok. “We’re not your kind. Not kind at all. You crossed our path, and that requires you pay me. One way or the other,”

Aker squeezed his face up like a lemon, and then said, “Let me give it a shot.”

The fox pulled an arrow out of his quiver and shot it so quickly that within a blink of the eye, Anzok's stein shattered in his hand. He spun around with a look of shock, which abruptly gave way to anger.

"I prefer you look at me when I'm talking to you," said Aker, defiantly. "That's better. Ah, now seeing you in the light, the other way was better."

"You smartass, you're all dead!" yelled Anzok.

Hearing the armadillo-man's words, every creature-kind in the entire place gritted their teeth collectively and rushed towards the three protectors.

"Good job, idiot," said Sahti, sarcastically.

The snake, dragon and the fox got into the formation of a circle, literally having each other's backs, as one after another creature was lunging at them.

The beams holding up the pub almost seemed to give way from the numerous creatures being thrashed into its support structure. It seemed the protectors had fought their way through half of the patrons lined up to take them on, when a voice called.

"Enough!" demanded Anzok. "It's my turn!"

“Oh hell,” said Aker, as he saw the armadillo-man tuck his head within his shell. With no time to do anything but watch, the three protectors were stream rolled over by a leathery curled ball.

The pub’s roof could not take it anymore, and a good portion of it, just above the protectors, came crashing down upon them. Between being flattened by the armadillo, and taking shots from century old beams to the head, all three were knocked out cold, buried under the rubble.

As light began to break through the black, the flames were the first thing Wizlon saw. Torches were in the hands of the creature-kind from the pub. The dragon-man felt something tight around wrists and feet, as he realized that he was bound to rope and being dragged through the dirt street.

“Sahti, wake up, protector,” said Wizlon. “Wake up.”

Slowly the snake-man’s eyes opened. He looked about him, accessing the situation. Sahti then looked to his side and saw Aker unconscious as his body was kicking quite a cloud of dust as it was being dragged down the main pathway out of town.

“Aker, Aker,” called out Sahti.

The fox-man came back to consciousness.

“Where are we?” Aker asked still blurry eyed.

“We’re right in the middle of the mess you created,” replied Sahti. “Thought you should be awake to enjoy it.”

Wizlon looked around and spotted a large chasm and several cave openings along the ridges.

“I do believe they are taking us to the *Ruins of the Damned* mining hole,” said the dragon-man.

When they stopped being dragged, several hands instantly gripped the protectors, lifting them to their feet.

“Well trespassers, we brought you here so you can find your friend,” said Anzok. “We heard she’s buried somewhere in the mines. So I’m doing you a favor… you can go look for her on the other side. Kill them!”

A gorilla-man named Gork, a one eyed jaguar-man, called One Eye, of course, and a vulture-headed man, Tund, stepped forward with long machetes in hand, as Anzok and the large gathered crowd looked on.

Sahti using *skull-speak* asked urgently, *Wizlon, Aker, what’s the plan, fellows?*

“Don’t worry, we got them just where we want them,” grinned Aker, as they moved him in front of what one would assume is meant to be the fox's final resting place. Sahti and Wizlon stood in front of their make-shift graves, too.

"Maybe, it's time we forget about that, not allowed to use magic thing," said Sahti under his breath, though he would have rather been using *skull-speak.*

"It would be my pleasure," replied Wizlon. "Or at least let me spit a little fire their way. That's not magic, is it?"

"Agreed," said Sahti. "It's just you. Dragon through and through."

"Hold on," said Aker. "Patience fellows. Just a moment or two more."

Robur had specifically warned them that using magic would bring the entirety of *the Outlands* and its citizens down upon them.

However, with the three creature-kind with blades raised high above their own heads, readying to strike them dead… it sort of felt as though that was happening now. That being said, the choice of *whether or not* to break the forbidden rule was no longer really a choice.

But before a spell could be cast, or a law be broken, the sound of rustling through the trees could be heard, off to the side of the chasm. The noise was loud enough to get the attention of the blade wielders, as well as several others standing around the protectors.

"Ah, just on time," grinned Aker.

From out of the darkness, two red glowing eyes approached fast. The vulture-headed man instantly saw that it was the crow-woman and soared up to meet her. As Tund did so, with blade in hand, he was met with two burning hot rays that seared right through his wings. Directly before Anzok, fell the bird-man in three separate parts; two wings, one torso.

"What the hell is this?" asked Anzok.

Just then the black crow touched down and transformed into full form a crow-woman.

"I was told you were dead, crow; buried right here under the red soil," growled the armadillo. "Well, I guess if you want to make sure the job gets done, you have to see to it yourself."

Anzok gestured to the Gork the gorilla and One Eye the jaguar, to leave the protectors for the moment, and advance on the one they knew as Hathor. However, before they could do so, a voice stops them in their tracks.

"Not so fast," said Aker as claws came bursting out of the top of his hands and discarded the ropes that bound him and those around the other two protectors with ease.

Sahti looked at him as the ropes fell.

"So you could have done that at any time?"

Aker just winked at Sahti, and said, "Let's do this!"

The fox tore through One Eye in a manner more fitting of Lore than of Aker. Sahti slid towards Gork, who was much larger than the snake-man, though the gorilla went flying through the air, all the same, when Sahti landed a devastating uppercut punch.

Seeing this happen, the crowd, which was made of a variety of creature-kind, rushed towards the protectors and the crow-woman. Wizlon stepped forward in front of the others, and blasted the storming creatures with a steady stream of fire that protruded from his stretched open dragon snout.

Several of the creature-kind began to flee at this point, most with their fur singed. A few unfortunate souls were still on fire as they fled; some with wings even took to the air, as their ember lit bodies disappeared into the night.

However, Anzok and a handful of his most loyal stood their ground. Just so happens that the crow-woman suddenly recognized a few of the creature-kind beside the armadillo-man. It would seem they might have been the ones who had a run-in with her before.

"You tried to kill me before. You buried me, and obviously I let you believe that you'd killed me," said the crow-woman. "That was only because I wanted it that way. Now I see you are here again, and this time with creature-kind that I know and know well. So I will give you, what you never give another… a chance to run. Trust me, you should run."

Instead Anzok let out a battle cry, and rolled himself up into the hard leathery ball and began rolling towards them, in a steamroller manner. Flanking the armadillo were the last few of his men. They would quickly come to regret not taking Hathor's advice.

The crow's eyes brightened as if powering up, and from out of them, she zeroed in on the ones who had buried her. When her red beams found them, they were instantly turned to dust. Aker and Sahti were about to spring into action, when Wizlon put his hand on their shoulders.

"I got this," he said, as the massive rolling boulder of skin was bearing down upon them. Wizlon put his hand to his mouth and made a high-pitched whistle call.

From out of the tree line emerged Wixaki, the dragon that had carried the protectors to *the Outlands*. His large body filled the night sky behind Hathor and the protectors. The large beast breathed in deep and then exhaled a stream of fire that soared just over their heads and struck the rolling ball and those running alongside, turning them all into piles of ash.

“Damn, big fella,” said Aker impressed. “Remind me never to get on your bad side.”

“Well, at least we didn’t use magic,” said Sahti, as the embers of their foes were still glowing bright red as they floated on the night air.

The snake-man’s gaze then found Aker.

“You let all this happen, didn’t you?”

“Well, let’s just say I didn’t stop it.”

Sahti looked puzzled, “But how did you know they’d take us to the mines, and that the crow-woman would appear?”

“Well, when we took the detour to the Hercana, you know, the *Island of Debauchery*, I asked around,” said Aker. “It seems that ole Rollie Pollie, had quite the reputation for planting unwanted visitor trees right here in these mines. When I asked about a crow-woman, I heard that she’d met that very fate in this very same hole in the ground. Naturally I didn’t believe that. The crow-woman I knew as Hathor would never be taken down by the likes of these two bit lowlifes. And it seems I was right.”

The fox then gestured towards the crow-woman, with a respectful yet playful grin. The snake-man turned his head in her direction as well, but not making eye contact. Not just yet, anyways.

"Lady Zalika," said Sahti, with a bow, showing respect, being he was once her protector. "It is good to see you."

She nodded her head.

"It feels odd to my ear, to be called that name," said the crow-woman. "But this who I am, whether I deserve to be or not."

"Well, *what* or should I say, *who* are you these days?" asked Wizlon, who was Eshe's protector. He was still saddened at the loss of his charge… and at Hathor's hand. It was her spell cast upon the *Fountain of Life* at Katherzine's christening that led to her death.

"That is a good question," replied the crow-woman. "In truth, I do not know the answer. I have made many, many mistakes, of which, I will never be able to make right. Hathor made those mistakes, but she was me and I was her. I bear the sins of Hathor."

She paused, as the weight of her guilt was felt by all. She then spoke.

"I am Zalika Granxor."

The crow-woman lifted her chin, "Now I have a question. Why are you here?"

"For you," Sahti replied. "The *Dark One* is using a vision of you being held hostage, to lure Katherzine into danger. We needed to see if the vision was true. And it is good to see that it is not."

"The princess needs all the help she can get," added Aker. "You have both risked your life and given your life to save her, before. That is how I knew you would come out to help us. I believe as your protector Sahti does, that a good loyal heart beats inside of you. Your niece needs you, now more than ever. We all sense it… even the wizard."

The crow-woman turned and looked towards the tree line surrounding the mines. Her face showed that she was deep in thought, torn even.

"Everything's different now. I'm different too."

Just then, a brilliant light slowly floated towards them from out of the surrounding forest. As the glow came ever more into focus, before them was a beautiful creature hybrid. She appeared to have the face of a fairy, on the body of a woman with firefly wings. As she neared the crow-woman, her wings seemed to become even brighter.

"This is Fadessa," said the crow-woman with a subtle smile that none of the protectors had seen on Hathor or Zalika's lips before. "She's saved me in more ways than I can ever repay."

The protectors stood still and in shock, but all remained speechless, even Aker. The crow-woman took a deep breath as she held both of Fadessa's hands as she returned to the ground at Zalika's side.

“After Katherzine used the chimes, I assume to find me… her visit and use of magic was detected by those who run this land. Those like Anzok. Their fears were that I would attract others to this place with magical abilities, and they were right.

While my niece saw me deal with the devil-man and his cronies, from the pub in town, what she didn’t see was what came after that. The rulers of *the Outlands* wanted me dead, not for killing, but for magic… for bringing it here. So I decided to pick a fight I knew I’d lose, and let those cronies believe they’d killed me. I let them bury me. Being dead was the only way Anzok, and the long list of others like him would ever leave me alone.

What I didn’t count on, was that once I was buried I didn’t want to leave the grave. See, I am not just Zalika, and I am not just Hathor. I am both. The same way Katherzine brought trouble to my door, I am that for her. Lady Eshe, my own mother, died as a result of my jealousy. I was blinded with rage over my sister finding love… the very thing that has for so long eluded me. That kind of stain never leaves your soul. No matter what name you take, a darkness like that stays with you forever.

That being said, I truly believed Chaparral, Katie and everyone I have come in contact with would be better off, if I just let the dirt keep me.”

A tear, one that glowed, could be seen welling up in each corner of Fadessa's eyes. The crow-woman smiled and then continued.

"That's when I felt the scraping away of the ground that covered me. As I lay there, I thought the thugs must be back for some reason, and they wanted to dig me up and do it all over again. But when the dirt was pulled from my face, the most radiant light blinded my eyes. When the blurriness gave way, I saw Fadessa and I fell apart. She took me in and nursed me back to health… body and soul. She accepted me as I am… Hathor and Zalika."

She paused again and looked at Sahti, so without Hathor I'd never be who I am today. And today I am someone who found something to live for, again."

The protectors were very moved by the crow-woman's journey, but also surprised by the version of her that stood before them now.

"I am very happy for you," said Sahti. "But we need you and so does your niece."

Zalika looked deep in thought, torn.

Then surprisingly a sweet soft voice spoke.

"Come," said Fadessa. "You are our guests. Come."

The fairy-like woman lifted off the ground, with wings gently flapping.

"This way."

Zalika spread her wings too, and together with the three protectors and Wixaki, the dragon filling the sky behind them, they all followed the glow deep into the forest, quite a distance away from the mines.

As they came to the top of a ridge looking down into a valley, Fadessa stopped, pausing in midair. At first when the protectors viewed the pathway before them, it appeared to be heavily overgrown vegetation. But then, the firefly-woman said a few words unknown to anyone but her, and her kind. As she did this, her glow became more intense with every flap of her wings. As if by magic, a curtain of plant-life fell away. In the same spot that was just overrun with shrubbery, it now showed a vibrant valley of green well-kept forest; in the treetops above sat a home that was supported by thick branches. The outside walkways that connected to different parts of the large home were illuminated by several warmly lit lanterns.

A stream ran just below, with a make-shift washing board and hanging station for clothes. All in all, it looked like a cozy home in the forest, which it was.

"You are welcome as our guests," said Fadessa. "Here it is safe, against *the Outlands*, worst."

“Wait a minute, I thought magic is not allowed,” said Wizlon.

“It’s not,” answered Fadessa, with a mischievous grin.

“How -” started Sahti.

Zalika sensing what the snake-man was going to ask offered the answer in advance.

“It’s old magic that predates whatever guards the rulers put in place.”

“Can you use this magic to contact the wizard and let him know we found you?” asked Wizlon.

“Sorry, it is only spells that work here,” replied Fadessa. “My kind doesn’t even have villages anymore, as we did many moons ago. Because of attackers, it is the only thing that has kept us safe from the darker elements of t*he Outlands*. Today we have been forced to have our homes spread throughout the forest concealed by this ancient magic.”

“So you deeply can understand the need to protect those we care about from dark forces,” said Aker. He then looked at the crow-woman, “This is why we need to get back as soon as possible with word. Your niece is counting on us. In truth, maybe she could use her aunt by her side, too. ”

“We’ll talk more in the morning,” said Zalika, sensing the fox-man’s loyalty as a protector rising up. “For the hour’s late, and much needs to be considered.”

"Agreed," added Sahti. "It's a conversation for the morning."

With that the protectors, Zalika, and Fadessa all turned in for the evening. Wixaki, the large dragon, found a clearing and after a few times going round in circles, plopped into the ground, shaking several nearby trees, even freeing some weathered branches.

However, when the crow-woman was out of earshot, Wizlon leaned in close to Aker and Sahti, and said in a hushed tone, "We will still take turns standing guard. Let us not forget, this is still the crow-woman that tried to kill us for several years. Forgive me, if I take this new version with a grain of sand."

Aker nodded in agreement. Hesitantly, Sahti agreed as well.

"I'll take the first watch," said the dragon-man.

The night passed uneventfully. As it gave way to morning Zalika and Fadessa were up early. They made sure to have to plenty of food for the protectors; they even had a large stock of meat for Wixaki.

"I trust you had a good night's rest," said Fadessa as Sahti, Aker and Wizlon pulled up a seat at a large table that sat on the ground, just below the house and trees.

"Yes, thank you," said Sahti, politely.

The snake-man then turned his gaze towards Zalika.

“I wanted to talk to you about -” started Sahti, but he was cut short.

“I’m not going with you,” said Zalika. “My home is here, now. My life is here, too.”

Fadessa smiled lovingly at Zalika, as the crow-woman continued.

“However, I do wish you all the best, in this fight, as well as a safe journey home.”

She paused, looking a bit sheepish about refusing to join their ranks.

“Please do give my niece, my love,” said Zalika, while not making eye contact, and instead looking at the trees and shrubbery that was laid out before her. “I thought about it all night, and in the end, I know that I’m no good for her. I would only make things more difficult. I’ve made too many mistakes. Wronged too many. The things I’ve done, you can’t just put down and pretend they didn’t happen. It seems that wherever my wings carry me, I carry this curse with me.”

Sahti couldn’t hide his disappointment, but he grinned at his former charge and offered some heartfelt words.

“I was there when you were but a child taking your first steps. And I was there when Katie came out of the battle in the caves with Osiris, and informed all of us that he had ended your life. I have seen you walk through it all. That said, if you have found peace, then I am forever grateful to the Great Spirits for that. Little Zalika Granxor desires it. You are not cursed. You just took the wrong path, a few times, while on this journey. Haven't we all?"

Zalika kept looking towards the forest, so that no one could see the tears that were trickling down from her eyes.

"Well then," said Wizlon breaking through the intense moment, "we do need to get making our way back to our princess."

"Agreed," added Aker. "At least we can confirm that you have not been taken by the *Dark One*. Katie will be pleased to hear that you are doing well."

"Let's grab our belongings," said Wizlon, and then he called out to the large dragon who was chewing on a large bone that was picked of any meat. "Wixaki, are you ready to take to flight old friend?"

The dragon, who was known to be of few words, just offered an affirming nod.

Zalika and Fadessa went with the protectors and Wixaki as they made their way to the translucent border that concealed their home.

"Many thanks for giving us shelter," said Sahti.

"I am the one in your debt," replied the crow-woman. "You believed I could change. That is more than I can ask of anyone."

Fadessa rose up several feet off the ground and once more her wings began to become brighter and brighter with each flap. As they did so, the curtain fell away revealing the outer world, and much more.

"Over here," called a voice, which seemed to emanate from above in the treetops. "We spotted them!"

Unknown to Zalika and the protectors, when they were following Fadessa's glowing wings, as she led them into the forest, they were not alone. Also following the light was a short in stature, creature-kind, named, Rotel, who had the features of a meerkat, mixed with a weasel. Being his size was short, it aided in him being undetected as he saw the firefly-woman open the cloaked perimeter and then reported back to the rulers of *the Outlands*.

Quickly Fadessa began to rise up into the air, attempting to trigger the spell once more and conceal her home. However as she started to get her wings to illuminate, she was hit by a large rock in the head rendering her unconscious.

"Fadessa," cried out Zalika, as she caught the firefly woman before she hit the ground. Blood was trickling down from her forehead. The crow gently placed Fadessa down. As she lifted her gaze her eyes had a familiar red glow that the protectors had seen before. It had now returned.

Zalika lifted up into the air with wings spread wide. She spotted Rotel high up in a tree, clinging to its branches. Immediately a blast shot forth from her eyes. Two red beams ripped through the treetop, sending it with the weasel attached, to the ground below.

Rotel scurried away towards the top of a nearby ridge, with Zalika hot on his heels. As the crow bore down upon the weasel, readying to end him, he crossed over the ledge, and there was a small army of creature-kind all standing shoulder to shoulder.

"Kill the crow!" screamed the top boss of all of *the Outlands*. His name was Gruntok. He had the head of a wildebeest, with a disposition to match.

All of the creatures roared out loud as they stormed through the forest heading towards where Zalika and Fadessa's home had just been uncloaked.

The crow instantly turned around midair and was flying as fast as she could back towards where she left Fadessa. Entering the sky and closing in on her, were two winged creatures; One with the appearance of a buzzard, another with that of a hawk.

"It's an ambush," cried out Zalika as she was nearing the protectors' location.

Wizlon lifted into the air and instantly spit a blast of fire, which roasted the hawk-man that was just about to reach the crow. He then spun around in midair and grabbed onto the buzzard-man as they swirled, spinning in a downward spiral crashing into the trees, striking one another as they did so.

Swiftly Zalika swooped in and grabbed Fadessa.

"Cover me, while I get her to safety, please," said Zalika, with great concern for her partner.

"You got it," said Sahti. "Go! We will hold them off as long as we can. Afterwards, we'll find you."

Zalika flew off in a direction that led deeper into the forest.

There was no other option for the protectors. They had to stand and fight, as the wall of creature-kind was barreling down upon them. Gruntok was leading the pack.

"The disrespect!" he yelled. "Come into our land and kill one of our rulers. I will make an example of you for all to see!"

As he said this, the wildebeest grabbed Sahti and threw him through the air like a ragdoll.

Enraged, after seeing this, Aker slashed his way through the two creature-kind men who had the features of oversized wombats.

“Try that with me, tough guy!” said the fox-man,

He leapt up and used his razor-like claws to leave a deep slice across Gruntok’s face. Aker moved too quickly for the wildebeest to get his large oversized fists onto him. The fox tore into him left and right, arms digging into the big boss.

Wizlon was up in the air giving the fox-man cover, blasting any who got close with a wall of fire. However the numbers were too great and a large condor creature hybrid slipped through, and plowed into Wizlon, knocking him out of the sky. The two hit the ground hard, exchanging blows as they rolled in the dirt.

With the dragon-man down, several creature-kind rushed Aker all at once, pulling him away from Gruntok. Three creature-kind hybrids - a baboon, a hyena and a warthog - together, pinned the fox-man to the ground, holding him so that their ruler could exact his revenge.

“I’ll teach you what happens when you dare raise a hand to me,” said the bloodied wildebeest, as he lifted his massive foot overtop Aker’s face.

Just then a forked tongue, like a lasso, sprang forth from out of the brush where Sahti had been thrown. It wrapped itself around Gruntok’s neck and squeezed tight as it lifted the large ruler off the ground. His face started to turn an odd purplish blue, as he gasped for air. This action diverted the attention of the three holding down Aker just enough so that the fox broke free from their grasp, and not a minute too soon either, as a bore-man hit Sahti in the side with a rather thick tree branch, which caused him to lose his grip on Gruntok.

Wizlon, now was not only battling the condor, but also a hybrid with the face of a badger, as well another creature with the features of a rat. And there seemed to be more rapidly coming down the hill towards them.

"Oh hell," said Aker, "this does not look good, seeing the hordes of angry *Outlanders* looking to have their heads.

Just then a shadow fell over the protectors, as well as those they were fighting. In the air above was Wixaki, with Zalika by his side. It seems that he wanted to make sure that the crow-woman got Fadessa to safety. So he followed. It would seem they arrived back just in time.

The large dragon of few words had a look on his face that said it all. But he spoke anyway.

"You not hurt, friends," said the dragon, with a deep voice that shook the forest.

"What he said," added Zalika.

From out of the dragon's mouth shot forth a stream of fire that scorched several in the mob which were advancing. Zalika swooped down and with blazing red beams incinerated the three that were holding down Aker, turning them to ash.

However before the large dragon or Zalika could focus their attention onto Gruntok and those who had been fighting Sahti and Wizlon, several large jagged rocks began hitting Wixaki, piercing his thick dragon skin, which caused him to roar in pain. He was their ride back to warn Katie and the protectors knew it.

"We need to get out of here, while we can," called out Wizlon.

"You three and Wixaki go, I will do my best to hold them off while you escape," said Zalika still fighting fiercely, as one by one the creature-kind continued to break through the tree line, advancing upon them.

"We can't do that; there are too many," replied Sahti, still fending off objects being hurled his way, as well. "You will be killed."

"I'm not leaving Fadessa or our home," replied Zalika. "Go now!"

The crow-woman's tone left no room for debate, so the protectors leapt onto the back of Wixaki and began to soar upward. As Sahti looked down he saw his former charge fighting for dear life. Her glowing red eyes with black feathered wings spread was a sight to behold indeed. Though, it all seemed futile, as there appeared to be no end to how many creature-kind were lining the forest, all swarming the very spot the crow-woman and Fadessa called home.

The snake-man's heart might have been filled with sadness, but it quickly turned to rage. There below him, as Zalika was busied with holding off the onslaught, Sahti saw the slimy little weasel, Rotel, grinning as he put torch to wood, setting the home Fadessa and Zalika had made for themselves, ablaze.

"No!" shouted Sahti. "I am still her protector, and protectors protect, whether she likes it or not! Dragon, take us back down, now!"

Downward Wixaki flew at lightning speed; it seemed that he agreed with the snake-man's decision. It was another stream of fire that made it to the ground first, paving the way for the protectors to get to Zalika. Aker and Wizlon gave cover for Sahti.

The crow-woman had fallen out of the sky and was now surrounded and badly bruised and beaten. Yet, she was still fighting.

"I said go and save Katherzine," muttered Zalika, bent down on one knee, barely able to speak, about to collapse.

"Not without you, Zalika," said Sahti.

The snake-man almost slid to where Zalika had fallen. Sahti's forked tongue found those who had been unloading on her, and split them in two.

"I am now and forever, your protector," said Sahti as he picked her up into his arms.

She looked at him with tears in her eyes and gave a slight smile, struggling to not lose consciousness; her last word before giving in to the darkness was softly spoken, but heard all the same... "Fadessa."

"Hurry," said Aker as he and Wizlon leapt back onto the back of Wixaki. The fox reached out his hand to the snake-man. With one arm interlocked with Aker's and the other holding Zalika tight, Sahti was heaved aboard.

"Wixaki, find Fadessa," called out Sahti, as sharpened rocks whizzed by his head.

The large dragon let out a fiery roar and off he flew in the direction of where he had followed Zalika earlier. With those below now tracking the protectors and dragon's every move, time was of the essence. Once at the spot, Wizlon leapt off of the dragon's back while he was still airborne. Wizlon spread his wings and soared to where the still unconscious firefly-woman was and scooped her up into his arms, and returned without the need to have the entire party touch down. No need to waste any time getting back to Katie, being they had a month of travel ahead of them, and not mention this time, they would be carrying two very injured travelers with them on this journey.

Without haste they flew upward into the sky above, leaving the hordes of angry *Outlanders* below, and doing so without offering so much as any sort of parting gift. Well, unless you consider what fell out of Aker's mouth a gift.

"Dammit," said the fox, spitting.

"What's wrong?" asked Wizlon.

"Ah, nothing it's just a tooth, and a back, at that. Won't even miss it," said Aker, through a crimson red grin. "Besides isn't this the way you're supposed to look after a relaxing trip to *the Outlands*?"

Sahti looked over at his friend and fought hard to suppress a grin. Instead he just muttered something under his breath.

"Dumbass."

CHAPTER EIGHT
"DON'T GO OUT TONIGHT"

After the meeting of *the Seven*, Simon, stayed true to his word, and informed the girls of the protectors' journey to determine the crow-woman's whereabouts. It seemed to pacify Katie for the time being, even though she was still being plagued with disturbing visions of her aunt being tortured. She could now turn her attention and her mind towards her studies, which on this morning was demanding in no uncertain terms that she do so.

It had been no more than a day or two since Wizlon, Sahti and Aker had set out on their journey to *the Outlands* in hopes of finding Zalika, when the enchanted parchment which contained Katie and Eshe's class schedules, had escaped from inside the locked chest and seemed to have an urgent message.

The girls were both very tired from their midnight on the dot, *History of Magic* class with Professor Toohasi, when the enchanted parchment, as it had done before, unfurled itself floating mid- air at the foot of their beds. It was shaking feverishly like a flag blowing in a hurricane. This was not a pleasing sound to the ear upon waking… whether the ear is human or feline.

Green Eyes actually tried to claw at the thing, which caused the scroll to roll itself back up, just briefly enough, to crack the slumbering cat over the head.

Both Katie and Eshe read the words together as they appeared.

"The Special Skills and Knowledge of Ancient Enchantment class begins in 10 minutes. All permissions have been forwarded to any

professors of classes that stand in conflict with said scheduling. Tardiness is next to ungodliness… so kindly, HURRY."

With the wave of her wand, Eshe drew both their toothbrushes to them. As they were readying themselves getting dressed and grabbing their belongings, the brushes followed them around floating in midair, brushing away.

"Time's short," mumbled Eshe, with half a mouth full of paste.

"Right," replied Katie, with the muddled sound.

Even without using *skull-speak,* they were both in agreement. Katie's brush had barely made it out of her mouth when the two of them leapt out of the window and onto their brooms. It saved quite a bit of time getting to the atrium by way of flight across the courtyard.

"What do you think we'll be taught today… another history lesson?" asked Katie.

"Who knows?" replied Eshe. "Maybe today's trip down memory lane will be recalling the time that Osiris asked Hopingráve to the prom or something and Robur crashed their date."

The two of them snickered as they approached the glass ceiling of the atrium. To their surprise a spell shot right between them almost knocking them off their brooms, and then another and another.

"What the -" started Eshe, as she grabbed her wand in hand.

"Where is it coming from?" called out Katie.

"I think someone is firing at us from inside the atrium," replied Eshe. "Let's go in for a look."

"Careful, Osiris knows we're here. He attacked us once; could be him again," said Katie.

The two soared towards the glasshouse using their best broomstick maneuvering to get close. However just as they neared an open glass shingle, if you will, a blast hit Eshe hard in the chest, freezing her solid. "Eshe," cried out Katie, who raced after her as she began to plummet towards the atrium rooftop.

"*Cush-a monad!*" yelled Katie, as a spell shot forth from the tip of her wand that followed Eshe as she smashed through the glass ceiling. As the shards of glass exploded everywhere, the spell snuck through to the ground just before impact creating an inflated cushion for Eshe to crash down upon.

Katie then noticed a dark figure in a black robe, with face concealed by a large hood. In this mysterious intruder's hand was a wand. As Katie noticed it, the thing seemed to light up on his tip, noticing her, as well.

"Mummify!" said the crackly voice from under the cloak.

Before the spell reached Katie, she did a sort of barrel turn with her broomstick in hand. As the beam passed by, Katie came out of the maneuver; she cast out a spell of her own in reply.

"Rush-a-tonum!"

She conjured a full blown tornado and unleashed it upon the atrium. Every bit of glass that made up the atrium was all at once shattered into a million pieces.

The dark cloaked figure had cast a counterspell - *shield-amona* - just before the shards reached him. He stood with feet firm, wand in hand; using it like a knight would use a shield of armor. Under this make-shift dome, he remained safe and unharmed.

That is until a shadow leapt from out of the *Shadow Tree* and landed in the middle of the chaos.

"You wooden headed idiot!" said Professor Hopingráve. "Look at what you've done to my atrium!"

In an instant, the protective dome lowered and could conceal the mysterious figure's identity no more. He uncloaked himself.

"Robur?" said Katie, shocked.

"Well, Hazel," said Robur sheepishly, "it is our job to prepare them for battle, and they need to be on the ready at all times."

"Do have you have to destroy my entire class to do so?" replied Professor Hopingráve indignantly.

"Oh, it's not that bad," said Robur, lifting his wand and giving it a twirl. Immediately the bits of glass lifted into the air, and almost like a conductor leading a symphony, the wizard had the shards dance their way back into place. In the end, not a crack remained… might have even mended a few that were there before the day's events had occurred; at least that's what the wizard tried to sell to the enraged professor.

"And what about Miss Leota?" asked Professor Hopingráve, pointing to the stiff version of Eshe glued to her broom, awkwardly still, lying on the floor. "Is your desire to keep her like that for the entire class?"

"Ah yes, right, right," said Robur, having forgot.

He lifted his wand one more and said, *"Mendi-o-so!"*

Eshe instantly regained movement. First thing that moved though was her mouth.

"Robur! What the hell?" she said.

"Welcome back, Lady Eshe," said Robur with a kind grin as if he had not just froze her, made her fall out of the sky and through a roof. "Now there we are; everything is back to normal. Shall we begin? Or should I say continue our lesson?"

Katie couldn't help but let a smile escape as she watched the wizard almost cause actual steam to billow out of Professor Hopingráve and Eshe's ears. *At least it doesn't look like we're going to get another history lesson today,* Katie thought to herself.

"No you're not," said Professor Hopingráve being able to hear thoughts. "And just to note for the record, Osiris never took me to any prom… and neither has this bag of bones, with two left feet, either."

Katie and Eshe looked at each other, realizing that they'd forgotten what good hearing the professor, being part hare has.

"Alright then," said Robur, ignoring the professor's comment and getting back to the task at hand. "So Katie, Eshe, when under attack in a situation like you were just in, not knowing who is attacking you, or where exactly the oncoming fire is coming from, your decision was to move in closer and advance. What other options might you have considered?"

“Excellent question,” added Professor Hopingráve.

Katie and Eshe looked puzzled, as they considered what had just occurred. Katie was the first to speak up.

“I wouldn’t do anything different, at least not that I can think of,” answered Katie.

“But Miss Windsor, your actions saved Miss Leota, however the two of you decided to go into combat, without even knowing who your enemy was,” replied Professor Hopingráve. “Perhaps taking cover and letting your enemy reveal themselves would be better.”

“As well, you could learn their intentions,” said Robur. “When in a match of *Witch’s War*, the very best players don’t usually win in the first few moves. But so many overly eager players lose a match before it even begins.”

“How do you know when to fight and when not to?” asked Eshe.

“Well, trust your gut, but also listen to your head,” replied Professor Hopingráve. “It’s more about options and choices.”

“How about we have a do-over and see what happens,” suggested Robur.

From there the young witches went through the same scenario several times over, with different opponents. Each time having a different outcome and using different spells and charms.

Over the next few weeks the classes were a mix of history lessons and actual wizard duals. To Katie and Eshe's surprise, a few of the classes had guest professors join Robur and Professor Hopingráve.

Professor Bokor just so happened to attend a nighttime class. The subject matter was battling vampires and werewolves, of course. The professor fully changed into a bat and continuously swooped down upon Katie and Eshe as they did their best to hit him with spells.

Eshe struck him with a spell twice. Katie, just once. In the end, Eshe swore that he bit her at least four times. Katie seemed to have avoided any bites. Later that night Eshe woke up in a cold sweat.

"Are you sure," Eshe asked.

"Yes I'm sure," replied Katie. "For the last time, you are not a vampire."

Katie turned over hugging her pillow trying to get back to sleep.

When Professor Toohasi stopped by, he not only brought a fresh pot of his *Wild Brew* with him, he also showed the young witches some counterspells that had been passed down through his kind. What the girls found particularly helpful was the *invis-ie-onish* spell. The owl-like professor used his wand, pulling in energy from the night sky, and then cast out a spell, "*Moon-cloak-ess*."

This enchantment not only makes the witch, wizard or creature-kind who cast it, invisible, but if done at night, they can actually move through solid objects, like walls, trees and locked doors just to name a few.

Professor Montakha's time dropping by *Special Skills and Knowledge of Ancient Enchantments,* was an all-out free for all. Katie and Eshe got to use almost every spell they knew and the phoenix-like teacher knew how to defend against every one of them. By the end of Montakha's visit both Eshe and Katie were so exhausted they actually went back to the dorm, and slept through their next two regularly scheduled classes in their curriculums. One of these classes was Professor Montakha's very own, *X-chanted Warcery - The Study of Rivalry, Dueling and Combat* class, which made the fiery professor grin when he called out their names during roll call.

Though Katie was enjoying her time with Robur and Professor Hopingráve in this *not so secret*, secret class, outside of the class she was dealing with quite a bit of backlash from ruining the *Haunt-O-Wick Maze*, particularly from those in red robes. It seemed that Tamrah and

Kilmon had been doing their best to let every student know that all of the extra protections and additional rules were a result of the *"Princess of Chaparral."*

The *Stormanders* were demanding that Headmistress Valborga, expel Katie Windsor and Eshe Leota, being that they'd brought Osiris to the academy's doorsteps and therefor put all the student body in jeopardy, to which the headmistress let all know that not only was she not going to comment on whether or not a Granxor was attending her school, other than to say that the name, *Granxor*, does not appear on the current registry for the academy, and that she was not going to entertain expelling students because of, or based on, rumors or innuendo.

When, Tamrah and Kilmon, amongst others, held a protest in the *Great Hall*, Headmistress Valborga went on further to say, "Miss Badara, Mr. Kroy, as I told you on *Haunt-O-Wick Eve*, we move forward together as an academy. If not... divided, we will crumble under its foundation. If you insist on seeing students expelled for disrupting the educational process at this fine institution... well, I might just begin with the two of you."

After that, the protests seemed to have dwindled back down to just snide comments and hostile stares, as Katie and Eshe passed by in the hallways, entered class, breathed the same air, so on and so forth.

However, for Katie in particular, that was not the only thing weighing on her mind. Something dark and foreboding continued to sneak into her thoughts, her dreams, coming to her in the dead of night.

This nightmare would begin innocent enough, with a black feather floating in the wind. Katie would follow it as it glided through the woods. Deeper and deeper in the feather would go. Eventually it always found itself floating into a dark cave, and as Katie would almost touch and grab it… underground it would spiral, deeper and deeper still. Always Katie, even in a dream state, could feel her heart pounding, her breath shallow, and feet failing her, as she tried desperately to keep the black feather in her sight.

It had been several weeks since Aker, Sahti and Wizlon had left on their secret mission to *the Outlands,* and Robur had not received any word on whether or not they'd been able to locate the crow-woman. The wizard knew of Katie's concerns about her aunt… and he knew she'd had a vision. However, what he did not know was that on this night the dream became evermore real, at least to Katie it did.

On this night and this dream, something felt different about it right from the start. As she made it through the woods and into the cave, it seemed as though Katie was a step ahead of the previous dreams, a step faster. At the point when the feather usually spirals downward into blackness, Katie caught it. As she felt her fingers wrap around the feather, this time she twirled round and round with it. Her head felt light, eyes blurry, her stomach turning as she became dizzier with each spin. And then the ride stopped. Katie felt herself crash upon the hard stone beneath her. When her head stopped spinning and her vision settled into focus, she found herself in a dungeon, not unlike the ones under the castle at *Clarion's Peak.*

Across the heavily shadowed room was someone in shackles around their ankles and wrists. The light from the torch burning in the hallway just outside the cell, is seeping just enough to show Katie who it is being detained.

"Aunt Zalika," cries out Katie.

"Katherzine, is that you?" replied, Zalika. Her eyes are covered with cloth wrapped tight as to keep her in utter darkness.

"It's me," replied Katie, in a hushed tone trying not to alert whoever is keeping her aunt hostage. Though there is little doubt as to whom the person is.

Katie tries to get near her aunt to free her. However as she reaches her hand out attempting to remove the covering from her aunt's eyes, there seems to be an enchantment that is blocking her from doing so.

"I can't reach you," said Katie. "I need my wand."

"How did you find me?" asked Zalika, as she didn't know whether or not to trust her senses. "And how did you get into this locked cell?"

"I'm not sure," replied Katie. "I might be using the bells, without knowing it. I mean, I was dreaming."

This thought gave Katie pause.

"Am I still dreaming? This doesn't feel like a dream. Not at all," she reasoned to herself and out loud.

"Perhaps that is why you can't free me," said Zalika. "If you're here in spirit alone, I am grateful. But it will take flesh and bone to set me free from these chains."

"I don't how much time I have before I wake, so please tell me all that you can," said Katie. "Do you know who did this to you? How you got here? And where here is?"

"I would recognize this place anywhere. We're somewhere in the caves under *Clarion's Peak*," said the crow-woman through weakened breath. "Who else but the *Dark One* brought me here? Only Katherzine, you must not try to rescue me, it is a trap. He wants you dead… he needs you dead. You know this."

"How well has that worked out for him?" replied Katie defiantly.

Just then a scraping sound of a walking stick upon stone echoed throughout the cave.

"I smell that little brat's blood, even though you trespass in spirit, that Granxor stench stays upon you!" spat Osiris, as he lifted his staff high. It glowed a wicked yet brilliant blood red. His wrinkled, shriveled up lips cast forth a spell.

"Kill-a-gra-mona!"

As the word bounced off the rock walls, light from the staff became so blinding that for a moment, Katie thought that maybe she'd died.

However, the clank of her wind chimes against the floor at the foot of her bed let her know that it was not yet her time. She was still very much alive, breathing heavy, with night gown drenched from a cold sweat.

"You okay?" asked Eshe with Green Eyes and Vexika staring at her with concerning looks.

"No, I thought he killed me," replied Katie, waking from the fog of her horrific experience.

"Who?" asked Vexika.

"Osiris, once again," answered Katie as the events began to replay in her mind. Then abruptly a thought raced to the forefront. "Aunt Zalika? I think he used the killing curse on her. We've got to save her!"

"What did you see?" asked Eshe.

"He has her held prisoner somewhere in the caves under *Clarion's Peak*. I was talking to her, when he rounded the corner. Osiris sensed my presence. He lifted his staff and cast the killing spell and before I could do anything to shield myself or Zalika, I was back here."

Katie paused eyeing the floor deep in thought. She lifted her head. Her face bore a very serious expression.

"I am not going to wait any longer. If no one else is going to do anything, then I am going to try to save her."

Eshe grabbed Katie's hand and squeezed it tight.

"I understand Katie, believe me I do," said Eshe. 'In my blood I know that Osiris is just trying to lure you in. Robur and Professor Hopingráve are right. We need to stay within the academy's grounds. All of us are getting stronger every day, and soon we will hear from Aker, Sahti and Wizlon. Right, Simon?"

Eshe looked at Green Eyes, who meowed with a subtle nod of his head.

"I forgot that you are, well you, Simon… just inside there," said Vexika.

The cat looked around the room to make sure that no one was within earshot, and transformed into Simon.

"Eshe is correct Katie. We must wait before acting," said Simon.

This made Katie recall what Robur had told her in their class, when being attacked on the way to the atrium; when they retaliated without knowing who the attacker was.

Simon continued, "It is crucial that you do not chase after your aunt no matter what your visions might suggest," pleaded the protector. "I am sure that as soon as the protectors know something, and can get word to us, they will. Then together we will battle whatever Osiris throws our way. But we will do it on our terms."

"But you didn't see her," replied Katie. "What next… I wait behind these walls, while Osiris takes out every family member I have on this world? You wouldn't sit by if it was me being held, I'm sure of it."

“The Granxors are safe. Lore, Gennadius and Zoticus are seeing to that,” said Simon. “They are on constant watch over *Clarion’s Peak.* Rest assured of that. It is you and Eshe that we must keep out of harm’s way while all prepare for the battle that is foreseen and inevitable.”

Katie did not reply, but looked exhausted from the conversation.

“Let’s turn in,” said Vexika, breaking through the uncomfortableness. “We’ve got Voodoology at sunrise on the dot, and you know Professor Bokor takes yawning in his class quite personally.”

“That he does,” said Eshe with a grin.

With that, Eshe and Vexika returned to their beds, and Simon returned to cat form. However, Katie laid her head down on her pillow but sleep eluded her. She dreaded closing her eyes, because when she did so, the vision of her aunt lying dead was always there to greet her anew.

The next day Katie and Eshe attended all their classes as normal, however Eshe noticed something peculiar about Katie. She had a sort of mind to mind connection with her because of their shared ability to use *skull-speak*, yet today no wandering thoughts slipped through. If she didn’t know better, Eshe thought Katie was closing off her mind to all outsiders, and at this moment, that seemed to include her.

“Are you okay?” asked Eshe. “You don’t seem yourself.”

“I’m fine,” replied Katie, curtly. “Well not fine, actually. Sort of fed-up. I mean, no communication from Aker, Wizlon and Sahti. Really? They can’t send an owl? A carrier pigeon? Anything?”

“I agree, some word would be nice,” said Eshe. “It’s the stuff of legend, *the Outlands*, and how isolated they are from the rest of Chaparral. But that’s why Zalika went there. She didn’t want it to be easy to find her.”

“That’s the thing,” said Katie. “What if she didn’t go there at all? It would be awfully clever of Osiris to have me believe she was half a world away and in need. It divided the protectors, and quite frankly it’s dividing me too. My mind, my thoughts, my dreams, all have become something that I’m not sure I can trust anymore. And being told just wait is actual torture when everything in me is saying the opposite.”

“We can go to see Robur together and tell him how you feel,” said Eshe.

Katie let out a deep exhale, “What’s the point. I would just get told to be patient and stay put. Easy to say when you’re not the one being plagued with visions being drilled into your skull, via the *Dark One*.”

That night the dorm was dark with only the moonlight shining in. All the girls were asleep, save one… Katie. Even Green Eyes, was in a dream state, with his paws moving back and forth as if he was running through a forest. That always brought a smile to Katie's face. However tonight, she found no joy at all, as once again she tossed and turned unable to shut her eyes without the same dark images of her aunt begging for her was again filling her mind. If she wasn't begging, then it was her lifeless body hanging like a vile painting on a cave wall, with Osiris laughing as he admired his own handy work.

Katie sat upright in her bed. Under her breath she spoke.

"I've had enough. This has to end."

She eyed the clock and it was just under a half until midnight. Suddenly something flicked within Katie's eyes, and she knew what she had to do.

Quietly, as to not wake anyone, Katie made her way out of an open window and on to her broom with wand in hand. Upward she flew, seemingly towards the largest of Chaparral's moons. In truth though, she was headed towards Professor Toohasi's study. There was no *History of Magic* class scheduled for tonight. However it was just about midnight on the dot, and being it was a night off for the owl-like professor, she did not know if he'd be there or not, as it was known that Professor Toohasi did like to spend his time off by going on excursions every chance he got.

As she touched down on the perch of a landing that led to the professor's study, Katie walked softly as to not disturb him should he be resting, being the hour was late. She turned the knob slowly, to find it was locked. With not much force she knocked on the door.

"Professor?" Katie called out, in a hushed tone. But there was no reply. So she tried again. "Professor, are you in, by chance?"

Katie boarded her broom once more and flew to the rooftop of the study. There were several owls perched on beams just within openings which were designed to let them come and go as they pleased.

Moving her broom close to one of these flaps, Katie poked her head inside. She noticed the room was dim with no lighting other than what shone through by way of the moon. She did not hear the percolations of a coffee pot, and figured that she could safely conclude that the professor was not home. As she looked around, below her she could see the old grandfather clock just behind and to the side of Professor Toohasi's desk. It was just a few minutes until midnight at the dot.

To the dismay of a few awakened owls, Katie made her way in through the opening and down to the old clock. For a moment she stood and waited. Then when the moment was right, she lifted her wand and did as she'd seen the owl-like professor do so many times before and cast the appropriate charm to usher in the true *Witching Hour*. As it would do for the professor, so it did for Katie, and the grandfather clock shifted its numbers to include 13 o'clock.

The world wobbled as it always did when the true *Witching Hour* was ushered in. Katie got her footing and instantly leapt atop her broom and sailed out of the same opening in the roof she'd entered in through.

As she moved through the cold night air, she surmised that almost all of the world would be asleep and that being the case, this would be the perfect opportunity to see for herself, whether or not, her aunt was being held prisoner, though she knew that she only had an hour to do so before the spell would give way, and normal time would return. Not being at the face of the grandfather clock to reset this spell by hand, would indeed come with consequences. Katie did not know what these consequences were, being Professor Toohasi had never let the lapse of time occur. *Still,* Katie thought to herself, *it's worth the risk.*

Hurriedly, Katie soared towards the caves below Clarion's Peak. She was tempted to fly by her family's castle atop the mountainside just to glimpse her family, but thought better of it given the time constraints she was under.

Katie felt that she'd been kept away from them for so long, even after they reunited. *Seems cruel somehow, and rather unfair, really*, she thought. And then something she hadn't pondered before crept in… *maybe they don't want me around them… maybe I'm not princess-like at all… maybe I'm too, well, too me.*

"No time for all of that, right now," she muttered to herself as the caves were now coming into view.

Quickly Katie regained her focus, as another vision of Zalika's body displayed itself across her mind's eye. She could not ascertain as to whether or not she was alive. All she could see was a body motionless, chained to the stone cave wall. With wings spread wide and head slumped.

As she soared before the several cave entrances, Katie closed her eyes considering which one to choose. The deeper she went into her own senses; something began to occur, something familiar. Katie felt a burning pain coursing throughout her hands. Suddenly her fingernails began to stretch, elongate… hair began sprouting out of her skin… and when she moved her tongue over her teeth, they too had changed. They were now sharp. Without trying to, the were-witch had resurfaced for the first time in quite some time.

Looking up to the largest of Chaparral's moons, Katie muttered under her now gravelly voice, "Well it is a full moon, after all."

The tip of the broom entered a cave, almost as if it was a hunting dog sniffing out its prey. But it wasn't the stick; it was Katie on the hunt. Once inside, Katie moved by instinct, not unlike when she had chased Green Eyes through the woods back in Windermere. She could smell who she was looking for. She could smell Granxor blood. It had a familiar scent, and the scent was coming from around the next darkened bend. As Katie rounded the corner she saw the crow-woman from her vision.

"Aunt Zalika," called out Katie in a whispery voice, though it still had a raspy feral tone to it.

The woman being held prisoner offered no reply. In fact she made no movements at all.

Jumping off her broom, Katie quickly made her way to the woman, bending down to one knee, and gently lifting her aunt's head upward from under her chin.

"Aunt Zalika can you hear me?" she asked. "I'm going to get you out of here."

To Katie's delight, her aunt did regain consciousness and reply.

"Oh my dear, I knew you would come," said the crow-woman. "But you shouldn't have."

Just then Katie felt several hands grab her. One hand snatched away her wand, gripping it tight, while two others grabbed her wrists making sure that no spell would be cast. Katie thought to herself, *how could so many people sneak up on me without me knowing?*

The answer revealed itself, as Katie's gaze once again found the crow-woman. Her docile, almost comatose expression abruptly changed. It was as if a mask of wax had melted away revealing the spider-like face of Osiris.

"Yes, little brat, I knew I could count on you, to try to be the great Granxor savior," spat the *Dark One* who had used the shadows to conceal his extra appendages. Osiris now had Katie held tight within his grasp. "You played right into my hands. Now stop squirming. There's no escape for you now."

Katie began to say a spell, but one of the *Dark One's* hands suddenly had a wand slide out from its concealment, tucked inside his flowing robe and fixed itself tightly in the palm of his hand.

"Silenta!" demanded Osiris and his wand responded to his command as suddenly cross-stitching appeared atop Katie's mouth. Stitches burrowing right through Katie's skin, weaving in and out of her lips, until they were sealed tight.

"Now that's better," said Osiris with a maniacal grin.

Since she couldn't talk, through *skull-speak,* Katie tried another way to use her magical abilities.

"Cara-hoista!"

The spell should have allowed Katie to be able to use her fingers to toss the *Dark One* down the darkened cave, hoisting him along the way, like a puppet dangling upon its strings. However, instantly Osiris shut the spell down before any enchantment took hold.

In her eyes, surprise shone. Osiris saw it and the delight upon his face was terrifying to Katie.

Determined she tried another spell.

"Rush-a-tonum!"

Again, Katie thought that she could use the innate magical abilities she possessed, and once more Osiris killed the spell cold.

"Is something wrong?" asked the *Dark One*, his wicked grin never giving way.

When her attempt was thwarted twice, it caused another spell to take root, and this one was very effective, indeed. It was fear… and as that fear took over, the were-witch faded away and Katie quickly began to become less fierce, less feral. As her confidence waned, the girl from Windermere returned.

"Ah, now that's the Granxor brat I remember," said the *Dark One*.

Where is my aunt, thought Katie to herself. *I know I was tracking her scent, a Granxor's scent.*

"Good questions, all," replied Osiris.

Katie's eyes widened with shock.

"That's right I too can do that little *skull-speak* trick of yours, now. In fact I have all of your powers, thanks to the *Mother of Bones*… my mother," said Osiris, through clenched teeth as he pointed to a pile of bones in the corner of the cave. As if a veil was lifted, Katie began to realize that with more candlelight flickering and breaking through the shadows, this cave was the very cave that was in the *Witch's Glass*. But how, she thought.

"But how, indeed," responding Osiris. "See, Mother gave her life to bring me back. In her final act, she took that vile drop of Granxor blood from out of you and put it into me. There was one of your powers, in particular that Mother witnessed firsthand. It was your ability to heal that beast, Simon. Ah, but I am getting ahead of myself. More on that in a moment. Patience, little girl."

The *Dark One* moved in close to Katie's face and stared into her eyes, with such intent it seemed as though he would enter into her skull.

"Ah yes, the blood you were tracking was your aunt's, and your grandmother's and your very own. But now, it's my blood, too."

So pleased with himself, Osiris tilted his head backwards laughing maniacally. Katie looked away wincing at the thought of it all.

"And as for your aunt, the traitor… she is gone… and soon, so will all of the Granxors' line. When this is all over, the only one left standing with any of that vile blood in them will be me and one other. And no, it won't be you."

Katie gathered up every bit of courage she could muster and tried to lash out as she had in the great battle at *Clarion's Peak*, as she had at the schoolhouse in Windermere, as she had, when she felt as though the ground and sky would listen to her and obey... *I am the Tree…* she thought as pushed her hands forward, hoping to see Osiris knocked into and through the stone wall. But no, instead the *Dark One* just grinned and laughed, as the wave of energy hit him square in the chest, and then faltered, like a fly on a horse's back, before the tail swats it dead.

“No girl!” spat Osiris. “You are not the Tree, we are the Tree. Everything you think of to do to me, I hear it first. Every power you want to use on me, I have it, too. That blood, that damn Granxor blood.”

The *Dark One* laughed a good hearty laugh and then suddenly Osiris spun around with his staff raised high, and when he did so, Katie lifted into the air. He then whipped his hand towards the cave wall, and Katie followed his gesture, smacking into the stone. Chains suddenly appeared from out of nowhere and bound Katie’s wrists and ankles to the wall.

The pile of bones in the corner seemed to wobble as the *Dark One* said this.

“Oh yes, I almost forgot… the bones,” returning to his calmer, but no less sinister demeanor, “That’s the best part of it all. I want to make sure you’re comfortable, for this. You’re not going to want to miss any of it. See, you foolish girl, the *Mother of Bones* died right over there upon those bones. More important, is that she passed inside the *Witch’s Glass* within the *Witching Hour*. So her soul remained there, or at least bits of it… enough soul of what is required.”

Katie winced, not at all liking where this was headed. A previous conversation that she had with Professor Toohasi ran through her mind, where she had questioned if the *Shadow Tree* could restore his clock…

what else it could restore? As well, she reasoned, Professor Hopingráve came back in spirit form.

Osiris heard Katie's internal dialogue through *skull-speak.*

"Good question to ask… you are a clever girl, indeed," said Osiris, as he considered the wand he had taken from Katie, being it was carved from out of the *Shadow Tree*. "While you are tracing through your memories, might I suggest one of particular interest to me. When your tear drop brought the lion-man back from the grave, my mother noticed, though not for the reasons you might think. No, the *Mother of Bones…* had foreseen her fate, and that she'd bring me back. Bring me back by way of your blood."

The *Dark One* ran his boney fingers across Katie's face. His sharpened jagged nails dug into her skin, causing beads of blood to trickle out.

"There it is, the magical thing that binds us now and forever, little girl," said Osiris, as the blood pooled in his overturned long fingernail. He carefully walked over to the mound in the corner, and let the crimson drops fall overtop the bones.

"If the *Shadow Tree*, brought your professor's clock back, what else can it restore, is how you put it, correct, little girl? And might I add that if your tears also have restorative powers, would it not stand to reason that your blood would do the same? Shall we see together?"

The *Dark One* shouted out, *arise-amora*, as he pointed Katie's wand at the blood drops splattered upon the pile. Instantly the bones began to respond. One by one they rose up into the air, floating, awakening. Once the proper quantity had arisen, they started to fasten and connect to each other, creating something familiar. As the frame of a hunched over skeleton was completed, from out of the enchanted dust, trickling from the spell that had been cast, formed the skin of an old woman. It did not stop there, however, within mere moments she was draped in a black flowing cape, with a pointed rim hat, to boot. In short the witch was back, or as Osiris said…

"Mother."

"Well done, my boy," said the *Mother of Bones*. "Well done, indeed."

Osiris helped the newly reformed witch to a large stone, upon which she could sit.

"Here mother, you must rest, for it will take some time before you are fully whole again."

"Yes, my boy, we have all the time we need, do we not? We are still in the *Witching Hour*, correct?"

"We are, in fact, very much still in the *Witching Hour*, and we have the Granxor brat. Seems the princess snuck out of the academy by using the owl-man's old grandfather clock. No one knows she's here," said Osiris. "Since she came to us during the *Witching Hour*, at the hour's end, she's all ours… trapped in this realm until the clock is reset and the spell opens the doorway again. And no one knows she's within the spell, but us."

"Well done, Osiris."

Just then the old witch's head fell forward.

"Rest, mother, rest. For you too, will soon have all of the brat's power. That's why I used sap straight from the tree, instead of my own blood,"

The *Dark One* caringly saw that his mother was braced against the wall and as comfortable as she could be. Osiris then straightened himself upright.

"I will return soon, Mother. I have things to do to make sure everything is in place, when the time is right."

He then looked towards Katie, "See brat, I had hoped that you would have brought your precious wind chimes with you tonight. They are crucial to our plans. Fret not though, thanks to mother's foresight, I am to conjure just the right spell that will allow me to travel in and out of the

Witching Hour realm. No silly magic will stop the *Dark One's* reign from being ushered in."

Osiris pointed his staff towards the stone wall of the cave. He hid his face and spoke a few words of old, under his breath, not allowing Katie to hear them or even see his lips as the spell was cast. From the tip of his staff a light struck the rock and a portal opened.

"Now, together we will complete what we started. The tree that this brat declared was so strong will be destroyed as if it never was," said Osiris looking back towards his mother.

With a sinister smirk Osiris took one last look at Katie, as if he wanted to take in as much of her misery as possible. He then turned into a black mist and drifted into the portal, disappearing out of the cave. In his wake the *Dark One* left Katie alone with the newly reformed… *Mother of Bones*. In hind sight it would seem that Katie did indeed have good reason to ponder what else could be brought back from the grave by the *Shadow Tree* and its ilk, after all.

CHAPTER NINE

"HAS ANYONE SEEN MY PRINCESS?"

The next morning Eshe awoke to a feeling of unease. Resting on her pillow, with eyes still shut, she noticed just how quiet the room was, as well as the lack of chatter in her head. Usually by way of *skull-speak*, she would have already heard an unguarded thought that Katie let slip through, but not today. Instantly she opened her eyes and turned her head towards Katie's bed. It was empty.

"Hey, where's Katie?" Eshe asked.

Instantly Vexika and Green Eyes lifted up and peered around the room as if Katie would be hidden behind a chair, or cloaked by the window tapestries.

"I don't know," replied, Vexika. "Probably just went for breakfast."

The panther-girl paused seeing how concerned Eshe and Green Eyes were. She got out to bed, placed a hand on Eshe's shoulder, and then added, "I'm sure she's fine."

"I'm not sure about that," said Eshe. "I have a feeling that something is very wrong."

Eshe with Green Eyes at her feet, and Vexika by her side quickly raced to the *Great Hall,* which was packed with students bustling to make it to class on time. They searched the crowd as they went toward the table Katie liked to sit and eat her meals at, usually with a book in her hand. There was a black robed girl with a book covering her face.

"Katie, you gave us quite the scare," said Vexika as she pulled down a worn copy of, *A Guide to Magical Manifestation,* from in front of Lixa

Lupix, a *House Hallox* student, first year with hair not unlike Katie, but with the face of a doe deer.

"Hey, I was reading that," said Lixa, indignantly.

"Sorry, Lixa," said the panther-girl. "Thought you were someone else."

The three decided to head to the atrium and see if Katie had gone there, perhaps to see Professor Hopingráve. As they hurried through the hallways, asking those along the way if they'd seen Katie, suddenly a voice called out loudly for all to hear.

"Has anyone seen, my princess? Please, please, help me find my princess."

Eshe and Vexika looked towards the grand staircase and coming down it was Tamrah, Kilmon and a few other *Stormanders*.

"Well, well…" said Tamrah, "did precious Katie Granxor get herself kidnapped for a royal ransom?"

"Shut your mouth," said Vexika, her hairs standing on end. "You don't know what you're talking about."

"I don't, huh," replied the rhino-girl, "We all know the truth… and the Granxors have whatever is coming to them."

At this point a rather large crowd of students had started gathering, hearing the heated exchange. As to not let things escalate any further,

Eshe grabbed her friend by the arm pulling the panther-girl away from the red-robed bully.

"Come, on. They're not worth it."

Eshe, Vexika and Green Eyes started to continue on their way when the rhino-girl decided she had more to say, especially being that she had an audience.

"If you ask me," Tamrah said loudly for the entire crowd to hear. "I hope that Osiris did finally get her, and did away with her. At least then, we won't all be put at risk for a no good normal."

No sooner had the words left Tamrah's elongated snout, when Eshe had spun around, walked straight up to the rhino-girl and clocked her so hard, with a punch to the chin, that she knocked over the *Stormander* students behind her as she fell backwards.

"You ever say that about my granddaughter again, and they will be the last words you ever speak!"

The gathered students gasped in both surprise and shock. However the show wasn't over, not just yet, anyway.

"I knew it," said Tamrah through a bloody lip. "They are both Granxors! And they are putting us in danger! Get her!"

The group of *Stormander* students led by Kilmon began bearing down on Eshe. Within a second, Vexika had jumped to Eshe's side, as wands began to appear in several red-robed students' hands throughout the hallway.

Suddenly Green Eyes leapt into the air towards the advancing group of *Stormanders.* As he did so, the cat transformed. In an instant, the most feral fierce version of Simon the Protector filled the gap standing between Eshe and any wishing to do her harm.

"You want to hurt Lady Eshe," growled the cat-man, with sharpened claws looking directly into the eyes of Kilmon, "then you have to go through me,"

The croc-boy decided to press his luck, as he and the three *Stormanders* flanking him, lunged towards the protector. With a roar that shook the entirety of the hallway, and several swipes of his claw, Simon sent the red-robed bullies through the air, smashing into the walls that surrounded them.

"Let's get out of here," cried out Kilmon stumbling to get up.

All the *Stormanders* took off running down the hallway, as Simon stood firmly planted in front of Eshe and Vexika.

"This isn't over," cried out Tamrah as she disappeared out of sight.

Eshe looked at Vexika and Simon with an appreciative expression.

"Well, I guess the secret's out," said Vexika.

"Yes it is," agreed Eshe. "Now everything changes."

Simon's eyes tightened.

"Katie, she needs us," said the protector.

Leaving several open mouthed, stunned students in their wake… the three hurriedly made their way to the atrium.

As they entered, there was no *Magelic Botany* class in session. The glass house study was empty, save the plant life. However, as Eshe glanced towards the row of mausoleums with the *Shadow Tree* overlooking, and overshadowing them all, she realized that someone was probably always there.

"Professor Hopingráve, we need to speak to you, please," called out Eshe.

A voice emanated throughout the entire atrium.

"What is the matter, Miss Leota?"

The words were followed by a shadow that leapt out of the oak tree. From overhead a gush of wind blew Eshe's hair back, and within a mere moment, the ghostly professor was standing directly before them.

"Professor, Katie is gone, she's missing," said Eshe.

Professor Hopingráve was about to speak, when she noticed Simon the protector. Her eyes widened, taken aback.

"About that," said Eshe, "by now, I'm sure the entire school knows our secret, and who Katie's cat really is."

Eshe paused before continuing, "Who we… Katie and I, really am, too."

"I see," replied Professor Hopingráve, not seeming too surprised, but still wishing to keep a stoic demeanor. "Then they will know the truth, and we will take it from there."

Professor Hopingráve lifted her chin and straightened her stance, to display to Eshe, Vexika as well as to Simon that she was in perfect control of the situation.

"Has Robur been alerted?" the professor asked.

"Not yet, professor," replied Vexika. "We wanted to see if we could find her first."

"Simon, would you let him know?" asked the professor. "The *Shadow Tree* should do nicely as a window to Robur's *Great Oak*. In fact I know it is, with the right spell. I trust you are well-versed in this matter?"

Simon nodded and went quickly to the oak that the professor had just leapt out of.

•

"Miss Leota, Miss Vee, we need to make the other professors and the headmistress aware of what has occurred," said Professor Hopingráve, with her wand now at the ready. Her broomstick hurriedly twirled from somewhere nearby and landed obediently in the hand.

"You two with me," said the professor as she twirled her wand. Instantly two more brooms answered the call, each landing in the palms of their soon to be riders. "We ride."

"Is Simon coming?" Eshe asked.

"I have a feeling he will be busy with Robur and *the Seven*, until we get this matter resolved."

With that the three were off into the air.

First stop, Professor Montakha. Once the phoenix-teacher was told, he promptly added extra security measures to the already strong safeguards, essentially putting the academy in a high alert lockdown.

Next Professor Hopingráve, Eshe and Vexika, made their way into the darkened study of Professor Bokor. He seemed to get an alert from the cosmos, just before Professor Hopingráve was able to tell him the news. Professor Bokor excused himself; saying that he was informed that *time is of the essence.*

Eshe could see that the were-vampire of a creature teacher meant what he had said, as he feverishly flipped through books of spells and enchantments, while holding court with spirits that Eshe could not see.

Leaving Professor Bokor to the business at hand, the three, Professor Hopingráve, Eshe and Vexika flew upwards toward the top of the academy to Professor Toohasi's study.

When they reached the landing that led into the *History of Magic* classroom, as Eshe and Vexika knew it to be, they were surprised to find Robur, Simon and Headmistress Valborga standing alongside Professor Toohasi.

"Headmistress, Professor," said Professor Hopingráve, "I assume you have been briefed on the current situation, being Robur and Simon are present."

"Yes we have," replied the Headmistress. "Miss Windsor's whereabouts are unknown, and that is unacceptable."

"Those of us in the faculty, especially with empathic abilities, have sensed something dark is building… rising. And our Katie Windsor is indeed at the center of this coming storm," said the owl-like professor, in a much more serious tone than Eshe was used to seeing him display. "I asked the headmistress to meet me here in my study, because I could tell that someone was here last night, in my absence. The owls let me know as much, when I returned this morning from my journey to the village of Orbach, a few valleys to the north. I was there, having heard of a rare dagger that was rumored to have been used in *the Great Battle at the Krantiza Bridge*, that of course took place right here, before the gates of our academy."

Professor Toohasi gestured towards his desk where a brilliant gold dagger sat amid a beam of sunlight that was trickling in from the rafters.

"Is that *the Great Zabar's* dagger?" asked Professor Hopingráve.

The owl-like professor nodded *yes*.

"Astonishing," said Headmistress Valborga. "*House Zabar* would be delighted to know the magical blade does indeed exist."

"Yes, but to the point of why we are here," said Professor Toohasi, who tended to be very secretive about his out of academy activities. "When I entered my study, I instantly knew something wasn't right. The owls had been disturbed, frazzled… as if disturbed by an intruder. Yet, I could not find that anything had been taken. Odd, indeed."

Hand lifted, the professor gestured once more around the room, showing that all of his rare artifacts, oddities and various collections of antiques were still there and intact.

“When I contacted the headmistress to inform her about this, she had just been informed by Robur and Simon about Miss Windsor’s disappearance,” continued Professor Toohasi. “It is peculiar that both of these things occurred at the same time. Perhaps it was she who visited here last night. Miss Windsor might have wanted to see me for some reason, and found the study empty.”

“Perhaps,” added Headmistress Valborga. “Still, we have to consider all options until we have Miss Windsor found and back under our protection.”

“We have alerted *the Seven*,” said Robur. “As well, Simon has made us all aware, that the academy now knows that he is *a protector* and that Eshe and Katie are in fact Granxors.”

Professor Toohasi’s eyes widened much larger than normal, which made it clear that he did not know, that this information had been made public knowledge.

“Quite frankly it is time that secrets are put aside,” continued the wizard. “Osiris is coming to destroy any who stand in his way. The time we have prepared for is now.”

The wizard walked towards the opening leading out of the study with Simon by his side. Robur pointed his staff towards the blue morning sky and a portal formed.

"Where are you going?" asked Eshe.

"Simon and I are meeting with the other protectors, at least those who are able to," replied Robur.

"We need to hear from Aker, Sahti and Wizlon," said Eshe. "Katie was troubled by the visions of Zalika that the *Dark One* kept filling her head with. Does he have them both now? If he does…"

Overcome with emotion, Eshe stopped mid-sentence.

"We're going to get Katie back," said Simon.

Eshe gave Simon an appreciative smile, as together with the wizard they turned and leapt off the birdhouse like perch and into a portal window. It closed behind them.

Eshe had a feeling of hopelessness rush over her. *I need to do something, I need to find her,* she thought to herself.

Professor Hopingráve heard her thoughts, as she had a tendency to do.

"We are doing everything we can do," said the professor. "If this is Osiris, he is counting on us to panic. And that we can't do."

"You knew him," replied Eshe. "Were even his friend. Was he always, evil? Because I have only known him to be so."

"No, the Osiris I knew so long ago, was actually passionate about standing up for the rights of the oppressed. Somewhere on that journey, he crossed over into being the oppressor. Though, I am sure, it happened so subtly that he didn't even realize that it was even occurring, until one day… you greet the world as the very darkness you were trying to rid it of."

Eshe lowered her gaze and coldly spoke, "I know what I would do to anyone if they hurt her."

"And that is the same road that Osiris walked down," replied Professor Hopingráve, softly. "In my many lifetimes, I never have seen any who walked down that road reach a place that endures. The greatest witches and wizards know this to be true. Only one spell, which I know of, truly lasts forever. And it's not born of hate."

"What spell is that?" asked Eshe.

"It's *the Forever Spell*," replied Professor Hopingráve.

Eshe had more questions about the spell, but just then, a group of students arrived upon the owl-like professor's perch. Word of Katie's and

Eshe's secret had clearly spread and some students wanted more than just answers… they wanted retribution.

"We demand that Eshe Leota or Granxor or whoever she is, be expelled immediately," said Tamrah, who still sported a swollen nose, from Eshe's punch.

"If you don't throw them out, we will!" demanded Kilmon.

The *Stormanders* were united in their outrage. However someone else still ran the academy.

"Demand, do you?" said Headmistress Valborga. "Miss Badara, Mr. Kroy, I decide who can and cannot attend this academy, and you would do good to remember that."

"Our families have pull as well, and you should remember that!" barked back Tamrah.

Collectively the students behind the rhino-girl continued their support of their spokesperson.

"Maybe all of our families should pull their support of this academy until we get a new headmistress, one not in the pocket of the Granxors," said Tamrah, seeming more than furious. She was determined. The rhino-girl decided to even take it a step further. "Osiris wasn't wrong in his desire to fight back against the normals. It is their hatred of creature-kind that has caused us to live like second class citizens for centuries. Now their princess wants to take the one school they banished us to, as well?"

"You speak from ignorance, child," said Professor Hopingráve, stepping in between the crowd of *Stormanders* and the headmistress. "Hatred will lead to more hatred, as it has for my many lives. The solution is not further isolation and fear. Now go to your dorms, before you carry this too far, Miss Badara."

The rhino-girl looked directly at Eshe with a murderous glare.

"This isn't over, Granxor! We are not going to keep this quiet. No one is going make us bow down to you!" Tamrah looked at the headmistress and reiterated, "No one!"

The rhino-girl turned and walked off with all of the *Stormander* students following in her wake.

*

A liquid window appeared before King Ragnar's throne, which caused Lore, his protector, to bare his teeth for a moment. The ape-man's face relaxed just a bit when Robur and Simon stepped out of the portal.

"*Your Highness*, I have troubling news," said Robur, as he and Simon bent down to one knee before the King and Queen of Chaparral.

"It is good to see you both," said King Ragnar with a nod to the wizard and the lion-man protector at his side. "Please speak."

"Thank you, *Your Highness*," continued Robur. "Princess Katherzine has disappeared from the academy and we are searching for her as we speak."

"Do you know if she ran off, or if it was something else?" asked Queen Bellzonna.

"*Your Majesty*, we are not for sure, but there was an incident where the *Dark One* attacked the academy on *Haunt-O-Wick Eve* and attempted to lure Katie and another student off grounds, away from the protections we have put in place."

"Osiris is back?" asked the queen.

"It appears so," replied Robur.

Just at that moment Gennadius and Zoticus came into the Throne Room. It seems they were on alert through *skull-speak*. Both bowed and then nodded to Simon and the wizard.

"We need to hear from our brothers in regards to the crow-woman," said Zoticus.

"Is it confirmed? Is Hathor alive, as well?" asked King Ragnar.

"That is the word we are awaiting," replied Simon. "Aker, Wizlon and Sahti should let us know one way or another any day now."

Simon paused before speaking, considering what he'd say next.

"Princess Katherzine was having dreams that showed her Aunt Zalika, being tortured by Osiris. Often she'd wake in a cold sweat with her heart racing. I saw with my own eyes how bad she was being tormented by these visions. It would not surprise me if she decided to try to rescue her aunt. I think she may be the one who went after Osiris."

The king stroked his chin, which he was known to do when he was deep in thought.

"I know you have kept certain details about our long-lost daughter from us for her protection," said King Ragnar. "However, it seems the time for secrecy is over. You mentioned that there was another student that Osiris was trying to lure out. Who would that be?"

The protectors and the wizard exchanged glances through lowered heads. It was not unlike being called into the headmistress' office at the academy thought Zoticus. Robur agreed, having heard that through using *skull-speak*.

"Well, we didn't want to tell you because you knowing could cause irreparable harm to the kingdom and to Chaparral."

"How so?" asked the queen, chiming in, intrigued.

The wizard took a deep breath before answering.

"A person from the past came into our timeline to aid in helping Princess Katherzine control her abilities, as well as giving her support as she makes her way through the academy."

"Someone from another time period?" asked King Ragnar in shock. "And you thought this was a good idea?"

Robur looked somewhat sheepish at hearing the king ask the question that he'd been asking himself for quite some time. His only refuge was that Aker was not there to forever remind him of this moment.

The king continued, "Well, who is this person? And remember this is your king asking, so no more clandestine replies. I want the full truth. This is my daughter, and I don't want to lose her again."

"It was and is Eshe Granxor," replied Robur. "Only it is, my lady, at the same age as Princess Katherzine is today.

A gasp fell over the entire chamber. The moment of stillness and shock felt like an eternity to the wizard. Then the uncomfortable silence was broken with a very loud response.

"Are you mad?" yelled King Ragnar. "She is gone and you bring her back in this way! Not to mention the risk to our entire bloodline should she die. I am no wizard, but is that not the way that kind of sorcery would work?"

The king actually got up off of the throne and walked towards Robur in a manner he'd never done before.

Aggressively he continued, "How dare you, risk my family's future, Katherzine's future. I should burn that cursed oak to the ground and its ashes and what's left of you thrown in the dungeons!"

Abruptly someone stepped in-between the king and Robur almost cutting off the king mid-sentence.

"How dare you!" growled Simon. "It is Robur and *the Seven* who have put our lives on the line over and over again for your family. I died for Princess Katherzine and I would do it again. I've been there by her side, as she cried many a tear. Meanwhile, after you were freed from the frozen spell that kept you from your daughter, what did you do? You sent her away… again! And now you talk about family? About putting those who watched over Princess Katherzine…" he paused and then called by her preferred name, "…Katie, in a dungeon?"

The lion-man stood up tall before continuing.

"Well, *Your Highness*, if you try to harm one white hair on the wizard, then you will have to go through me."

The king took a step or two backwards. He then looked around the room expecting someone to be appalled, to step in. Yet, no one did.

"Are you going to let someone speak to your king like that?"

One by one, King Ragnar looked at the other protectors in the room. First he eyed Zoticus, yet the Minotaur stood tall. Then his gaze found Gennadius and the grizzly lowered his snout and offered a look of defiance. Finally the king looked at Lore.

"You, as well," asked King Ragnar. "My faithful servant, you will not defend your king's honor?"

The ape-man stood upright, which added several feet to his height. Once fully extended and with chest inflated outward, the protector who once had literally had cut his own hand off, spoke.

"Me Lore. Me owned by no one. Katie and *the Seven* are Lore's family."

The throne room was silent while the powerful words of the bravest protector that Chaparral had ever known soaked into the walls of the once frozen castle. Finally a voice broke through and shattered the awkward standoff.

We have her.

However the words were not voiced in the room, at least not at first.

We have her.

"You hear that?" asked Zoticus, looking in Robur's direction.

"Yes, I hear it, too," suddenly growled Gennadius.

The King and Queen looked puzzled, not sure what was occurring. Someone was speaking to the wizard and the protectors using *skull-speak.*

The wizard abruptly lifted his staff and waved it in a circular motion, causing a glassy window to appear. In it were the faces of Aker, Sahti and Wizlon. The fox was the first to speak.

"What did I miss?" asked Aker, before realizing where Simon, Zoticus, Gennadius, Lore, and Robur were.

"Is that?" started Aker, noticing the King and Queen. However, before the fox could offer up formal addresses, Robur interjected.

"We heard your message, who is it that you have?" asked Robur.

"We have the crow-woman," answered Wizlon. "But she is badly injured. We just arrived here, on Hercana Island. The local doctor is seeing to her and Fadessa's wounds. "

"Who is Fadessa?" asked Simon.

“Let’s say, she saved Zalika, in more than one way,” replied Wizlon.

The mention of the name, *Zalika*, however, made the King and Queen, gasp.

Wizlon could tell from the tone and mood of Robur and the others that something was off; he started to get the sense something very wrong had occurred.

“You asked who we had. Who else would we have had?” asked Wizlon.

“Katie is missing,” replied Robur.

“Missing? How?” asked Aker. But before anyone could reply, the fox said, matter-of-factly, “We are on our way.”

The call abruptly ended.

CHAPTER TEN
"HOMECOMING"

The fox was good to his word. As it were, Aker and Wizlon returned in less than two weeks. Zalika and Fadessa were too ill to travel, so Sahti stayed behind so that both of them could fully heal. Not to mention, that as a protector, it was the snake-man's charge to keep watch over the Granxor bloodline. Indeed the crow-woman was still very much a limb branching out of that particular tree, a tree which Osiris was dead intent on upending.

However, in staying behind, it left Sahti with a real predicament. How would they all get back home? That would have to be a concern for another day. Presently, Katie and her safe return was all that mattered.

Wixaki, the large dragon, flew as fast as his wings would carry him, which was considerably faster, than it would have been with Sahti, Zalika and Fadessa added to his cargo. The fox insisted that they waste no time on their journey back. Neither Wizlon nor Wixaki, dared to challenge Aker on this matter. They'd never seen the fox so determined... so serious. It would seem that Lore was not the only one who thought of Katie as family.

During the two weeks, no one had had any success in locating Katie's whereabouts. The abduction of the long-lost princess was on the lips of everyone at the academy. Some were kind and voiced concern, while others were not.

“Can you believe she lied about who she was the entire time?” said Tamrah. “Meanwhile, the other Granxor girl, whoever she really is, is allowed to stay!”

The rhino-girl was riling up the group of *Stormanders* in the courtyard where Professor Montakha’s class was about to commence.

“Seems to me, that the professors and the headmistress are in the pocket of the royal family,” continued Tamrah. “My father told them as much, when he found out, about what they have allowed to occur here. He pulled all of his funding, until there is a change of leadership.”

Just then Professor Montakha appeared, landing behind the gathered group of red robed students. His head was all ablaze as phoenix heads sometimes tend to do, especially when enraged.

“Who am I in the pocket of, Miss Badara?” asked the professor.

But before the shocked student could answer, the fiery professor continued.

“Did you ever consider that the way you are acting and behaving right now, is exactly why you weren’t told who Eshe and Katie really were?”

The rhino-girl was taken aback by Professor Montakha’s sudden appearance, however she regained her composure enough to keep that defiant glare upon her face that she’d become known for.

“This academy is for creature-kind and not pampered princesses and normals!” she spat back.

“No, this academy was formed to teach magic to those who had been shunned by others. Do you see the irony in that, as we stand here today, with you speaking your words of division, Miss Badara? How about you, Mr. Kroy? How about any of you? This is how you would want to be treated, not for what you have done, but rather for things you have no control over… like your bloodline, or your last name?”

Vexika and others in black, silver and purple robes straggled in as the professor spoke.

“No, professor,” said the panther-girl with her chin up high. “I would not like to be judged on anything other than my character. Maybe that’s what the problem is for some.”

Vexika looked right at Tamrah and Kilmon.

“I agree, Miss Vee, I agree,” said Professor Montakha. “Shall we proceed with class, Miss Badara, Mr. Kroy, or is there more you’d like to say?”

The red robed students seemed to collectively roll their eyes and mutter a few inaudible comments, though the class did proceed. Noticeably absent from this, what would have been her first class back since Katie’s disappearance was Eshe. That was for good reason, though. As she reminded Robur, the Wizard, when he said once again that she should stay at the academy and wait for word, "*Katie is not only my best friend, she is my granddaughter, or will be, however you want to say it... and I will go with you and the Seven, thank you very much. Or you can try to stop me from going out on my own. Either way, I am going to search for Katie.*"

The wizard could see flashes of Katie in this young teenage version of Eshe, and he knew better than to say anything but, *"Yes, Miss Eshe. Shall we be off, then?"*

And they were.

Robur had informed Eshe how things went with the visit to *Clarion's Peak.*

"I assume another visit to the Granxor castle is out of the question?" asked Robur.

"I don't see the point," replied Eshe. "I have older me's memories, however they are not triggered until something relative to the said memory causes them to be recalled. That said, it is clear that just because we were a royal family does not mean we were perfect by any means. I can sense older me's frustration with her family's love of their own position in society."

Robut nodded as if this was not altogether unknown to him.

Eshe continued, "As well, I wanted say that I am not innocent of that trap, either. Or older me… well you know what I mean. Still, I think bypassing the big family reunion right now, is probably wise."

"Agreed," said the wizard.

"When Katie was recounting the visions that Osiris was showing her of Zalika, they seemed to be in the caves under *Clarion's Peak*. She thought so, and so did I. I'd swear it was more than an educated guess, I believe it was intentional. Let us start there."

The wizard nodded and then lifted his staff. Eshe raised her lantern and from out of it shot a beam of light which when it poured over the stick of the wood, opened a portal. Together Robur, using his staff which led him through the air not unlike the rusty handlebar, and Eshe on her broom, soared into the opening. When they exited, the two of them were at the edge of the forest in the *Great Valley*… above them were the *Forbidden Caves*.

The sun had set when they found themselves hovering before the caves. A few of Chaparral's moons could be seen even though the sky dusked only moments earlier.

Eshe held her lantern with an outstretched arm, guiding the light onto the openings. She closed her eyes and let her senses intertwine themselves with the light. Deeper and deeper her six senses awakened and before she knew it, she heard a growling sound fill her ears.

"Miss Eshe," called out Robur, "your face?"

She had transformed into a white furred were-witch, like her granddaughter before her had done in this very spot just a few moons ago. Suddenly her eyes widened as the lantern's light seemed to pull her arm like a fisherman with a bite on the line.

"This way," she growled.

Following the light downward into the cave, Robur and Eshe were led to a somewhat open cavernous space with rock formations that looked very familiar to Eshe.

"It seems like I've been here before."

Just then, something crawled into Eshe's ear and rattled around inside her skull.

“Eshe? Eshe? Is that you?” asked the faint voice possibly through *skull-speak.*

Eshe tilted her head struggling to determine where the voice was coming from. Cautiously she tiptoed around the corner, letting the light from the lantern lead the way.

As the beam stretched across and over the stone wall, suddenly it exposed a silhouette of a figure chained and bound to the rock. Eshe made the light reach even further into the cavern, and as she did so, it revealed the hunched over figure of an old lady stirring a bubbling pot.

“What was that? Are you talking to someone, dearie?” spat the old woman. “Who’s there? Show yourself!”

As the beam crawled up and over her, the old woman acted as though the light was a snake digging into her skin, burning her every inch of the way. Even in shadow, Eshe and Robur could feel the old woman’s angry stare searching for an intruder, a trespasser.

Knowing time was of the essence, Katie’s shadow spoke once more.

”The witch’s -” started Katie, but the *Mother of Bones* pointed her wand and cried out, *“Silenta!”*

Katie was abruptly cut off, as if a spell got her tongue, for it had.

The skull to skull communication between Katie and Eshe was silenced. Instantly Eshe withdrew the lantern's light so that it only cast its beam onto the slab of stone to her side. After a moment, and having heard no further obscenities from the old woman, she decided to risk it, and slowly moved the beam back once again towards the open area. Inch by inch the light crept forward and then abruptly a dark figure came into view, seeming to fill the entire cave.

"I am Lord Osiris!" declared the voice.

The face of the *Dark One* with mouth open wide, made Eshe and Robur recoil. It almost seemed as if the shadowy figure would devour the light, lantern, and the two trespassers wholly.

"Your tricks won't save her this time, wizard. I want you and the family which you have so faithfully served, to know the pain you've caused me and mine. My mother had to choose between her own life and the life of her son. How fortunate that inside the *Witch's Glass*, just before she gave her life to save me… as she tossed me out through the opening, she told me how to bring her back, and so I was able to save her. Still, she died. She sacrificed.

Now it should be no different for the little girl who sent me into these caves so long ago."

The *Dark One* now spoke directly to Eshe.

"Better yet, Eshe Granxor, do the right thing, like my mother did, and freely sacrifice yourself to save your granddaughter. Or else you will slowly watch her die! This I promise you!"

As Osiris said these words, Katie began to cry out in agony, which filled the caves, alongside Osiris and his mother's laughter.

"Leave her alone, you monster!" said Eshe.

Robur started to cast a spell, but the *Mother of Bones* beat him to it.

"Conceal-mentiosa!" demanded the witch.

Osiris added, *"Invis-ie-onish"* followed by, *"Rush-a-tonum!"*

Instantaneously Eshe and Robur were cast out of the caves; spit out as if they were gourd seeds in a *Haunt-O-Wick* carving contest. Whatever enchantment was further cast by the *Mother of Bones* and her son, ordered the rocks rise up and seal the caves tights, so that the side of the mountain looked whole… healed even.

"The *Mother of Bones* lives, now she and her son have Katie," said Eshe now returning to her non were-witch state. "They're keeping her in some otherworldly dimension or realm. What are we going to do?"

"In all my years, this magic is novel to me," replied Robur perplexed. "Though, that matters not, Miss Eshe. We are going to get her back."

The old wizard stroked his long white beard. Despite the fact the he was only of spirit, he appeared to be feeling his age at this moment. He took in a deep breath, while eyeing the mountainside.

"We need to get you back to the academy straight away," he said matter-of-factly. Before Eshe could utter a word in protest, the wizard continued. "Our unexpected visit caused Osiris to tip his hand just a bit. See, if he wanted to end Katie's life, he would have done it by now. Mother and son, want something else, and it would appear that you are the one they need to see that plan through to fruition."

"I get it," said Eshe, not at all happy about the words she was saying. "I need to stay within the protections."

Robur continued, "Killing you would no doubt cause a ripple effect throughout the Granxor timeline, but moreover it would erase many unpleasantries in Cassandra's and Osiris' own history, as well. I surmised that might have been the plan all along."

He paused, and then gave one last look at where the cave opening once was.

"They want a redo."

With that the wizard lifted his staff and pointed it towards the sky, and it carried him upwards. Mounted upon her broom, Eshe flew closely by his side the entire flight back to the academy.

*

The following day Eshe woke to see a dark robed figure with a black furry face with piercing eyes standing bedside, waiting for her eyelids to lift.

"About time you wake up," said the panther-girl. "What's going on? What the latest? Have you heard anything? Where did you and the Wizard go off to? Come on, spill it?"

"Vexika," replied Eshe still coming to, as the memories of the previous day's events came rushing back to mind, "it isn't good."

"What do you mean?" asked Vexika, concerned, even hesitant to hear the reply.

"I saw Katie, or at least a shadow of her," said Eshe, unsure. "It was in the caves under *Clarion's Peak*. Yet she was there, but she wasn't there. I only saw her by way of my lantern's light."

“Amazing that thing,” said Vexika, gesturing towards the chest at the foot of the bed, where the lantern was stored. “Go on.”

“Osiris and his mother, the *Mother of Bones*, have her,” continued Eshe, as the panther-girl let out a gasp. “Now that everything is out in the open, I can talk freely. She is who Katie and I were battling when the *Shadow Tree* went up in flames last year. We thought she was gone, but Osiris brought her back. Somehow they got Katie and we couldn’t get to her. We couldn’t save her.”

Eshe paused as she was choking up at the thought of leaving her best friend behind.

“We are going to get her back,” said Vexika, as she grasped Eshe’s hand as squeezed it tight. “I promise.”

Eshe smiled at her friend, and together they got ready for the first class that Eshe would attend since Katie’s disappearance.

The first class back would be *Voodoology*, which of course began at sunrise on the dot. Against Eshe’s better judgment, she listened to Robur, the headmistress and the other professors whom all urged her to resume attending classes while the search for Katie continued.

As Eshe and Vexika made their way skillfully up the staircase to Professor Bokor’s classroom, several eyeballs seemed to be staring a bit more than usual. In a hushed tone a few steps down from where the girls had just passed by, words carried to Eshe's ears.

"That's her. That's one of the Granxor girls," said a particularly loud set of eyes.

"I heard the *Dark One* took the other one," replied a more shifty set of peepers, nearest to the darkest corner of the stairwell.

"Osiris took the girl who stepped on you both," said a set of tight angry eyes. "The careless girl stepped on me no less than three times this semester and counting."

The voice paused and the angry eyes suddenly widened, almost as if they were smiling, as the voice added, "Well, not counting anymore, I presume."

The open lids seemed to get a good chuckle in… that is until, and just by coincidence mind you, Eshe dropped her stack of books, which were then followed by Vexika's books, as well. Even more curious was the fact that each corner of the books seemed to magically poke an eyeball as they tumbled down the stairwell.

The laughter was quickly replaced by moans and colorful epithets. As the books settled, every eye was fixed on the two girls standing at the top of the stairs.

"Oh, how careless of me," said Eshe.

"How careless, indeed," added Vexika.

"Revert-e-oso!"

The two girls lifted their wands… with a swoop of their wrists and a cleverly cast spell… the books lifted into the air and returned perfectly stacked into their owners arms.

"I might just be careless again tomorrow and the next day, and the day after that, if given a reason," said Eshe. "Do we see eye to eye, on the matter?"

All the wide open, yet watery and somewhat reddened bloodshot eyes, seemed to nod in agreement. They did so by a stairwell full of pupils that lifted and lowered up and down in unison, not unlike bouncing balls.

"Good," replied Eshe.

The two girls turned towards the classroom with a rather intense swoosh of the robes, which caused a gush of wind that made a few of the eyes blink. In their absence the stairwell became silent, which doesn't happen often.

As Eshe and Vexika entered the room more whispers could be heard. But no sooner had the finger pointing started, when a bat soared down from the rafters. Instantly as the bat neared the professor's desk, a figure in a long black robe emerged. It was indeed, Professor Bokor.

"Let's take our seats students. We have a plethora of spells to cover today."

Everyone's ears perked up with this announcement. Literally this happened for Vexika, being part feline and all.

"Recent events have no doubt emphasized the need for all students to be prepared to defend themselves."

He paused for dramatic effect and then, *"Ignitious!"*

Ever the showman, the professor spun round with wand in hand, and abruptly cast a spell that conjured a wall of fire, to which he then busted through, like a lion through a flaming ring in a circus.

"Should any of you be confronted by one who possesses great knowledge of the dark arts, knowing a few counter spells might save your life."

He then raised his hand searching the room, from student to student before landing upon Tamrah.

"Miss Badara, think a thought that you don't want me to know, and then guard it with all your might," said the professor.

Professor Bokor closed his eyes, squinted tightly, as he began to probe into the rhino-girl's mind.

"Is this your thought?" he asked, as he gave his wand a twirl, and the professor appeared in his underwear dancing on the academy rooftop under the moonlight, like a ballerina. Tamarah remained silent, even embarrassed, as the entire class erupted into laughter.

"You will need to do better than that, Miss Badara, though I do look good in that particular lighting, I must say," said Professor Bokor, not bothered at all by the imagined thought. He moved from student to student, letting each of them try to hide a thought or memory, as he would seek it out. In the end, only a few were able to deter him from collecting said memory. Eshe was one of the ones that passed the test. The other two were Vexika and to everyone's surprise, Kilmon. Vexika surmised that it was because the croc-boy had no thoughts in his head to find, just a lot of open space.

The professor was so entertaining that for the rest of the class, all the students were absolutely fixated on every overly exaggerated move and hung on every grandiose word that he spoke. Even Tamarah and Kilmon, remained so enthralled that they did not even cast a single dispersion or unflattering comment, Eshe's way. None were happier about this than

Eshe, who for an hour or so, found some refuge from the nonstop thoughts of Katie. However, that refuge was short lived.

After class Professor Bokor, dismissed all the students, but asked if Eshe might stay behind for a moment.

"Miss Leota," started the professor, not sure if he should address her differently now that the secret was out, though in the end he decided to stay with the familiar until told to do otherwise, "I wanted to ask if there has been any word on Katie's whereabouts?"

Eshe didn't know whether to divulge all the details of what she and Robur had learned or not. Professor Bokor, could sense her hesitation.

"Well, we do believe that the *Dark One* has her," started Eshe, when the professor suddenly winced. He turned his head to the side as if he was once again receiving a transmission from the great beyond, as he was known to do.

At first Eshe started to roll her eyes, as the thought, *here we go again*, came to the forefront of her mind, then the professor began to speak, and that thought quickly vanished.

"Are you going to just let her die?" asked the professor in a creaky, crackly voice.

"Professor?" asked Eshe, backing away from him apprehensively.

"I would have thought that the little girl, who stood so arrogantly in that church, in the *City of Gold*, and sent me to the underworld, keeping me imprisoned for so many years, would be braver than to retreat. Hide in your academy, as your precious future granddaughter wastes away. Shame, shame, shame."

Just then the professor winced once more, as he seemed to come out of a trance that he didn't even know he'd been in.

"Sorry, Miss Leota, I guess the class took more out of me, than I knew. Well, I just wanted to make sure you continue to protect your mind against any intrusion. You did well today, but don't let your guard down."

"I won't," replied Eshe, still shaken.

"Are you okay, Miss Leota?" asked the professor. "You look like you've seen a ghost."

"No, I'm fine," replied Eshe, while suppressing a thought, *I didn't see a ghost, but I seemed to have just talked to one.*

Professor Bokor titled his head as if he is might have heard an echo of that thought she had just conjured.

“Thank you for your concern,” Eshe said quickly, to divert the professor from digging any deeper. “Just gotta hurry to my next class. Professor Hopingráve does not like tardiness, so… thanks.”

Her feet moved so fast that Eshe hardly remembered exiting the class or if she stepped on any eyeballs as she made her way down the stairwell. As she rounded the corner which led into the *Great Hall*, Eshe saw a furry black tail standing out above the groups of students. It was rapidly moving in her direction. Vexika had been waiting for Eshe, as good friends tend to do.

“What did Professor Bokor want?” asked Vexika.

“He wanted to help me, but,” started Eshe, but got choked up thinking about the words that Osiris had just said.

“What happened?” asked the panther-girl, seeing that Eshe was becoming emotional.

“The *Dark One* came though the professor,” said Eshe, “and he’s going to hurt Katie, unless I give myself to him.”

Vexika hugged Eshe and held her tight, and then whispered, as everyone seemed to watching them.

“That is not going to happen. You know he would kill you both,” she said, and paused. “We are going to get her back. Again, I promise. And I never break my word.”

As Eshe’s head was on Vexika’s shoulder, something suddenly caught her eye. Hanging in the main hallway every few feet were flyers with Katie’s face on them. They read…

A Normal is Missing

Princess Katie Granxor

Wanted by *the Dark One…*

And No One Else.

Good Riddance!

Standing in front of one of the flyers was Tamrah, Kilmon and several *Stormander* students laughing. Eshe walked straight at Tamrah; suddenly her wand appeared in her hand.

“You think torturing someone is funny?” asked Eshe. “Then how about I show you what it’s like!”

“You wouldn’t dare,” said Tamrah.

Before she could finish the thought the rhino-girl found herself floating defenselessly upside down.

“Help me! Someone stop her!” cried out Tamrah.

Kilmon rushed towards Eshe, but with the swipe of her hand she cast him into a wall knocking him unconscious.

"Anyone else?" asked Eshe looking at the red-robed students who had so recently been laughing maniacally. "I didn't think so."

Suddenly a cloud of red smoke appeared. From out of the mist stepped Headmistress Valborga.

"Miss Leota, put Miss Badara down!"

Eshe looked at the headmistress stone-faced. Now it was Eshe who seemed to be entranced. She wasn't. No, Eshe was enraged.

"I said," started the headmistress, and then she noticed the flyer which was hanging on the wall. Headmistress Valborga straightened her back and lifted her chin and calmly walked over to Eshe. She put her hand atop of Eshe's and gently encouraged her to lower the wand, which she did.

The rhino-girl crashed to the floor with a thud. Instantly Tamrah leapt to her feet and rushed at Eshe.

"Mummify!"

With the wave of her wand, the headmistress froze Tamrah in her tracks. Sadly her mouth still could move.

"You cast a spell on me? I'm the victim, here," protested Tamrah. "I demand you release me. And that you finally expel that Granxor girl or my father will have your head!"

"That is the last time you will threaten me or my position as headmaster."

Headmistress Valborga moved closed to Tamrah. Once she was only inches from her face she looked her dead in the eyes. The headmistress raised her hand, and as she did so, one of the flyers ripped itself from the wall and flew into her grip.

"Now speaking of my job, I want to know just who littered my academy with this filth. Do you know who it was, Miss Badara?"

"I have no clue, Headmistress," replied Tamrah with a smirk.

The headmistress twirled her wand between fingers coming to rest perfectly positioned to cast another spell, which it did.

As everyone watched, a window of smoke materialized, not unlike the mist that the headmistress had emerged out of. Upon the vapors the hallway appeared. The recollections of memories seemed to be replaying an event that had taken place the night before. The vision went on to reveal that it was Tamrah, Kilmon and a few other *Stormander* students hanging the flyers in the hallway. The group of red robed students who were shown in the video all happened to be standing nearby. One of course, was very close by… in fact the headmistress could hear that Tamrah's heartbeat had quickened as a result of being caught red-handed, as it were.

"Since you've demanded that someone be expelled, several times now, you finally get your wish," said Headmistress Valborga. "You and all the students who hung this abhorrent flyer up in *my* academy… are expelled."

The chins of several students in red robes dropped, while quite a few grins appeared on students from the other houses. It would seem that many in the academy saw this flyer and the antics that surrounded it as a bridge too far.

"You can't do that!" said Tamrah.

"Yes I can, and I did," replied the headmistress. "Have your things packed and ready to go by dawn tomorrow. Your parents can pick you up right here in the *Great Hall* in the morning. Now you can have plenty of time to spend with daddy."

Tamrah looked both shocked and yet defiant.

"Don't worry, though. All is not lost, take this time and learn a lesson from it, and some manners. You can apply next semester, with an apology to Miss Windsor, for what you said here today. Only then, will I consider reinstating you."

The headmistress turned and started to walk away into a cloud of red mist, when Tamrah once more drew her attention.

"That apology will never happen!" said the rhino-girl now loosed from the spell that mummified her.

"What did you say Miss Badara?" asked Headmistress Valborga, now as red in the face as the misty cloud that still lingered near to her.

"If the *Dark One* has her, she is not coming back," said Tamrah with her head held high, not backing down at all. "Katie Granxor is as good as dead. Whether you like it or not, I have the right to say it."

Headmistress Valborga actually seemed too angry to reply to the hurtful cold words. Instead she took in a breath and spoke calmly which was more frightening than if she had screamed at the top of her lungs.

"Tomorrow morning, all of you… right here… bags packed. See to it."

The headmistress disappeared into the red cloud, leaving Tamrah, Kilmon and the other red robed students standing in the midst of silver, black and purple robes.

"What are you looking at?" barked Kilmon, as they made their way through the crowd.

All eyes stayed on the group of *Stormanders* until they exited towards their dorms in shame. Even some from their same house stood defiant against them. Eshe took no joy in their expulsions, but she was not sad about it either.

The bell for the next class, *Magelic Botany*, had long since rang out, It would seem that several of the students were running behind because of the incident in the *Great Hall*, so Eshe and Vexika would not be alone in being late. As they entered the atrium they were happy to see that Professor Hopingráve was not yet present before the class. However just as they made it to the center of the glasshouse, a familiar shadow stretched across several of the rows of plants, before landing with a thud before the gathered students.

"Good day, everyone," said Professor Hopingráve, as she adjusted her pointed hat. "I understand we had quite an ugly event take place in the *Great Hall*, so I delayed the start of class until all who will be attending, could do so. There is no place in this academy for such undignified actions as what I was informed happened. None, whatsoever."

The professor then gave a look towards Eshe, and offered a bit of a comforting grin, before continuing.

“That being said, I see that Miss Badara, Mr. Kroy, Mr. Lox, and Mr. Uxmok will not be attending today or anytime in the near future. So be it. Let’s get down to business. We do indeed have a lot to cover.”

The ghostly professor turned around facing a certain section of her garden. With her back turned to the class, she continued speaking.

“Protective charms and potions… and the specific herbs one needs to make them.”

Suddenly her eyes appeared, poking out from in-between the strands of hair that covered the back of her head. Like two gumballs sitting in a candy machine dispensary, the eyes sort of rolled around as the professor spoke.

“Can anyone tell me how to make a potion that allows you to appear to be a certain creature or person?”

Vexika spoke up first.

“That would be the clonipidus plant. Its magic properties have long been known to allow its taker to act somewhat as a chameleon. As well, it can allow you, for a short period of time, to… as you say professor… take on the appearance of another.”

“Very good Miss Vee,” replied Professor Hopingráve. “Very good, indeed.”

Eshe leaned over and whispered, "I'm impressed, Vexika."

The panther-girl leaned in and replied, "As children we would use it to play tricks on my mother, all the time. She'd kiss one of us goodnight, only to walk down the stairs, and see that same child walking in through the front door. She thought she was going mad."

After the class was over, just as it happened with Professor Bokor, Professor Hopingráve asked for Eshe to stay behind, though she also asked Vexika to stay, too.

"Miss Leota, I wanted to speak to both you and Miss Vee. I spoke to Robur who is with *the Seven*. Aker and Wizlon have just arrived at *Clarion's Peak*. I know this is hard, as evidenced by the actions of this morning's events, but patience is required. Osiris is counting on us to act rash. He is cunning, and will act only when he knows every piece is lined up in his favor. I know him well. You say Katie is alive. You saw that, with your own eyes. That is only so, because it serves him, to keep her alive. You both must not be led out from the grounds for any reason. I can sense that is exactly what the *Dark One* wants."

The professor gave a kind smile of sorts, somewhat like a smirk and said, "I don't claim to be on the same level of the cosmic superiority as Professor Bokor, of course, but connected I am, indeed. We are nearing the end. And in that end… we will need to all be standing together. That is our strength."

Suddenly the professor looked as though someone or something inside the oak was calling to her, wanting her attention.

"I must leave you now," said the hare-like professor and sprung up into the air, her shadow trailing her as she disappeared into the *Shadow Tree.*

*

At that moment high upon *Clarion's Peak… the Seven* and Robur were reunited in the courtyard of the *Granxor Castle.*

"Any word on Katie?" asked Aker, before any pleasantries.

"Katie is being held by Osiris and his mother, Cassandra, in some otherworldly realm," replied the wizard. "We've yet to figure out how to reach her. However, I have a feeling it won't be long until they reach us. The *Dark One* wants Eshe in exchange for Katherzine. It would seem that since his return, it is her that has been his target."

"What exactly did you see?" asked the fox.

Hesitating to tell the already agitated fox-man, Robur carefully replied, "Katie was bound and unable to speak, except through *skull-speak.* Even with that she only got a couple of words out before the *Mother of Bones* became wise to her efforts."

"What did she say?" asked Wizlon.

"The witch is," replied Robur. "She was trying to tell us that the witch is back. Sadly the *Mother of Bones* heard her, and us, and before we knew it, we were cast out of the *Forbidden Caves* below this castle, and they sealed themselves, completely."

Simon added, "We've searched every inch of the dungeons looking for a way into the cavern. But there is no way that we can find. No portal, no trap door. It is as if, they are there but not there at all."

"Let's try again," demanded Aker.

"We will," said Robur. "Still it is Eshe that he wants. It might just be advantageous to us to be prepared should he blink… and come for her."

"And let Katie go on being tortured?" said Aker through gritted teeth, "over my dead body! Let's move!"

Aker looked more like Lore, the ape-man, than the jovial fox to which all the protectors had come to know. No one questioned him. No one dared.

*

After Eshe and Vexika left Professor Hopingráve's atrium, they retreated to their dorm. They had only one other class on schedule which was *History of Magic* at midnight on the dot, as *X-chanted Warcery* was dark this day on the calendar. It would seem that Professor Montakha had other academy business to attend to… it was something to do with shoring up the defenses around the grounds.

This gave the girls a bit of time to rest before they had to fly up to Professor Toohasi's study. The normally loud and vibrant sleeping area was now noticeably subdued and still. The very walls themselves were missing Katie and Green Eyes, and so were Eshe and Vexika.

"I feel like there has to be something more I can do," said Eshe, disheartened.

"All of *the Seven*, the professors, and the headmistress are all doing their best," said Vexika, as she gave Eshe a hug sitting on the side of her bed. "But right now let's get some rest before Professor Toohasi's class; I think we could both use it."

Within mere moments, the two exhausted girls were fast asleep. It would seem the panther-girl was spot on about them needing sleep. Meanwhile at the same time a few floors down, another student was wide awake and fuming with anger.

How dare that damn, normal sympathizer, expel me, a true creature-kind, she thought to herself. *I wish we could throw them all off the Krantiza Bridge, and let only those with true creature blood through these once hallowed doors!*

"My, my young lady, those are big words, but are you willing to act on them, Tamrah?" asked a voice that seemed to come from inside her own skull as well out of the floor her feet rested upon, the ceiling she was under, and the walls that surrounded her.

"Who are you?" asked Tamrah out loud. Then she thought to herself, *Am I going crazy?*

"No, you are not touched in the head, my child," replied the voice hearing the rhino-girl's inner dialog. "Still the question remains… are you willing to act?"

"Yes I am," replied Tamrah. "But what can I do, I've been expelled."

"Child this is bigger than the academy and that vile trader of a headmistress," decried the voice. "This is your moment to stand up, to join a bigger cause."

The voice paused.

"Ask the question that won't leave your mind, my child."

Tamrah, most certainly knowing the answer, dared to ask it.

"Who are you?"

"I am Lord Osiris!"

The rhino-girl fell off of the bed she was sitting on the side of and crawled backwards in fear.

"Get up, my child, come to me," said the *Dark One*. "The *Mother of Bones* and I have a job for you to do."

The room suddenly became dark.

The candles which had been flickering wildly, since the omnipresent voice crept through the once impenetrable gates, one by one extinguished themselves. Osiris' voice embedded itself nicely within the rhino-girl's skull, and relayed his instructions.

Up a few floors from Tamrah's room, Eshe and Vexika had just awoken from what the panther-girl liked to call their catnap before the moonlit midnight on the dot class. No matter what alarm the girls set, it always went as follows.

"For crying out loud," said Vexika, as she lifted her head and with a quick lunging bite, snatched out of the air, the bewitched squawking bird that had been flying in circles around her pillow, trying to wake her up. "That damn malfunctioning alarm, was supposed to get us up ten minutes ago."

The panther-girl let out a rather large yawn, as she did so a feather or two, left over from her alarm clock, fell from her mouth. She looked over at a still lump not too far away, and cried out, "Hurry Eshe, we're going to be late!"

The lump pulled the cover over its head.

"There's going to be fresh cup of *Professor Toohasi's Wild Brew* waiting for you," Vexika said intringuinly.

The covers seemed to jump into the air by themselves. In fact, they may have, being Eshe was already fully dressed with wand in hand.

"Does the trick every time," grinned the panther-girl, as she noticed Eshe fully ready to go. "Damn girl, you sleep in them."

"Why not?" replied Eshe. "It's two minutes sooner to me getting that hot cup of coffee."

Eshe summoned her broom, which soared across the room and came to rest in her outstretched hand. With a twist of her wrist, the window threw itself open, and within a mere few seconds Eshe was outside in the cold night air, waiting under the moonlight grasping a wand while her broom floated impatiently underneath her.

"You coming?" she asked.

"Alright, alright," said Vexika, "just let me grab my things."

A moment or so later, the two black robed bunk-bors were soaring upwards towards the owl-like professor's study, high above the rest of the academy.

From a window not far away, seemingly waiting in the shadows, someone eagerly watched as they flew.

"Now, my child," said the voice in Tamrah's head. "I sense your hesitation, your nervousness. Fret not, my mother and I will guide you."

The rhino-girl did as the voices in her head told her to do. She crept up the staircase and waited until the hallway leading to Eshe and Vexika's room was empty. Once inside their dorm bedroom, she stood at the foot of Katie's bed, as the conversation within her skull added yet another voice to the mix.

"This is the one," said an old lady's voice.

"Yes, Mother, I can sense it, too," replied Osiris. "The wretched Granxor blood, now within me is a secret spiller indeed."

"Now listen carefully, girl, and repeat after me," said the *Mother of Bones. "Um-fi-id-na-suma... Um-fi-id-na-suma... Um-fi-id-na-suma."*

As the old lady in the cave spoke, the very same chant passed over Tamrah's lips. The spell opened the memory lock. As it unlatched itself;

it grew wings and hovered before coming to rest on the floor next to the chest.

"Get the pipes, dearie, and keep them wrapped, so that no sound escapes. This is very important… no sound can emanate from those chimes. Wrap them tight," directed the *Mother of Bones*. "Now hurry, on your broom and fly!"

Tamrah started to leave when the witch cried out, *wait, the chest.* Once again she spoke through the Rhino-girl's voice and spoke.

"Um-fi-id-na-suya… Um-fi-id-na-suya."

Instantly the memory lock received the command and obeyed, reattaching itself to the chest, so that none were the wiser as to what had just occurred.

Upwards Tamrah flew on her broom towards Professor Toohasi's study. When she arrived class had already begun. The rhino-girl, instructed by the voices in her head, flew to the rooftop and peered into the room below, through the bird nesting overhang.

The owl-like professor had just finished giving everyone their cups of his famous *Wild Brew.* Even though she was on this special mission Tamrah could not help the cravings that seemed to be rushing over her, just by smelling the perfectly percolated coffee.

“Focus, dearie,” said the witch’s voice in her head. “Be patient. When I tell you to do so, you must get inside the classroom, without anyone seeing you. Understand?”

Tamrah nodded her head yes, even though it was inside her head that the entire conversation was taking place.

With a classroom full of empty cups now resting on desktops, the students were about to journey out, for the night’s lesson. Fascinating thing about the *Wild Brew,* even though it is steaming hot when put in a student’s hand, there never seems to be any to be found, after forty-five seconds, a minute tops. Some have actually been known to have to visit Mrs. Moons’ infirmary with tongue burns after consuming a cup too quickly, and yet the next day be right back at it, bandage and all.

With everyone sufficiently wired, Professor Toohasi made his way to the old grandfather clock to begin the ritual that all of his students were very familiar with. With the lifting of his wand, and a somewhat secret spell cast, the timepiece shifted its numbers to now include 13 o’clock. The professor moved the hour hand back from 13 to 12 ushering in the *Witching Hour*.

“Move dearie, but be silent as a mouse,” said the *Mother of Bones*. “Be careful not to spook the owls. You must be inside the room to be covered by the spell.”

Tamrah dismounted her broom and had it affixed to her back. In one hand she had the chimes wrapped tight in cloth, with the one hand she was gripping the rooftop beams, doing her best to navigate the few owls that were perched and not out on a nightly hunt.

Down below Professor Toohasi had gathered everybody in the center of the room as he commonly does, just before he opens the roof.

Tamrah saw this and hurriedly rushed into a shadowed section of the rafters.

“Retracto!” demanded Professor Toohasi with his wand pointed upwards.

The owls abruptly flapped their wings at being disturbed, as they often do, but something caught Vexika’s attention. After all, being part feline, the panther-girl is well known for her exceptional hearing. In Tamrah’s haste to be concealed in the shadows, there might have been the slightest of clanks of the wind chimes against a bit of the wooden perch, even though the pipes were wrapped.

"Alright everyone, follow me," said the professor, who boarded his broom and soared through the openings of the rooftop. One after the other, the students followed the owl-like professor out into the night. Among the last to leave the room was Vexika and Eshe, though.

"Did you hear that?" asked Vexika.

"Hear what?" replied Eshe as they soared past the rafters of the study and out into the night air.

"I swear I heard a metal thud when the roof opened… one that I had not heard before in Professor Toohasi's class," said the panther-girl. "Though I have heard it before, and I do not forget a smell or a sound. It's a cat thing."

"Where did you hear it before?" asked Eshe.

"When Katie woke from her dreams, and her pipes fell to the floor. I know I just heard Katie's chimes," replied Vexika. "Follow me."

Stealthily, the panther-girl with Eshe by her side, trailed behind the group, before dropping down out of the moonlit sky, sneaking away from the class. The two girls looped around and flew just above the treeline headed back down towards the classroom.

As they neared the tower heading back up towards the owl-like professor's classroom, they saw a figure on a broom soar out of the rooftop heading towards the edge of the forest.

"Someone was there," said Vexika. "And there it is again! I can hear the clanking of the pipes. It's subtle, but it's there. I am sure of it. "

"We have to follow! If that thief has the chimes, we have to stop'em," replied Eshe. "Let's go!"

Trusting the panther-girl's hearing and sense of smell, much like a cat stalking its prey, Vexika and Eshe followed the mysterious figure as she soared out of and beyond the school's grounds. They were careful to stay far enough behind, as to not be spotted.

As good as Vexika's hearing was it could not hear the conversation taking place inside the rhino-girl's head, but it was taking place all the same.

"Come, dearie," called the *Mother of Bones*. "Follow my voice. Let the broom lead you to Lord Osiris."

As Tamrah came to edge of the forest in the *Great Valley,* she was instructed to stop at the foot of where the *Forbidden Caves* used to be. Eshe knew exactly where the stranger was going to. As Vexika and Eshe neared to the rider they'd been chasing, it was the panther-girl's extraordinary night vision that allowed her to be the first to realize just who it was.

"Is that Tamrah?" asked Vexika. "I'll be damned, it is."

Eshe's face turned red as she literally bit her lower lip, though a few words still seeped out.

"Why that no good, backstabbing, sack of –"

"Shh…" motioned Vexika to Eshe. "She's going to hear you."

Just about at that very moment, the rhino-girl had just been given the spell to unseal the opening to the cave that Katie was held captive in.

"Laever-lla!" shouted out, Tamrah, as she held out her wand and gave it a twirl of the wrist.

Instantly the mountainside obeyed. The dirt concealing the cave, crumbled away. Tamrah flew upward to where the new formed doorway had been made. Without hesitation she flew inside.

"We gotta know what she's up to," said the panther-girl.

"I think I got a pretty good guess," said Eshe. "Come on; let's go before it seals itself back up."

"Alright, but let's make sure to stay hidden," replied Vexika. "Cause, if your guess, involves who I think it does, then we're going to need more than just the two of us."

As they lifted off the ground on their brooms, Eshe raised her wand.

"Invis-ie-onish!"

Under the moonlight's glow, the two girls disappeared from view just before they disappeared into the cave's opening.

Vexika nodded towards Eshe with a gesture that suggested, *good thinking*. Even though they were invisible to the outside world, this particular spell, if done correctly, allows those under the spell to see one another, if so desired. Eshe had, of course, performed it perfectly.

Ahead, Tamrah had just turned the last corner that led to a spacious cavern where Osiris, the *Mother of Bones* and Katie were.

"Ah, dearie, come," said the old woman standing at the *Dark One's* side. "Come and meet Lord Osiris."

Tamrah dismounted her broom, and instantly bowed down to one knee. She turned her head ever so slightly to the right side and glanced at Katie who was chained to the wall, and seemed to be unconscious, and under some sort of spell that kept her that way.

"Lord Osiris, I am humbled to be in your presence. It is an honor, my lord," said the rhino-girl, who if she was honest with herself was more frightened than honored.

Osiris seemed to care not about the pleasantries, for he was indeed single-minded.

"Do you have it?" he asked with a creaky voice that actually sounded older and gravellier than his mother.

"Yes, my lord," replied Tamrah as she reached for the makeshift cloth satchel that she had the wind chimes in, that was fastened to her torso. As she did so, the slightest of clanks occurred between a couple of the pipes.

"What was that?" barked Osiris, enraged.

The *Dark One* lifted his staff, which caused the rhino-girl to lift up off of her feet and instantaneously soar directly towards Osiris. Before Tamrah knew what was happening, the *Dark One's* boney sharp nailed fingers were wrapped around her neck, squeezing it tight. Though he was old and frail in appearance, his strength did not match that image. Within that mere moment, his other six arms dislodged themselves from out of his side. Still, with but his one free hand, he held up in the air the sizeable rhino-girl.

"You were told to wrap the pipes tight so that no sound could be heard! Were you not?" asked Osiris in a terrifying manner, which literally had Tamrah shaking. Eshe and Vexika could see it from they were hiding.

"Yes, my lord," struggled Tamrah, through a breath that was heavily constricted. "I'm sorry, my lord, I thought I had."

Eshe was readying her wand to cast a spell, which had Vexika close her eyes, thinking that they were about to enter a fight that they had very little chance of surviving. The panther-girl also knew that was just who Eshe was… someone who was going to try to save someone else, no matter the cost. However, just when Eshe was about to intervene, the *Mother of Bones*, spoke.

"Now there, dearie, all is not lost; you did bring us something very crucial to our plans. Without these wretched pipes we cannot enter the academy. With these in our possession, so many things are possible."

Tamrah seemed relieved, and actually let out a sizable exhale, when Osiris released his grip and let her feet once again touch the ground.

The *Mother of Bones* turned around abruptly… "Still you did not obey! Kill her!"

With that two of Osiris' arms gripped the rhino-girl's shoulders, while two more of his arms gripped her waist. Instantly she was lifted back up into the air. Not unlike a spider advancing on its webbed prey; it was clear as two more of the *Dark One's* eight arms moved towards Tamrah's head, she was going to die.

Within a single heartbeat, Eshe exploded out from under the invisibility spell. However the Eshe that entered the cave was not who was standing in her shoes now. She had fully transformed into a were-witch, with a wand in one hand and sharpened claws ripping at anyone who neared with the other.

In fact it was Eshe's clawed hand that ripped across a few of Osiris' arms causing him to drop Tamrah, as her body hit the stone floor with a loud thud. Injured, but she was still alive.

Quickly Eshe grabbed the rhino-girl, as Vexika shot a spell at the *Dark One*. Osiris and his mother were so caught off guard by the surprise intruders that it gave Eshe and Vexika mere moments to get out of the cave with their lives.

As Eshe in were-witch form drug Tamrah around the stone corner and onto her broom, she heard a familiar metal clanking.

"Dammit, the chimes," cried out Eshe in a gravely voice. "They fell out! We've got to get them back!"

"There's no time," shouted back Vexika, as she kept casting spell and counter-spells at the *Dark One* and the *Mother of Bones*, as they were now advancing on them. "We've to get out of here, now, while we can. The *Witching Hour* is almost up!"

“After them!” screamed the *Mother of Bones*. “I’ll get the chimes and guard the girl! You capture them now, my son, and we can end this tonight!”

Eshe knew her bunk-bor was right, if they didn’t make it back they could be trapped in the *Witching Hour* until the next time someone opened the portal again.

Quickly Eshe and Vexika, on their brooms were soaring through the cave, hoping to make it back to the opening before the *Mother of Bones*, had time to seal it once more. It was a good thing that Eshe was in her were-witch mode, because it gave her the strength to hold on to the injured rhino-girl as she flew.

“He’s gaining on us,” said Vexika, as she looked back and saw the black mist drifting rapidly towards them. Inside the smoke you could see the eight armed alchemist gripping the rocks, like a spider zeroing in on its prey.

“The opening is just ahead,” said Eshe. “We can make it!”

As they neared the entry to the cave, they could see the moonlight peering in. Then suddenly the rocks started to fall from the ceiling above, and they seemed to be sealing the opening.

“Hold tight!” said the panther-girl as they made it through the slightest of slivers left between the rocks. “Good it sealed him in.”

Just then the *Dark One* busted through the stone barrier, as if several sticks of dynamite had been ignited.

“Ah, hell,” said Vexika, seeing the maniacal look upon Osiris’ face.

“We have to make it back to the academy!” shouted Eshe. “He’ll catch us if we fly high. Our only chance is through the forest.”

The girls flew as fast as their brooms would take them. The black mist behind them was indeed slowed down by the trees, but not by much. Osiris continued to use his eight arms like oars on a rowboat, pushing off of rocks and trees, anything that the *Dark One* could get his grip on to propel him forward.

“I don’t know if we are going to make it,” cried Vexika.

She could feel the cold mist touch upon the tips of the straw upon the back of her broom. The panther-girl winced preparing to be knocked onto the ground with Osiris wailing onto her.

Instead, as they made it just out of the forest line and into the clearing, the black mist faded. When they turned around they saw Osiris standing with eight arms stretched out and several hands touching the invisible dome of protection that surrounded the academy. The murderous look upon his face, now more than ever resembled a spider… one that just saw its prey free itself from his web. There was no time to waste even though they just barely made it back onto academy grounds within the *Witching Hour*. Now they had to get back into the classroom. As their brooms passed through the opening of Professor Toohasi's study, the owl-like professor and the rest of the students were already inside.

"Where did the two of you disappear to?" he asked. "And… oh dear, is that Miss Badara?"

Eshe disembarked from her broom with tears in her eyes, "She's badly hurt. They almost killed her."

"Who did this?" asked Professor Toohasi.

"The *Dark One* and the *Mother of Bones*," said Vexika. "And…"

The panther-girl started to tell more but saw the tears in Eshe's eyes.

"We had to leave her," said Eshe, with a lump in her throat.

"Who?" asked the professor.

"Katie," sobbed Eshe. "I just… I just left her there."

CHAPTER ELEVEN

"TRAPPED IN THE WITCHING HOUR"

Word spread about what had happened between Osiris and Tamrah, throughout the academy. While many *Stormanders,* particularly Kilmon wanted to hear the tale firsthand from the rhino-girl herself - which could not happen until she recovered and was released from Mrs. Moons care – it did seem that the mood of the academy was changing. It went from, *did you hear that Katie and Eshe are Granxors,* to, *someone has to save Katie, she's one of us*. Even the *Stormanders* got the massage. As the one red-robed student with spider features not unlike that of the *Dark One* himself, put it, *if Osiris would kill Tamrah he would kill any of us too*.

Salex Spix was right.

Osiris and the *Mother of Bones* were of single mind, with a single goal. All of this world, as it was known, would become but a memory, that only they would remember. As far as they were concerned any poor soul in their way, were but pawns on a chess board… just pieces to move and sacrifice, as they saw fit.

"The time is at hand, my son," said the *Mother of Bones*, inside the cave.

"Yes, it is," replied Osiris. "They now know we're in the *Witching Hour.* So we must strike right away."

The old witch slowly creaked by Katie who was still unresponsive, in a trance, chained to the stone wall. The *Mother of Bones* made her way to a make-shift table with a glowing orb sitting atop a tattered cloth.

"Rest assured that Robur and the professors are plotting an attack against us at this very moment," said Cassandra as she circled her wrinkly hands round the glass of her orb. "Oh yes, I can see it is so. They are gathered before the clock, waiting for the 13th hour to be ushered in. We need to move within the *Witching Hour,* as well, and that hour is indeed, at hand, now!"

With that, the *Mother of Bones* waved her wand around in the air, and a small tornado sprung forth from out of the tip, and swirled around Katie. Instantly the chain shackles cracked open and fell to the ground. The twirling wind then lifted up their prisoner as she remained unconscious. Like a puppet on a string, the old witch guided Katie down the tunnels leading out of the cave. Osiris led the way, with his staff held out in front of him. The old weathered stick had a bright light emanating from its tip. As they turned one corner, the *Dark One* pointed his staff at a particularly large section of stone wall.

"Reveal-mentiosa!"

The wall instantly morphed into a doorway that lead out to what appeared to be somewhere in a darkened forest. Osiris, the *Mother of Bones* and Katie with her wind chimes, both hanging in midair like kites being pulled by invisible strings, stepped through the portal and into the dark of the night.

*

Meanwhile, at the same time, Robur, Simon, Aker the Fox, the headmistress, Professor Toohasi, Professor Hopingráve, Professor Montakha and Professor Bokor, all had assembled before the owl-like professor's old grandfather's clock waiting for the *Witching Hour* to strike, as well.

Having been quickly briefed on what had transpired with Eshe, Vexika and Tamrah… Headmistress Valborga assembled a rescue party straight away. All were alerted, though some of *the Seven* had to stay in their protector positions to make sure that no one else was targeted by the *Dark One*. Eshe and Vexika, were told that they must stay within the grounds, for their own protection. It was too risky for them to attempt anymore off grounds ventures, for like Katie they were almost taken hostage… or even worse.

That said, all that were gathered in the study atop the academy, had their eyes fixed on the minute hand as it approached its mark. When the timepiece did reach the desired time, Professor Toohasi conducted the ritual that he had done so many times before at the beginning of the *History of Magic* class, and as expected the numbers did their dance until 13 o'clock, reached its position on top of the circle of time. The owl-like professor then pointed his wand at the rooftop of his study, and the beams, as they were now used to doing, opened up and let the moonlight shine down into the room.

The moonlight revealed something else too; two students were hiding in the shadows out of view from the rest of the rescue crew. Eshe and Vexika, stepped out into the light.

"We told you both that you were not going to leave the grounds," started Robur.

However, as Eshe put it in her own words, "Try to stop me, from saving my best friend… or better yet, try to stop the grandmother in me from saving her granddaughter. In short, let me make this very clear, it isn't going to happen, old friend."

Eshe said this, while standing an inch or two taller than she normally does and staring right into Robur's eyes. The wizard knew when he had been bested and acquiesced.

Robur grinned as he looked at this young brave girl, who also happened to be, as she just stated his *old friend.*

"Have it your way, Lady Eshe."

The wizard then turned around and pointed his staff onto Simon and Aker, and said, "This might help us along."

Robur cast an enchantment, *"Soar-i-ona."*

Wings grew out of the cat-man and the fox-man's backs and lifted them upwards. Picking up on the cue, the headmistress abruptly turned into red mist, while Eshe, Vexika, Professors Toohasi and Hopingráve all boarded their brooms. Professor Montakha, spread his wings which were blazing red and rose up as the phoenix, while Professor Bokor spun around and out of the gust flew a bat with glowing red eyes.

"Let's go get our girl," said Aker.

Eshe nodded with a grin of appreciation at the fox-man.

The wizard lifted his staff and let it pull him out into the night air, leading the way towards the *Forbidden Caves*. Behind him flanked this motley band of *magixians, witches, wizards* and *creature-kind.* This was exactly the ominous warning that the *Mother of Bones* was seeing form through the mist in her orb, just before she and her son exited the cave through the portal. *Cassandra the Enchantress* still had the blood of a fortune teller running through her veins.

The rescue crew arrived at the exact place where, in the *Witching Hour*, Eshe and Vexika entered the cave that led to Katie. Once more, like it was when outside of the *Witching Hour*, Eshe and Robur got tossed out of this cave, the entrance was sealed shut.

This time though, Robur was in the enchanted hour, and he came prepared with spells to make sure that he would not be tossed out again.

"Devasta-nix!"

From the tip of wizard's staff shot forth a beam of light that struck the sealed opening and caused an explosion that rivaled any mining hole filled with several sticks of dynamite. The debris filled the air, but Aker did not wait for the smoke to clear.

"Katie!" he cried out, as the fox stormed down the passageway.

Simon, though silent, was no less intense, as he ran right on Aker's heels. Professor Bokor was still transformed as a bat, and soared overhead. Behind them was Professor Montakha whose fiery wings cast a glow that illuminated the darkened tunnel. Eshe and Vexika with their hands fastened to their broomsticks floated just behind the fierce protectors as they seemed to be hunting down their prey.

As the fox-man using his sense of smell turned the corner to the cavernous opening he paused, near to the large stone wall where Katie had been shackled.

"They held her here," said Aker, pointing to the rock, though the chains were no longer present.

Eshe nodded with a sad gaze and a lump in her throat.

"They're gone, now," said Simon. "They've moved her. They must have known we'd be coming for her."

His upper lip lifted and his teeth were bared, as he let out a growl that shook the entire cave.

"We will find her," said Robur now catching up with them. "We disrupted their plans, and caused them to flee. This is a good thing."

"A good thing?" barked Aker, sounding more like Lore than the normally jovial fox that all were used to. "The only good thing will be seeing that spider and his mother's heads on spikes. It is time we end this once and for all!"

Robur placed his hand on Aker's shoulder.

"We will get her back, but on the way to doing that, don't lose who you are, my friend."

"One hair," replied the fox. "They harm one hair on her head, and I will show you who I truly am!"

With that he stormed back down the passageway, back towards the cave's opening, all the while trying to keep track of Katie's scent. However, the fox lost the trail before he ever got there. As he turned a corner by another rather large stone wall, the scent completely evaporated into thin air.

"I lost it," said Aker. "It's like she disappeared right here."

A red mist floated in, and out of that mist suddenly appeared Headmistress Valborga.

"They used a portal," said the headmistress.

She then took out a wand and cast a spell at the stone wall.

"Reveal-mentiosa!"

An opening started to materialize, but then sealed itself once more.

"Ancient spells have been transfigured on this one, indeed," said Headmistress Valborga, as she whipped her wand around and gave it another go.

"Clan-desti-onis!"

This time the opening held, but only if the headmistress kept the stream of energy coming from her wand fixed on the opening. Gripping her wand tight, she struggled to maintain the spell.

"Go!" cried out Headmistress Valborga, "I will hold it open as long as I can."

Straightaway Professor Montakha and Professor Bokor flew through the portal first, being they had wings and scouted instantly for dangers, abruptly followed by Aker, Simon, Professor Toohasi, Eshe, Vexika and then Robur. Professor Hopingráve lingered until last.

"Give me your wand, Valenteen," said the spirit professor. "I am already dead you know."

"What I know is, that there are still ways to separate you from us," replied the headmistress, "and that is something I am not willing to have happen, again."

"Then together, old friend," said Professor Hopingráve.

"Together, Hazel, always," agreed Headmistress Valborga.

Both their hands gripped the wand as the portal began to shrink. Starting from her boots and twirling upwards, the headmistress' body began to transform into the red mist. She encircled Professor Hopingráve, now it was only one hand on the wand. The rabbit-like professor, with the red mist clinging to her, leapt through the opening just as the portal dissipated.

Professor Hopingráve landed onto the dew covered ground deep inside the forest. From out of the red mist that was rising off the professor emerged Headmistress Valborga.

"Thank you," said the headmistress.

With a grin and a nod, Professor Hopingráve acknowledged her longtime friend, and then quickly looked around. Not too far away she spotted the rest of the rescue crew. The professor got ready to call out to them, when she suddenly got the urging from inside her spirit to remain silent.

As they neared the rest of the group, whom all appeared to be staring at something in particular, Professor Hopingráve noticed a familiar site through the trees, as well.

"The portal led us to the academy?" she questioned. "That means…"

"Yes," added Robur, "that means Osiris has entered the grounds."

The wizard then lifted his wand to the sky and shot forth a beam of light that filled the night sky with a blast that looked like a thousand fireworks exploding at one time.

"What was that?" asked Eshe.

“I sent the signal to *the Seven*, that they are needed.” replied the wizard. “It seems the final battle is at hand.”

“But we’re in the *Witching Hour*,” said Eshe. “How can they get to us?”

Robur glanced towards Headmistress Valborga and Professor Hopingráve.

“It is quite astounding what three well-seasoned and yes, aged minds can do when they come together,” said Robur. “Centuries of spells and enchantments between us all. And yet we still seem to find something new, to hide up our sleeves.”

Just then like shooting stars falling out of the sky, the other of *the Seven* landed within the woods at their side. One by one.

Lore, the Ape-Man.

Gennadius, the Grizzly.

Sahti, the Snake.

Wizlon the Dragon.

Zoticus, the Bull.

They joined… Simon, the Lion and Aker, the Fox.

The Seven stood together as one, ready for battle, just on the other side of the *Krantiza Bridge*, which leads into the academy.

“You summoned us, master,” growled Lore.

"Yes, I did," said Robur, as he put his hand on the ape-man's shoulder. "But not master, friend. I called you because Osiris has entered the academy grounds, and he has Katie prisoner."

*

Meanwhile, at the same time that the rescue crew went to the *Forbidden Caves* to try and save Katie… Osiris and the *Mother of Bones* escaped through the portal, which led to the forest right outside the academy.

Up until this time, the *Dark One* had not been able to enter the grounds because of the protections placed around the school. That was all about to change.

"Ah, my son, this is it," said the *Mother of Bones,* as they came into the clearing in the forest that led to the *Krantiza Bridge.* "This will do nicely."

As the old witch said those words, the wand in her hand, guided Katie's wind chimes as they floated through the air, and hovered before the foot of the bridge.

"Yes, we can finally bring down that damn wall, which has hindered us for so long," said the *Dark One*, through gritted teeth. "Finally we can end that little brat Eshe Granxor and set things right. Finally Chaparral will be ours the way it was meant to be, before that fateful night in *the City of Graves!*"

Osiris ran his boney fingers through the wind chimes as they dangled before his face. The melody that resonated from the pipes sounded dark and eerie, with a distinctive high pitched nails scratching across a chalkboard mixed with the melody.

The chimes revealed a cloaked dome, which then began to wobble and disintegrate.

"Finally, indeed," muttered Osiris, as he stepped onto the bridge.

"Come along, Katie Granxor," said the *Mother of Bones* as she guided Katie still entranced, with her wand. "Let's find that grandmother of yours!"

It would seem that when the old woman looked into her orb she did not notice that there were two people hiding in the shadows when all were gathered in Professor Toohasi's study. That however, was not the only thing that these two trespassers did not notice. When the chimes broke through the protective barrier spell, they might have also pierced the spell that was cast upon Katie, holding her in a trance-like state. For at that moment when the chimes rang out, just the slightest of twitches occurred on the bells owner's fingertip.

As Osiris and the *Mother of Bones* crossed the *Krantiza Bridge,* the *Dark One* struck the pipes again; this time he ran the tip of his wooden staff through them, causing another ominous melody to ring out. The second strike caused another dome to emerge, which took form just after they entered inside the grounds; its purpose, to keep others out, while keeping the students, who are all fast asleep, in.

Reaching the other end of the bridge, Osiris paused and looked upon the school's creature logo of sorts, a giant creature skull with horns, which leads to the *Great Hall*. The *Dark One* lifted his staff and instantly the doors to the hall blew open.

"The Granox girl should be asleep in her dorm," said Osiris. "Let's find her and end this!"

The mother and son practically glided through the empty hallways and to the staircase leading to the girls' dorm. Once more, even though this time it was not intentional, the pipes clanked into one another. When they did so, again Katie twitched, this time it was her entire hand that moved. Inside her skull, her thoughts began to return to her. It seemed that the cursed spell that had been put upon her, entranced her mind, paralyzing it, as well.

With the return of even a spark of freewill, Katie… or her soul found itself in a black box of sorts, when it heard the chimes melody break through.

“I’m in here, help me,” Katie said, feeling like she was buried in a grave, without actually being deceased. “Please, get me out of here.”

In the distance Katie heard the pipes again, but they were so far away. Then in the darkness, a light, small at first appeared, not unlike a ship lost in the mist, but suddenly closing in on the shining beacon fixed on a rocky shore… the light became brighter and brighter until, the walls of darkness collapsed.

“Give me your hand, child,” said an older woman carrying a lantern.

“Eshe, is it you?” asked Katie.

Then two other voices spoke, from behind two other beams of light.

“It is us,” said the *Lady in White*, which Katie had once chased after in a maze under the *Coliseum of the Giants*, and the spirit of younger Eshe Leota that was her best friend.

“We have been and will always be with you,” said Grandmother Eshe.

Katie got to her feet inside this room filled with light inside her head. Even though she knew Aker's words about being needy, she couldn't help herself, and threw her arms around each one of them and gave them a hug, with tears filling her eyes.

"I thought I'd died," she said, and then paused as a thought rushed over her. "Did I die? Is this what there *is*.... after everything?"

"No child," said Grandmo ther Eshe. "This is the light that dances in-between everything. It both lasts forever and fades quickly."

Katie looked puzzled but somehow understood. Then the *Lady in White* reached out and wiped away a tear from Katie's cheek.

"What is it that you need to voice, my child?"

"I can't do it," said Katie.

"Do what?" asked the *Lady in White.*

"I can't defeat him," said Katie choking up once more. "I'm going to lose everyone I love."

Katie looked directly at younger Eshe.

"He's too powerful," cried Katie. "I just can't."

Grandmother Eshe took hold of Katie's hands and gripped them tight.

"No child, he is not more powerful than you. You are more powerful than you know. Like the light, some things are forever. Love is forever. Nothing is more powerful than that. Some call it… *the Forever Spell*."

Katie's eyes widened as she recalled Professor Toohasi telling her about that being the most powerful spell he'd ever known in his many travels. But before she could ask anything more about the spell, there was another clank of the chimes. This time, it was not an accident. Something had enraged Osiris and he had smashed them against a wall.

"Time is short Katherzine," said Grandmother Eshe. "We are going to need you to fight, my child. It comes down to you. You are the tree. But you are not alone. There is *another* we will visit tonight. Hold tight… help is on the way. You will know what to do, when the time is right!"

"We are with you, always," the three Eshes said in unison.

In an instant, Katie once again had full control of her senses. However, the words of Eshe echoed in her soul… *when the time is right*. With all the training she had done with the professors of the academy, she closed her mind and kept secret what had just occurred and made sure a certain witch and her son were none the wiser.

"Dammit!" spat Osiris, as he just knocked the wind chimes to the floor with his staff. "Where is she? Where is Eshe Granxor?"

The *Mother of Bones* looked dejected and enraged, as well.

"How? How did she slip through our fingers, yet again?" said the old witch, as she reached for her orb.

Waving her hand over the glass the enchantress began speaking words of old, until a vision appeared.

"Curses!" cried out the *Mother of Bones.* "She is with them in the *Forbidden Caves*. Tricky little brat, indeed, but all is not lost, my son. We have the academy and we have something they care deeply about… and *we have time*."

Precipitously Osiris exhibited a maniacal grin upon his wicked face, as he contemplated the words of his mother… *we have time*. He pointed his staff at the chimes and guided them as they rose up off of the floor to once again hover in midair.

"To the clock," said the *Dark One*.

Abruptly, Osiris, the *Mother of Bones* - with Katie and her wind chimes trailing behind not unlike balloons on short strings - took to flight without the aid of any brooms. Within seconds they were before the grandfather clock.

"This should do it," said the enchantress, as she pointed her wand at the face of the timepiece. *"Froz-a-mora!"*

The clock turned to ice, as the spell covered it over.

"Now let's wake the dead, so to speak," said the *Mother of Bones,* as she pointed her wand at the hovering wind chimes. *"Arise-fa-nora! Studentaceo!"*

The pipes of the wind chimes rung out like the old Windsor school bell. The walls of the academy shook as the students all began to awaken from their slumber. The spell conveniently did not wake any of the staff or professors on grounds.

"Shall we greet the student body, before our guests arrive?" asked the *Mother of Bones,* as she once again waved her hand over the orb, which showed that the rescue party had just made it out of the portal and were in the forest, adjacent to the *Krantiza Bridge.*

"We shall," replied Osiris, as he took to flight soaring down from the high tower, where Professor Toohasi's study was perched, and coming to rest in the *Great Hall*. His mother and Katie flanked the *Dark One* as he did so.

Gasps could be heard as Osiris stood in the middle of the *Great Hall,* his eight arms stretched out like a spider wanting to welcome in its prey to the web. Many faces filled with horror were fixed on Katie Windsor's apparent lifeless body hanging in midair next to her floating chimes.

"I am Lord Osiris, and I have come to set you free! Freedom comes at a cost, as all things worth having, do."

Many students were hiding themselves behind the staircase poles or peaking around corners, while many *Stormanders* seemed a bit steadier in their footing, but nervous all the same.

"Your obedience is demanded. Give it to me, and I and the *Mother of Bones* will remember you when the *Great Reset* occurs. Do not bend the knee right here and now, and when creature-kind's reign begins you will be remembered as a traitor."

One *Stormander*, Salex Spix, who also had eight arms and spider features stepped forward and dared ask a question.

"What is the *Great Reset,* sir?"

"Sir?" screeched the *Mother of Bones*. "That is Lord Osiris, to you! And bend your knee, now!"

The enchantress used her wand to make Salex bow down. His knees hit the marble floor with a crack that sounded like the bones contained inside the skin might have snapped in two.

"Sorry, Lord Osiris," said Salex, writhing in pain.

"Good question," replied Osiris, ignoring the student's groaning. "Many moons ago a certain Granxor girl interfered with the creature-kinds fate."

The *Dark One* turned and gestured to Katie, as she hovered, suspended before the gathered crowd.

"No, not this one," spat Osiris, "though she has done as fair amount of meddling where she didn't belong as well. The girl I am speaking of is Eshe Granxor or Eshe Leota as you know her. This brat's grandmother, you see. It was her who banished me to the underworld and stopped what would have been the rise of creature-kind. Then decades later, her granddaughter like a disease did the same."

The *Dark One* spat on the ground at Katie's feet.

"So tonight, here in the *Witching Hour*, we are going to reset history, so that the meddling little brat never lives to see her bloodline carry on. In so doing, Katie Windsor or Katie Granxor will never exist. Kill the tree down, by cutting it at the roots!"

More gasps filled the *Great Hall*. Still no one saw Katie's finger twitch, but it did. Still inside Katie's mind the words lingered, *when the time is right*. "Now, I have graciously answered your question, so now it is your turn," said Osiris. "Do you pledge your elegance to the *Dark One*, right here and now?"

The injured red-robed student stammered a bit, "Well, I'm not sure. I heard what happened to Tamrah, and if you tried to kill her, then who's to say, you won't kill me, too?"

"Good point," said Osiris, within a blink of an eye, one of the *Dark One's* arm rose up with a wand in it pointed directly at the spider-like boy slumped over on his knees. *"Kill-a-gra-mona!"*

*

Half a world away, Katie's Aunt Zalika was lying in a hospital bed next to a still badly injured, but healing slowly, love of her life, Fadessa. The crow-woman had mostly healed from her own injuries, yet was determined to stay at the firefly woman's bedside until she was well again. On this night though, that was about to change.

Days earlier, the medicine man of sorts whom was seeing to their healing, a creature-kind known as Vooden the Raven, found an interesting discovery when tending to Zalika'a wounds. Underneath one of her wings, was an old scar, which had healed over, yet it was causing the crow-woman significant pain. When he pressed around the scar tissue, he got quite the surprise. Out of the scar, a shard of glass ripped its way out from under the skin.

When Zalika asked the medicine man about the shard of glass, he was puzzled, saying, "It was as if the glass had re-formed itself under the surface, because there is no way the skin bound itself overtop such a sharp shard."

The bit of glass just happened to be on the tray next to Zalika on this very night when Sahti, the Snake, leapt to his feet as Robur's call went out to *the Seven* to reunite immediately. The wizard's signal not only lit up the skies above, it also came beaming into each protector's skull.

"What is it? What has happened?" asked Zalika, as she was taken off guard by her protector's sudden change in demeanor.

"They know where Katie is. Osiris has taken over the academy and he has her hostage. She needs all of *the Seven,* and she needs us now!"

Rapidly the room filled with light as Robur's spell engulfed the snake-man, making him translucent. Like a ghost, he was lifted through the solid walls and ceiling and into the sky. It showed just how powerful *Robur, the Spirit in the Great Oak*, really was.

Zalika wanted so badly to join the fight to try to help save Katie, but was torn. *How could I even get there in time being so far away,* she pondered*? Robur didn't send a summoning spell for me and why should he? After all, I am the one who killed him.*

It was recalling these memories that made it so hard for Zalika to ever move on from being Hathor. However, it was for that very reason, she, Zalika, knew that she needed to go.

If only there were a way, she thought.

Just then, a light reflected off of the shard of glass next to the crow-woman. Zalika thought that maybe it was caused by a stray beam that lingered after Sahti's exit. But he was gone. Then in the glass she saw what appeared to be someone she had not seen in a very long time. The familiar face bought a tear to her eye. It would seem the lantern that the older woman was holding in her hand caused the reflective beam that drew Zalika's attention. As quickly as the image appeared it faded.

The crow-woman wondered why this visitation had occurred and then the answer unveiled itself.

In the bit of mirror shone the old grandfather's clock that Hathor had used to enter the academy. She didn't know how or why, but a piece of the *Witch's Glass* had indeed reformed and it was beckoning for her to use it, once again, only this time with very different intent.

Katie's concerns earlier in the year were valid, after all. As she put it, *if the Shadow Tree could restore your clock, what else could it restore? It would seem that it could also restore parts of the Witch's Glass!*

Zalika looked over at Fadessa who had been heavily sedated. Her eyes opened slightly due to the loud commotion.

"Sweetie, Katie needs me, but I don't want to leave you," whispered Zalika softly. "I could never forgive myself if anything happens and I'm not here."

Fadessa smiled and looked deep into Zalika'a eyes, and said softly through strained voice "You have to go, it's your niece and she needs you… both of you, Zalika and Hathor. I will be here, when you return. Promise."

Zalika softly kissed Fadessa, and reached for the shard of glass. She looked inside at her own reflection and took a deep breath, turned to Fadessa and said, "I will return, soon. Love you."

Fadessa smiled and said, "I know you will."

With that, the crow-woman gazed into the glass and then was drawn into it fully.

As she had done less than a year earlier, from out of the grandfather clock sprang a black crow. Only this time the timepiece was frozen over, so the bird's entry sent bits of ice gushing down all over the owl-man's study.

Straight out of the high perched tower soared Zalika in through an opening and into the *Great Hall* she flew, arriving right at the moment Osiris bellowed out a certain evil spell.

"Kill-a-gra-mona!"

Cries of shock rang out as Salex Spix's body fell flat to the cold marble floor. Only he wasn't dead. A red beam from the crow's eyes had deflected the blast. The power of the counterspell sent the spider-like boy backwards.

Katie's hand lifted up, but then she realized, that a certain bird had just arrived. At that very moment, something else came though, in her mind's eye she somehow saw the signal that Robur, the Wizard had just sent up into the night sky. She felt *the Seven* were near.

Again, the words echoed in her mind… *when the time is right.* Another thought followed that one… *Just hold on until the bridge*. It was the kind of message she'd get through the branches of the *Great Oak*… a message sent by a certain wizard.

At that moment as the student scrambled for cover, an enraged Osiris and *Mother of Bones* paid them no mind. They had their sights set on one black feathered object, which seemed to have cast a spell and caused one's blood to boil. The bird's spell was working.

"Kill that damn bird!" shouted Osiris. Don't let that traitor get away!"

"Kill-a-gra-mona!" spat the *Dark One* and the *Mother of Bones*, trying desperately to hit the crow as it swooped, rose, twirled and evaded each deadly blast. It dodged every cursed spell, until the red-eyed bird had led the casters with wands in hand, right out the front doors of the academy.

High into the air the crow soared, before disappearing from sight. The *Dark One* and the *Mother of Bones* were looking for it, when suddenly they realized that they were standing at the foot of the *Krantiza Bridge.*

As they looked across to the other side of the divide, they saw a group gathered, standing steadfast and tall. It was Robur, *the Seven*, several professors, the headmistress, as well as Eshe and Vexika.

It appeared that a new battle was about to take place upon the *Krantiza Bridge*.

CHAPTER TWELVE

"THE BATTLE AT KRANTIZA BRIDGE"

"There you are, Lady Eshe," said Osiris, in a mocking tone, as he spotted Katie's teenage grandmother standing on the other side of the bridge. "We came for you tonight, and you weren't home. Nevertheless, here we are now. You've got a front row seat to watch us kill your precious granddaughter right here on the steps of your precious academy. That is unless you have reconsidered our offer, and want to surrender yourself to us. Your life... for hers."

Clandestine thoughts swirled behind the wall Katie had formed in her mind. *Is now the right time,* she wondered? *I want to fight! I want to shut his vile mouth!*

But before Katie acted those thoughts someone spoke to her saying, *Not yet! Hold on! Hold on!* She assumed it was Robur talking through *skull-speak*, even though the voice was cloaked so that no one else could hear the conversation, or even know that it was taking place.

The *Dark One* turned towards Katie as she dangled in midair, and with his staff pushing from under her chin, he caused her head to lift up from its slumped state. Next with the tip of his sharp pointy fingernail Osiris moved Katie's hair back from off of her face, and then slid his finger down her cheek, cutting open her skin. The *Mother of Bones* laughed as the blood began trickling down, splatting on the hard rock surface under their feet.

"I will kill them!" said Lore!

“Not if I kill them first,” said Aker the Fox as he pulled out one arrow after another from his quiver, shooting it at the heart of Osiris. Each arrow flew on a direct path towards its target, until they’d reach the bridge, at which point the arrows would hit an invisible dome, snap in two, before shattering into several pieces cast upon the ground.

The *Dark One* looked at the protectors and laughed with a wicked, maniacal grin plastered across his face.

“Futile, all of your attempts, are futile,” he said. “The only one I will allow to cross that barrier is you, Lady Eshe. Otherwise, you all can stand there and watch your long lost princess die!”

Osiris’ staff abruptly sent a stream of electricity out of its tip, straight into Katie’s head and all throughout her body. She writhed and shook in agony, all the while, she continued hanging in midair.

“Stop!” shouted Eshe, “That’s enough. I’ll do it.”

All the professors, the headmistress and *the Seven*, all echoed the same sentiment.

“Lady Eshe, you cannot do this,” said Wizlon.

“Eshe, absolutely not,” demanded Vexika with her hand on Eshe’s shoulder, with tears welling up in her eyes. “He will kill you.”

“Then so be it,” replied Eshe. “But I will not stand by and watch our best friend, my blood… my Katie… be tortured.”

Eshe put her hand atop of the panther-girl’s hand, “Please understand, I have to do this.”

Osiris withdrew his staff and watched as Eshe walked towards the foot of the bridge. He pointed the stick in his hand towards her, and instantly an opening formed for her to step through. As soon as Eshe walked inside the protective dome it quickly resealed itself, which was tested by Lore who tried to break his way through right after she entered to no avail.

Slowly as Eshe walked towards Osiris and the *Mother of Bones,* you could almost see them licking their lips readying themselves for the kill.

“Finally,” whispered the *Mother of Bones,* to her son. “Finally, we get to reset everything, reset it all to the way it should have been all along.”

“Yes mother, I say end it now and finally destroy that loathesome *Granxor Tree*,” agreed Osiris under his breath, and quiet so that Katie couldn’t hear every word.

The *Dark One* raised his staff and with all his might braced his feet and shouted the killing curse… *“Kill-a-gra-mona!”*

But to his surprise a black crow swooped in from what seemed out of nowhere and spread its wings wide as it hovered just above Eshe as she stood on the bridge. From out of the crow's eyes shot two red beams that met the *Dark One's* spell and was holding it at bay in a back and forth match of wills between its casters.

"The bird," spat Osiris. "We forgot about the damn crow! Kill it, mother!"

The *Mother of Bones* let the chimes drift out of her sight as she spun towards Eshe and the crow, readying her wand to strike.

"Two Granxors, one strike! It all ends now!" declared the old witch and began to cast forth a killing curse of her own to reinforce the *Dark One's* attempt. "*Kill-a-gra-*"

Before the *Mother of Bones* could complete the spell, a blinding light struck the old enchantress right in the face causing her to wince, and shield her eyes as she looked away. With the slight wave of her hand, Eshe called her lantern to come forth from out of the chest in front of her bed, as she had done when fighting Tamrah and Kilmon in the *Ring of Fire* a year earlier.

Now Katie, said the voice in Katie's head. It wasn't Robur after all. It was Eshe; all three versions of them actually.

When the *Mother of Bones* tried to regain her sight, a voice from behind her spoke out, with a voice that was loud and clear. The *Dark One's* mother peered through squinted lids to see just who was speaking to her. She was not at all pleased with the answer.

"I am the tree!" said Katie, "And you messed with the wrong Granxor!"

Instantly Katie leapt from her midair hibernation, and grabbed the chimes as she did so. When she landed on her feet she held the chimes upward, as her free hand shot forth a blast of energy that hit the pipes and caused them to ring out. The discharge was so strong that it knocked Osiris and the *Mother of Bones* to the ground.

As the wind chimes melody reverberated throughout the academy grounds, it felt like a massive earthquake had stuck. Eshe held tight to the railing on the side of the bridge. All the students took cover as well, as bits of roof shingles, and some loose stone from the school walls dropped onto the pavement below. The invisible dome that was keeping the academy hostage wobbled and shook, as well, before it too, all came tumbling down.

Immediately *the Seven* and Robur, the Wizard stormed the bridge. Those with the ability to fly took to the air, by wings or broom; those on foot were running as fast as their feet would carry them towards the fight. Either way, they were on the attack!

"Vexika, stay close to me," said the headmistress, with authority.

Headmistress Valborga, the panther-girl and the professors were next to step across the barrier that had just fallen... given way. Instead of rushing into battle the headmistress had other plans. However, so did Vexika. The panther-girl snuck away as Headmistress Valborga lifted her wand to the sky, busied with re-casting a protective spell.

"Protect-o-sempra!"

The owl-like professor lifted his wand next, and followed suit.

"Shield-amona!"

Professor Bokor had transformed from his bat-like state, though he still resembled that creature all the same, especially under the moonlit sky. He added his wand to the circle next.

"Invis-ie-onish!"

The phoenix-professor with wings ablaze added his wand next, though he seemed very eager get through these semantics, and enter into the battle. Still, he followed through with his obligations, all the same.

"Conceal-mentiosa!" called out Professor Montakha.

And as it was on *Haunt-O-Wick Eve*, the last to add to the protective enchantment was Professor Hopingráve. She lifted her wand and unlike on that night in the *Haunt-O-Wick Maze*, this time she did not conceal the spell from the naked ear, instead she yelled her contribution out loudly.

"Evera - Amora!"

It was indeed… *The Forever Spell!*

Rapidly the dome reformed; only this time it was not just keeping any intruders out, it was also keeping two particular intruders trapped within.

On the other side of the bridge, Osiris abruptly made it back to his feet, and began wildly casting defensive spells into the air in all directions. His mastery of the dark arts allowed his mother to regain her footing as well. Together they formed a shield around them as they stood before the opening to the academy. Katie was lying on the ground somewhat shaken by the spell she'd just cast as well. She was still inside their grasp and behind their fire line.

"You will pay for that you little brat!" said the *Mother of Bones* while fending off countless spells being sent her way by *the Seven* storming the bridge. "Osiris, strike the brat before she gets away, while I hold them off!"

However before the *Dark One* could get a spell cast, a black robed shadowy figure came in from out of nowhere, it seemed, and grabbed Katie, and leapt out overtop the charging protectors… getting the *Princess of Chaparral* back behind the line. When Katie turned to see who had grabbed her, it made her grin.

"Vexika," said Katie fighting back tears.

The panther-girl had obviously disobeyed the headmistress and raced ahead of *the Seven* across the bridge, dodged all spells, and came round the backside of the *Dark One* and his mother, all in order to save her and Eshe's best friend.

"Hey bunk-bor, it's been quite boring without you," smiled the panther-girl. "Don't ever do that again."

Together, Katie, with chimes in hand, and the panther-girl, made her way to where Eshe was at on the bridge. They hugged each other tight, but just for a moment, as spells were still being cast all around them. Quickly Katie took her spot next to her young grandmother who was gripping her enchanted lantern tight, and Vexika just behind them. Overhead, in crow form, Zalika guarded the two Granxor girls and the panther-girl below her.

The *Dark One* proved every bit of why he was so feared throughout the world of Chaparral. Wizlon and Professor Montakha together flew at Osiris and his mother, spitting fire balls that would incinerate any normal wizard. However, Osiris, just caught the blasts with his staff and turned them right back upon their senders, knocking both the dragon-man and the phoenix out of the sky.

The grizzly, Gennadius, and Zoticus, the bull, rushed the *Dark One*, but brute strength alone, as fierce as it was, was not enough, as Osiris froze them in midstride. The *Mother of Bones* then cast them both to the side. The bull-man and grizzly's body smashing into the stone wall with a thunderous crash.

Sahti, the snake, and Professor Bokor, who had reformed back into a bat, attacked next. The snake-man slid down the side of the academy wall trying to strike from behind, as Bokor, the bat, flew at them from the front. Again, the *Mother of Bones* and her son proved to be too much, as the enchantress used a spell that lifted the snake-man out of the shadows and tossed him directly into Professor Bokor, causing both of them to fall into the opening off of the bridge, falling into the water below.

With no time in-between attacks, it was one strike after another. Lore, the ape-man and Simon, the lion roared from each side of the *Dark One* and the *Mother of Bones* next. The ape-man, with his twirling metal spiked spheres where his arm used to be, actually broke through the defensive spell cast by Osiris and struck him knocking him backwards. Instantly, seeing her son being struck enraged the *Mother of Bones*, who blasted Lore, sending him so high and far into the air, that he actually hit the invisible protective dome, before collapsing back to the ground.

As the enchantress handled the ape-man, Osiris, while down to one knee, was able to see Simon about to strike the old witch, and shot forth a spell from his staff that sent the lion-man soaring almost as high as the ape-man.

As Osiris was getting back up to his feet, arrows began piercing through his garment. Aker, the fox, was attacking the *Dark One* and the *Mother of Bones* straight on. He was walking on the bridge directly at them, firing at will, showing absolutely no fear whatsoever. Professor Toohasi was flying, using his wings and not on a broom, as he usually was known to do. The owl-man was protecting the fox, by deflecting the spells Osiris and his mother were casting in their direction.

"Ah!" cried out the *Mother of Bones* wincing in pain, as one of the arrows sliced through her upper arm.

When either mother or son was injured, it caused the others blood to boil. Furious, the *Dark One's* anger exploded. He twirled his staff in a manner that sent every arrow back at the fox-man and the owl professor. One arrow struck Professor Toohasi in his right wing, causing him to fall to the ground. Without the protection provided by the owl-man, a spell cast by the injured enchantress struck Aker knocking him backwards halfway down the bridge.

“We can do this for eternity!” screamed Osiris. “You have but one option… give us Eshe Granxor or die!”

The endless casting of spells and attacks abruptly stopped as Robur, the Wizard, Professor Hopingráve, and Headmistress Valborga stood facing the *Dark One* and the *Mother of Bones.* Standing by their side was Eshe and Katie, with Zalika in crow form perched on Katie’s shoulder.

“It has been awhile, Osiris,” said Professor Hopingráve stepping forward.

“Hazel Hopingráve,” said Osiris, searching his memories. “It has been awhile, indeed.”

“Osiris, you need to end this peacefully,” said Professor Hopingráve. “All of us, all of creature-kind understand what it is to be shamed, to be outcast, but you’ve let your anger, as justified as it may be, change you into something you are not. I know, because I knew you before all of this.”

“That is the point Hazel,” replied Osiris. “With the *Great Reset*, I can be that version of me again. It was her and her kind that created the *Dark One*. How could I be anything else when cast into the underworld for countless years?”

As Osiris and Professor Hopingráve were speaking, slowly one by one, the other professors and all of *the Seven* made their way back up to the bridge and took their place alongside the others.

"Resetting time, just changes the time, not you," said Professor Hopingráve. "You can change today, just choose to let go of all the hate. Your kind are all right here, standing in front of you. We are all outcasts. Can't you see that?"

"Don't listen to this nonsense," spat the *Mother of Bones*. "Everything we've wanted is right at our fingertips. You just have to take it!"

As his mother finished her statement, she sent a blast at Professor Hopingráve and though Robur blocked most of the blast with his staff, a fraction of the spell struck her right in the chest. Even though she was in spirit form it weakened her.

The exchanges between the *Dark One*, the *Mother of Bones* and *the Seven*, Robur and the academy faculty commenced once more. As strong as the gathered creatures, wizards and witches were, it was clear that Osiris and his mother were indeed too strong. The spells they had used in coming back from the other side, had made them even more powerful than before, including having all of Katie's abilities. Nevertheless, the fight waged on.

“You cannot defeat me!” screamed Osiris. “I possess every power you have! Even you wizard!”

The *Dark One* shot a blast at Robur which he was barely able to deflect. With every deflection, *the Spirit in the Great Oak*, was growing weaker, as was Professor Hopingráve.

“We will outlast you!” laughed Osiris. “I can feel it!”

“Yes, my son, victory is near! Send word to the Salixion Dragons!” suggested the Mother of Bones. “Let’s burn this academy to the ground!”

“Agreed,” replied the *Dark One*. “A dagger to the heart would do nicely.”

However when Osiris tried to call in reinforcements, by sending up a signal into the night sky, it failed. As the stream of light went upwards, like a flare from a ship at sea, it could not reach a level that would achieve its goal. The signal hit the invisible dome and exploded in dissipating embers.

“It matters not, that you sealed us in. It’s just a matter of time! And patience is something that the countless years being cast in the underworld by you, Eshe Granxor, taught me,” spat Osiris. “I can feel your weakness, and its growing evermore. You have but one option… give us Eshe Granxor or die!

Just then, Katie again heard the spirit of the three Eshe's in her head. Zalika and the younger Eshe at Katie's side heard the same message, as well.

Together, you are stronger, said the voices. *There is one spell that Osiris and his mother know nothing of. Search your heart, you know the spell. Use it now.*

Katie stepped to the frontline of the battle, which took *the Seven* by surprise, and not in a good way.

"Katie, what are you doing?" shouted Simon.

"Trust me," replied Katie.

Grins grew on both Osiris and his mother's faces. They instantly turned their focus onto cursing Katie. They raised their wands and shouted…

"Kill-a-gra-mona!"

At the same time Katie raised her chimes in one hand and wand in the other and cast a spell that met the killing curse midway between them.

"Evera - Amora!"

Katie's spell held the two spells in check.

Eshe then raised her lantern in one hand and wand in the other. Both she and Katie'd hands summoned their wands from the chest by this point. She too, uttered the words of old.

"Evera - Amora!"

The spell began to move back towards the *Dark One* and the *Mother of Bones*, ever so slightly.

"Evera - Amora!"

The crow flying overhead landed and transformed into Zalika. She too, having heard the three Eshe's, withdrew her wand and added to the connecting steams with a shout of…

"Evera - Amora!"

Professor Hopingráve and Robur, the Wizard, then followed suit as well.

One by one, every one of *the Seven*, the professors and Headmistress Valborga all raised their wands each speaking aloud, the spell…

"Evera - Amora!"

The stream was slowly crawling its way back towards its casters.

"What magic is this?" asked the *Mother of Bones*.

They both, mother and son, pushed back as hard as they could, but the spell cast by Katie and crew to counter their killing spell was just too powerful to upend.

"We can't stop it! They're going to rebound the killing spell upon us!" declared Osiris.

Just before the boomeranging cursed spell reached them, Osiris whipped his staff around in a way that broke the connection. Simultaneously his mother uttered a spell and created a wall of smoke which the two of them used to flee into the academy, escaping into the *Great Hall*.

CHAPTER THIRTEEN
"THE FOREVER SPELL"

After Osiris and the *Mother of Bones* made their way inside the academy, it was clear that shock was setting in. Up until this point, they had their way with any who attacked them. But now, this mysterious spell had them confused and quite frankly, knocked back on their heels.

Moving as one, the professors, *the Seven*, the headmistress, Robur, Eshe, Katie, Vexika and Zalika, took to a line formation as they pushed forward upon the *Dark One*. It was a wall of spells being cast at Osiris and his mother. But it was *the one* spell that did what no other had done before. It caused doubt to creep into its recipients' minds.

"We've come too far to lose, now," cried out the *Mother of Bones* to her son. "We must fight another day."

"There is no choice," said Osiris. "We fight till we die!"

"No, there *is* a way," suggested, his mother, having something creep into her wicked mind. "It should be unguarded. Upward! We must go upward!"

The two of them floated up the staircase in the *Great Hall* as the back and forth continued and ascended to the next floor of the academy.

The professors were aiding the students who were running for cover, as the battle crept past them. It was a grave concern, to not let any student be used as a hostage.

At the top of the stairs on the second floor was a grand mural of the four founders of the academy. As the *Dark One* stepped in front of the stained glass he lifted his staff overhead and smashed out the window, sending shards flying throughout the entire hall. The bits of mural were not the only thing that would be soaring, though… as the *Dark One* took hold of his mother and the two took to flight, as well.

Following after them, giving chase were the professors, *the Seven*, the headmistress, Robur, Eshe, Katie, Vexika and Zalika. As moonlight shone down, the battle lifted itself to the highest point of the academy, the birdhouse-like study, which housed Professor Toohasi's *History of Magic* class.

As they landed upon the landing perches the *Mother of Bones* quickly entered the study and headed straight towards the center of the room where the professor's desk sat. Behind that desk, was just what the enchantress was searching for.

"Ah, as I suspected," said the *Mother of Bones,* seeing the clock was no longer frozen over. "This is how Hathor got inside the academy, and our way out!"

The enchantress pointed her wand at the clock hand and made sure to reset it, so that the *Witching Hour* held form at 13 o'clock. Osiris stayed on the perch battling to keep their pursuers at bay, and not let them inside the room.

"Listen my son," cried out the *Mother of Bones*. "All we need is Eshe Granxor! We grab her, and we can escape though the clock. We kill her in the *Witching Hour*, and that's where her bones will forever be."

"Yes, and the Great Reset will be our new reality!" added Osiris.

Just at that moment though, the rooftop to the study opened as it would often do. In from rafters came the entire academy faculty, *the Seven*, Robur, Katie, Eshe, Vexika and the crow-woman.

"There's no way out, Osiris," pleaded Professor Hopingráve, "and I don't want to see you die."

"Speak for yourself," said Lore, as the ape-man, leapt towards the *Dark One* striking him with his spinning metal spheres, knocking him backwards. Osiris shielded himself just enough to keep his head attached to the rest of his body, though it rattled the spider-like sorcerer.

One of the *Dark One's* eight arms lifted his staff and sent the killing spell directly at Lore, but the ape-man was able to use the sword in his hand to deflect the curse enough to keep himself alive, though it rattled him as well.

"Osiris, this has to end," pleaded Professor Hopingráve. "The back and forth will go on forever and no one wins."

“It ends when you give us Eshe, and we make this world what it should have always been,” replied Osiris.

“Changing the past, will not change the future,” said Katie, speaking calmly as she stepped forward with Eshe by her side. “It was wrong how the Granxor, my family, treated your mother and you.”

For a moment the *Mother of Bones* and Osiris looked puzzled as if a carnival trick was about to be played upon them.

“What are you playing at, little girl?” asked the *Mother of Bones.*

“It is true,” added Eshe. “Our bloodline did live in castles and watch while others scraped by and even starved. And yes, all of Chaparral embarrassed the out-casting of creature-kind. But it will never end if we keep fighting one another. Resetting the clock doesn’t erase anything.”

Eshe paused before stretching out her hand.

“Only *change* will do that,” she said extending herself forward, in a gesture of goodwill.

The room was silent. Even the owls that usually rested on the beams in the rafters did not make a sound. In this moment everything had a chance to indeed, change.

And then, a reply was offered.

"Get her!" screamed the *Mother of Bones,* and she cast a blinding spell and stunned all that were gathered.

The enchantress reached her boney hand forward and grabbed Eshe by her arm. Likewise Osiris acted in kind, and he too latched onto her, using a beam of energy from out of his staff, which acted like a hook pulling Eshe towards the old grandfather clock.

"I will have both your heads for this!" roared Lore, and readied himself to attack, when Katie stopped him in his tracks.

"No, Lore, you cannot win this alone!" she shouted, in a voice that sounded like thunder. "We do this together!"

Katie lifted her wind chimes and her wand and shouted, *"Evera - Amora!"*

Quickly the entire academy faculty, *the Seven* including Lore, Robur and Zalika all uttered the spell, joining their wands to the stream.

The *Dark One* and the *Mother of Bones* were not deterred. They conjured every bit of dark magic they'd learned throughout the centuries, and used it to aid their efforts in this tug-of-war for Eshe Granxor's soul.

Inch by inch Eshe was being pulled ever closer to the open portal that had now appeared in the body of the timepiece. For a moment, it seemed as though all would be lost and perseverance had won the night for Osiris and his mother, when a small voice outside the classroom, hovering under the moonlight spoke.

"Evera - Amora!" said a voice on a broom.

It was Tamrah, the rhino-girl still injured but holding tight to her broom.

"Evera - Amora!" added Vexika.

The panther-girl had once again snuck off and enlisted the students to come and defend one of their own and their academy. Next to Vexika adding his deep gravelly voice to the spell was Rah, the tigerboy, fully mended and by her side to the end.

Hearing the commotion, Professor Toohasi made his way to the perch with wand raised. The owl-man's eyes beamed with pride.

Suddenly the entire sky was filled with students on brooms, and those who were standing in the courtyard below. All of them had their wands out and pointed towards the birdhouse-like study. All of them repeating the spell… *"Evera - Amora!"*

The Forever Spell!

The individual streams wound together and like a rope wrapped themselves around Eshe gripping her tight and holding her within the academy grounds.

"If we can't take you with us," cried out the *Mother of Bones,* "then we will kill you, where you stand!"

The enchantress looked to her son and gave the command, "Finish her!"

Osiris readied his strike, but for a mere moment his glance shifted from Eshe to Hazel Hopingráve.

"What are you waiting for?" asked the *Mother of Bones.* "Kill her, now!"

But within that moment, Katie moved her wind chimes within the stream from *the Forever Spell.* It immediately caused another beam to emerge which wrapped itself around the *Dark One* and the *Mother of Bones* lifting them up like ragdolls, tossing them into the opening in the old grandfather clock.

Inside the body of the timepiece, was a dark netherworld, almost exactly like that in what was in the *Witching Glass*. One could see the two trapped souls stuck inside.

"No!" shouted the *Mother of Bones*. "It's been bewitched! "

What the *Mother of Bones* didn't know was that the three Eshe's encouraged Zalika, when she traveled through the old clock, to speak words of old, which they conveyed to her, which in short, would make the next travelers using the clock… unfortunate travelers, indeed.

It was as if the three Eshes somehow had an idea just how things might play out, and planned ahead, setting a trap, should a wrong choice be made by said travelers.

As Robur, Professor Hopingráve and all those gathered looked at Katie, wondering what she'd do next, being that these wicked souls had tormented her for years, she reached over and grabbed Eshe's hand.

Katie repeated the words Eshe had just offered.

"Resetting the clock doesn't erase anything. Only *change* will do that."

The two best friends nodded at each other in agreement. Not as if they had spoken with *skull-speak*, though that might have happened as well.

Katie lifted her wind chimes up before the grandfather clock. Eshe then pointed her lantern at the pipes. When the lantern's light hit the chimes it caused a melody that reverberated throughout the grounds. Together their enchanted items caused the old clock to shake and wobble as it lifted up off of the ground. From out of the hour hand, which was set on 13 o'clock, a glow began small at first, before engulfing the entire clock.

And then it was gone.

The clock, Osiris, and the *Mother of Bones*, all had disappeared.

Outside the birdhouse-like study, the entire sky cheered with wands in the air. They would not move from their spots until they saw the two students who had so bravely defended the good name of creatures everywhere.

Out on the perch, at the highest point of the school, stepped out Katie and Eshe Granxor holding hands with tears in their eyes. If anything could have broken through the protective dome, it would have been the thunderous applause that these two witches and their merry band of outcasts got from their own kind… creature-kind.

*

The next day word of the second great battle at *Krantiza Bridge* had spread throughout all of Chaparral. Osiris and the Mother of Bones had risen again, and were once again defeated by the long lost *Princess of Chaparral* and *the Seven*, with the help from several others of course. No one would say they were dead because there was no body or collection of bones to display. That might just have been the way Katie and Eshe Granxor wanted it.

After a bit of time had passed, and wounds had fully healed, Katherzine Granxor and her young grandmother Eshe Granxor, were summoned to *Clarion's Peak* for a grand ceremony at the *Granxor Castle*. This would be the first time Katie and Eshe had seen their royal family in quite some time.

The courtyard was full as they arrived to a sea of cheers, a shower of flower pedals and trumpets being sounded to let all within earshot know, that the long lost *Princess of Chaparral* had returned.

King Ragnar, Queen Bellzonna, Prince Longrid and Princess Berenice, were on the *Grand Staircase* to greet Katie, Eshe, Robur and *the Seven*, as well as the faculty from the *Academy Of Enchantments and Other Magical Studies.* It was on the *Grand Staircase* where the day's ceremony was to take place, honoring all who fought and defeated the *Dark One* and *the Mother of Bones.* All would be receiving the royal medal of bravery for their efforts.

"Princess Katherzine, welcome back home," said the king, as he leaned forward with a polite formal bow. Likewise, Prince Longrid and Princess Berenice followed suit with formal bows, while Queen Bellzonna greeted Katie with a kiss on the cheek.

The family then eyed Eshe unsure just how to proceed. After a moment or two of uncomfortable oddness, the entire royal family chose to bow to Eshe. As Robur and *the Seven*, Vexika and the faculty from the academy stepped forward to take their places, the family did not bow, but rather stood stoic waiting for the bended knee to be given their way, as it was customary and what protocol required.

Not invited however, were Zalika and Fadessa, though they both were as brave as any standing upon those steps in Katie's opinion. The king felt that she was disqualified from having any royal honor bestowed upon her because of her past misdeeds. And so it was decreed.

"We are gathered here today to honor all of the brave people who defended Chaparral from one of the darkest, most vile forces this world has ever known. The second great battle at the *Krantiza Bridge* will go down in history for the bravery of our Princess Katherzine to defend Chaparral's most vulnerable. Yes, my beloved daughter, Princess Katherzine, is a shining example to all, that all kind matter, and even a princess of the highest order, can care about those from a different social rank. Queen Bellzonna and I are so very proud to be the parents of such a truly wonderful daughter."

The crowd made up of creature-kind cheered loudly as Katie stepped forward to speak.

"Thank you all," said Katie and then paused reflectively as she looked at Eshe with a smile, and then *the Seven* and lastly at her professors and headmistress. "It has been quite a journey these last few years. I didn't know who I was when my story began. And thanks to the wonderful souls standing up here with me today, I now know exactly who I am."

The gathered cheered wildly, and some had tears in their eyes.

"I am Katie Windsor, and this is Eshe Leota and Vexika Vee, and over here…:" she pointed at the protectors, "these are my friends, Simon, Aker, Zoticus, Gennadius, Wizlon, Sahti and Lore."

Katie then turned and looked in Robur's direction.

"And the kindly faced older gentleman in white, Robur, has been like a father to me."

The king made a noticeable grimace.

"And together with the wonderful spirits that watch over our wonderful academy," Katie said with an appreciative gesture towards Professor Toohasi and Professor Hopingráve, "These creature-kind are my family."

Murmurs of shock rippled throughout the crowd.

"See, I don't know you, *Your Highness*," Katie said to the king. "You weren't there when I fell out of the tree, scraped my knee, cried over being picked on, or when I was almost killed by an angry soul that also felt as much like an outcast as I did."

Kaite took the medal off, which had been placed around her neck.

"The only ones who were there for me when I needed them, was him."

And she point at Simon.

"And him."

And she pointed at Robur.

"And her."

And she point at Eshe.

"It was all of them," said Katie, as she pointed at all of *the Seven*, the faulty and her friends.

"Outcasts… witches, wizards, creature-kind, all just like me. Katie Windsor, *Creature-kind's Princess… Princess of the Outcasts…* and proud of it."

With that, Katie and her family and friends decided to bypass the chariot rides, over-the-top fanfare, and all the rest of the pomp and circumstance, and instead exit in a manner fitting the creatures' princess.

She boarded a broom, as did Eshe and Vexika and took to flight. Following behind them were a motley assortment of creatures, witches and an old wizard, all of them grinning proudly from ear to ear as they took to flight, as well. As the stunned crowd below was looking upward as the guests of honor flew overhead, suddenly several gold medallions unexpectedly rained down upon them. It seems the others decided to follow Katie's lead and cast away their medals, too. The royal family stood speechless upon the grand staircase as they watched their long lost princess fly back towards the academy that she now called home.

When the students heard what had happened on *Clarion's Peak*, Katie and Eshe, became just about the most popular students to ever attend the academy. Even Tamrah and Kilmon, said, *that was stand up of you both.* The rhino-girl then added, *I mean, as stand up as anyone from stupid House Hallox could ever hope to be.*

Enrollment in the academy soared in the next few months, as it seemed the school, and the events that occurred there, was all anyone could talk about. So much so, that Headmistress Valborga had to hire a new professor. A black feathered hybrid.

Professor Zalika Granxor became a student favorite as the teacher of the newly formed addition to the curriculum… *Magical Mastery: Controlling the Darkness Within.* The students were not just were thrilled with the frequent guest visits from the professor's firefly girlfriend, Fadessa, but also most known hybrids on Chaparral, would often drop in for guest lectures and demonstrations, like *the Seven.*

Even with all the changes, *the Academy Of Enchantments and Other Magical Studies* did eventually return to some sense of normalcy - as much as a school of creature-kind could ever be *normal.* Still, from time to time, questions about the *Dark One* and his mother's fate would surface amongst whispers in the hallways, or in hushed tone conversations within shadowed corridors.

There was still much curiosity as to whether or not there might someday be another attack, another battle… another return.

While nothing definitive confirming whether they lived or died was ever written on parchment or in stone… on the night of the battle, after all was said and done, one wizard, while accompanying a severely dehydrated and malnourished young princess to Mrs. Moons' infirmary, did ask a question that the *old sod* couldn't get an answer to from reading one's mind through *skull-speak*.

"Katie," started Robur carefully. "I want to ask you something, and mind you, you do not have to answer, if you don't want to… but what did happen to Osiris and his mother?"

Katie lowered her head and took a deep breath.

"I knew I could just destroy the clock with their souls trapped in it, and that would be that," she paused, before continuing in a serious tone. "But then it never ends. There would be another and another. The change had to start with me, and Eshe and Zalika. We are a new *Tree*… stronger than the old… stronger together."

The old wizard placed his hand on Katie's shoulder and smiled a loving smile at the girl he had cared for like a daughter all of these years.

"I've never been more proud of you, Katie Windsor," said Robur, with a drop or two mists building in his eyes.

"Alright, now, she needs her rest."

Mrs. Moons was about to pull the curtain around Katie's bed, when Robur turned with a puzzled, inquisitive expression upon his face.

"So what do you think happened to the clock?" asked Robur.

"I don't know," replied Katie. "Through the chimes, I directed it to be sent somewhere far, far away… buried where no one will ever find it. And *voila*, it was gone."

The wizard turned to exit, when Katie stopped him with a question of her own.

"Did I do the right thing?" she asked. "What if they do return?"

"Then there will always be a brave girl, like Katie Windsor to rise up and meet them," said Robur. "I'm sure of it."

*

A half a world away, in a place called *the Outlands*, where magic is forbidden, an old antique store is open for business. It doesn't get many customers, but somehow it has remained a fixture in these parts for what seems like centuries. In fact, one old local once said, that he could not remember that old shanty of a store, not being there.

On this day, a young lad came into the store with his elderly grandmother. Something stuck out as odd to the old shopkeeper. The boy had on a cloak that hid his face from view. The grandmother seemed particularly aware of anyone staring too long at the boy. Even without words the shopkeeper knew to divert his gaze.

As the only two potential customers in the shop, the owner was watching as they browsed the rows of old collectables and ancient items. Without her knowing, the boy's hand let go of his grandmother's hand and disappeared. She turned and looked back, seeing that he was not there.

"Orixor, where are you!" she cried.

Instantly this got the storekeepers attention. The grandmother and the shop owner began looking down the aisles, but the boy wasn't there.

"Where could he be?" cried out the grandmother. "Orixo!"

Just then, the shopkeeper looked to the back of the store, past the sign that reads… *"Do Not Enter! Customers Not Allowed!"*

In the stockroom, there stood the boy as if in a trance, fixated on an old grandfather clock. As the storekeeper neared him, he could see the boy's reflection in the glass upon the timepiece's door. He had features not unlike that of a tarantula, spider-like but hairier.

"Orixor," cried the grandmother, as she rounded the corner, finding the back stockroom. "You can't just run off like that!"

"Sorry, grandmother," replied the boy in an eerie hushed tone. "But I heard voices in there."

He pointed towards the clock.

"What are these items?" asked the grandmother. "You do know that magic in forbidden, do you not?"

"Oh, no Ma'am," replied the shopkeeper, "these are just old trinkets and attic junk. The only thing magical here, are the prices."

"I want it, please, grandmother, you promised," said the boy. "You said I could pick out one item, and that's it."

"What?" asked the grandmother. "Why do you want that old thing, Orixor? It doesn't even work… and some joker put a 13 on the top of the dial. "

"Now Ma'am, a promise is a promise," added the shopkeeper, smelling a sale close at hand. "Again, price is magical, to die for, actually."

"Fine, but we'll have to have it delivered," relented the boy's grandmother, as she and the shopkeeper walked to the front of the shop.

"So it's just an old relic?" asked the grandmother.

"Hasn't worked in years, if ever," replied the owner, as the chime of the cash register rang out. **"And… all sales are final."**

Just as the shop keeper said, *that all sales are final*, the grandfather clock's hour hand ticked onto the number thirteen. From under the cloak in the reflection of the old grandfather clock, a grin as wide as Chaparral appeared on the young boy's face. It almost seemed as though, the clock was grinning, too.

EPILOGUE

"HEAR WHAT, CYNTHIANA?"

"The End," declared Uncle Simon, as his three little grandnieces taking shelter from the storm with him cheered. "Well, I am glad you enjoyed it, ladies… and how about that… it sounds like the storm has passed."

Quickly the applause offered by the three sets of clapping hands turned to questions about the story they'd just heard, and a lot of them.

"Wait, wait, wait," said Cynthiana, adamantly. "What happened to Eshe? Did she go back to her time period?

"Yeah, and how about Katie?" asked Hailey. "Did she finish school, and did she graduate from the academy?"

"How about the biggest question?" asked Kadence. "Did Osiris and the *Mother of Bones* get out of the old grandfather clock? If so did they attack Katie, the Granxors or the academy again?"

"Whoa, whoa, whoa," said Uncle Simon, "That's quite a bit, so I'll answer them one by one. And then we need to get back to the farmhouse. I am sure your families are worried sick and want to know that you are okay."

The kindly old man, with a walking stick resting across his knee, pointed at Cynthiana, who had her cat, Midnight, poking his head out of the zip-up sweat and said, "You first."

"It's always her that gets to go first," muttered Hailey, to which Kadence offered a nod of agreement and a pouty lip.

"Did Eshe go back to her time period?" asked Cynthiana.

"I'm pleased to say, that she did not," replied Uncle Simon.

The three girls all gasped.

"How?" asked Cynthiana.

"Well, as you remember, Robur cast a similar *a mere shadow of one's self* spell upon Eshe as he had with Katie. The Eshe that became Katie's best friend reasoned she'd already lived all three of the Granxor Eshes' lives through memories, so she decided to let the *mere shadow of herself* that was in her time period live out all those memories, which had already occurred… and she would stay with Katie at the academy as Eshe Leota and live out her life in this time period. So that is what she did."

"Now, I have fifty more questions," said Cynthiana.

"Nope, just one," said Uncle Simon. "And next, will be you, Little Miss Hailey."

"Did Katie complete more years at the academy?" asked Hailey. "Did she graduate?"

"Yes, she and Eshe are indeed proud *House Hallox* graduates of *the Academy of Enchantments and Other Magical Studies.* In fact the year that they graduated was the year that Professor Zalika Granxor married her longtime firefly girlfriend, Fadessa, in one of the most glorious creature-kind weddings to ever be held in the academy's courtyard. Simply spectacular, indeed."

"Aww," said the three girls in unison.

"Now, did I miss anyone? I can't remember?" asked Uncle Simon, playfully.

"Yeah, me, me," said Kadence with her hand raised.

"Ah yes, Kadence," said the old storyteller. "What was that question again?"

"Did the *Dark One* and his mother ever get out of that clock?" asked Kadence.

But before their great uncle could answer a voice conveniently interrupted his response to the question.

"Cynthiana, Kadence, Hailey… girls, where are you?"

"Grandmother!" said Cynthiana.

The girls walked through the darkness and towards their grandmother's voice. As they followed her calls, up ahead of them appeared a light. Quickly they raced out of the darkness and into their grandmother's arms.

"Grandmother Katie, we're so happy to see you!"

"Thank goodness you are alright," said Grandma Katie, fighting back tears. "We searched everywhere for you."

Their grandmother then raised her chin and called out, "I found them! They're here!"

In the distance the rustling of leaves and brush could be heard, as footsteps were racing towards them.

“There you are,” said a kindly older woman, as she ran and threw her arms around the three girls.

“Aunt Eshe,” said Kadence, “we were so scared. The storm almost swept us away!”

Hailey then jumped into the retelling of the tale.

“We were playing by the *Great Oak*, when something grabbed us and put us inside the cave, I guess.”

Just then Hailey looked around with a puzzled look upon her face.

“Hey, where’s the cave?”

“Yeah, where’s the cave, Uncle Simon?” asked Cynthiana, who had just spotted her uncle standing next to the *Great Oak*. “You said that you took shelter in the old Winslow Salt Mine, and then you heard us talking and found us.”

“Did I say that?” asked Uncle Simon, in a coy manner.

“Yes, you did!” replied Cynthiana, having none of it. “And where is the opening that we just came out of?”

“I… I don’t know,” replied Uncle Simon, sneaking glances at Grandma Katie and Aunt Eshe, hoping they might throw him a life preserver.

“Maybe you all were just under a bunch of fallen branches, and it looked like you were in a cave,” said Aunt Eshe, to which Uncle Simon nodded his head, trying to help sell it.

“Or maybe we fell in a hole or something,” he added, to which both Grandma Katie and Aunt Eshe winced at his horrible suggestion.

“Or maybe we went through the bark and into the *Great Oak,* just like Green Eyes did,” said Cynthiana.

“I think it was that one,” said Hailey.

“Yep, that one,” added Kadence.

“Maybe, maybe,” said Grandmother Katie nodding her head. “What’s important is that you are safe. *My whole world* is the three of you.”

Katie Windsor hugged her granddaughters once more, squeezing them tight, as she fought back tears.

“Come on let’s go home,” said Aunt Eshe, taking Kadence and Hailey by the hand and together they started walking out of the forest.

Grandmother Katie walked over to Uncle Simon and gave him a hug.

“Thank you, old friend,” said Katie.

“Once a protector, always a protector,” replied the elder Simon.

Together they turned towards the path that led to the Windsor farmhouse, when they noticed that one little girl was not with her cousins, up ahead of them.

"Where is Cynthiana?" asked Grandmother Katie under her breath.

At that very moment, a distant yet familiar melody echoed just behind her and Simon. They both turned and saw Cynthiana standing before the *Great Oak.*

"Cynthiana, what are you doing?" asked her grandmother, trying to divert her attention. "Come on, sweetie, let's go."

In the leaves above, just out of sight of Katie's granddaughter standing below was an aged, weather-worn set of chimes. Their melody was subtle, yet eerie and beautiful all at the same time.

Inside the trunk of the tree, the little girl heard a voice, small at first, but definitely audible. It whisphered a name… "Cynthiana, Cynthiana."

"Did you hear that?" she asked.

"Hear What, Cynthiana?" replied Grandmother Katie.

Inquisitively, Cynthiana reaches her hand towards the bark, just as her grandmother had so many years ago. And just as her grandmother and her beloved cat, Green Eyes, had done, she too saw her hand enter into the tree.

“Did you see that?” asked Cynthiana.

“See what?” replied Grandmother Katie.

“My hand, it went through the bark, just like… yours did in the story, Grandma,” she said.

“Well, that’s impossible. One, because I don’t remember anybody saying that I was Katherzine, do you?” replied her grandmother. “Secondly, hands do not go through bark in real life. Your great uncle just likes to tell you girls make believe stories, here by the *Great Oak*. Sometines the magic dust from all those tall tales can get in your head. That or actually you really did get a bump to the head with all those branches blowing around in the storm.”

Katie took her granddaughter’s hand, gently guiding it away from the tree.

As they walked down the pathway home, something crawled into Uncle Simons’s ear and straight into his skull.

"It seems it’s time for *another* to write *her own story* and she will need help from a friend," said the voice.

Grandmother Katie glanced over at Uncle Simon with an appreciative, loving smile.

"The best friend an odd outcast of a young girl has ever known."

Uncle Simon gave a grin of recognition back towards the princess he'd watched over his entire life, and then drifted behind, as if he forgot something he needed to go back to recover.

Odd thing though, on the way to the *Great Oak*, the kindly old man changed, and as he did so his walking stick hit the ground. Stepping over it, were four snowy white paws that raced towards the base of the *Great Oak*, and like magic disappeared, as if they too, entered the tree.

13 O'CLOCK

CARNIVAL MUSIC SERIES

PRESENTS:

13 O'CLOCK / APP-D SINGLE

www.jazanwild.com/13.mp3

JAZAN WILD

IN WILD'S WORDS...
THE CHIMES IN THE TREE BOOK SERIES HAS BECOME A GYPSY-WITCH'S READING OF SORTS... COMPLETE WITH CRYSTAL BALL AND ALL.

AT THE END OF BOOK TWO IN THIS SERIES... YOU SAY WITCH LIKE IT'S A BAD THING, I WROTE OF THE MANY PARALLELS THAT HAD SURFACED BETWEEN THE CHIMES STORY AND MY OWN REAL LIFE; EVENTS THAT HAD NOT OCCURRED AT THE TIME OF WRITING THE BOOK OR WERE NOT YET KNOWN TO ME.

I SPOKE OF HOW A DNA TEST REVEALED THAT I HAD A FAMILY THAT I DIDN'T KNOW EXISTED... A GRANDFATHER, AUNTS, UNCLES AND COUSINS, THAT I HAD NEVER MET BEFORE. MY MOTHER HAD A FATHER SHE NEVER HAD THE CHANCE TO MEET, RAY.

SINCE THEN I CAN SAY THAT TODAY, AS I WAS IN THE PROCESS OF WRITING THE LAST CHAPTERS OF THIS BOOK, WHICH CONCLUDES THE SERIES, I DID HAVE THE PLEASURE OF MEETING MY AUNT RANELLE AND UNCLE JAY FOR THE FIRST TIME.

NOT ONLY DID WE MEET, BUT THEY TOOK ME TO WHERE THEY GREW UP IN CALIFORNIA AND WHERE MY GRANDFATHER SPENT MUCH OF HIS LIFE. I GOT TO SEE WHERE HE WORKED AND EVEN THE PLACE WHERE HE LIKED TO SIT AND GET A DRINK WHEN THE END OF THE WORK DAY BELL SOUNDED.

WE EVEN WENT TO A BASEBALL GAME IN THE SAME STADIUM THAT MY AUNT AND UNCLE WENT TO WITH RAY, MANY YEARS EARLIER. GO DODGERS!

LIFE IS STRANGE, TO THINK THAT, I - A KID FROM VIRGINIA WHO DREAMED OF PLAYING DRUMS IN A ROCK BAND, AND WITH THE ABILITY TO TELL IMAGINATIVE STORIES - LEFT A SMALL TOWN AND NOT KNOWING A SOUL IN CALIFORNIA, BOARDED A PLANE TO ATTEND A MUSIC SCHOOL IN HOLLYWOOD. ONLY TO LATER LEARN THAT I WAS NOT ALONE, NOT REALLY.

I HAD FAMILY JUST A SHORT RIDE AWAY DOWN THE 10 FREEWAY, I JUST HADN'T MET THEM YET. WELL, IN THIS SERIES YOU HAVE KATIE GETTING TO KNOW THE YOUNGER VERSION OF HER GRANDMOTHER THROUGH TIME TRAVEL.

SO I GUESS ANYTHING IS POSSIBLE...
THAT IS IF YOU ***BELIEVE IN MAGIC.***
(WITCH) **I MOST CERTAINLY** DO!

www.ingramcontent.com/pod-product-compliance
Lightning Source LLC
LaVergne TN
LVHW061218100826
845148LV00004B/792